# In This Moment

*Heart of Vallantine Book 1*

## Kelly Moran

## Praise for Kelly Moran's Books

*"Breathes life into an appealing story."*
Publishers Weekly
*"Readers will fall in love."*
Romantic Times
*"Great escape reading."*
Library Journal
*"Touching & gratifying."*
Kirkus Reviews
*"Sexy, heart-tugging fun."*
USA Today
*"Emotional & totally engaging."*
Carla Neggers
*"A gem of a writer."*
Sharon Sala
*"I read in one sitting."*
Carly Phillips
*"Compelling characters."*
Roxanne St. Claire
*"A sexy, emotional romance."*
Kim Karr
*"An emotionally raw story. A compelling read."*
Katie Ashley
*"I devoured the book!"*
Laura Kaye

*D*earest Visitors,

Welcome to Vallantine, Georgia, where the only thing sweeter than the Belle Peaches we're famous for are the patrons.

Founded in 1870 by William & Katherine Vallantine, our cozy, picturesque town is home to 2500 residents, and pocketed between Statesboro and Savannah. Quaint Vallantine is nestled beside the Ogeechee River. We have 3 inns and 2 B&Bs for convenience, or a hotel just outside the city limits. There are several family-operated restaurants for your dining pleasure to suit your palate or fancy.

On your visit, be sure to check out our main square. There're over 45 locally owned independent shops along the old-world cobblestone streets. Take a riverboat dinner cruise at sunset or a horse-drawn carriage ride through the historic plantation district. Enjoy a walking tour of the Vallantine Cemetery or Peach Park, where multiple statues stand in remembrance of important figures in history, and stroll among the hundred-year-old oak trees teeming with Spanish moss. You can even view parts of the original library, still standing, that William built in 1875 for Katherine, who loved books. Some say she never left, that her spirit can be caught reading one of her favorite volumes between the shelves while she idly waits to assist all who enter seeking knowledge.

You may have been drawn here for our annual Peach Festival or Pecan Fair, but our southern charm will make you never want to leave. Hospitality is our middle name. If you're so inclined, before you do depart, go say hello to Miss Katie—the first Belle Peach tree ever planted in town, named after the one and only Katherine Vallantine. It's legend around these parts that doing so will bring you good luck and a lifetime of love. She's also been known to grant a wish or two if she's in the mood.

Y'all come back now, you hear!

Gunner Davis, Mayor of Vallantine

# Chapter One

Today sucked. She'd had a lot of terrible ones in her twenty-eight years on Earth, more than half of those years in this very town, but today took the whole pig pickin' cake.

In the little black dress she'd worn to the funeral, heels dangling by the straps from her numb fingers, Rebecca Moore stood on the front lawn outside of her grandmother's modest home and chewed the inside of her cheek. She should go inside. Should get affairs in order and her life together. Both seemed like too daunting a task and beyond her ability. So, she stayed put.

Darn fibromyalgia pain was bad right now. The strangling achiness in her neck and shoulders, which never went away, was probably angrier due to stress and lack of sleep. She'd forgotten to take her vitamins this morning and do her stretches, too, which wouldn't help. Her own fault. Drugging weariness tugged at her, threatening to pull her under. Another fibro side effect, yet triple-fold today.

Sunlight beat down on her just to contradict her sour mood. Humidity was thicker than her first crush's head. Cicadas buzzed and a brown thrasher chirped its three-note whistling call from a nearby magnolia tree. The air smelled like rain from this morning, roses from her grandmother's bushes, and faintly of barbeque from a neighbor's backyard. A lawnmower ground a grating whine off in the distance. Children laughing and playing carried on the breeze from the other direction.

She wasn't supposed to be here. A short visit for holidays, sure. Not long-term. Not forever. Certainly not because she'd failed or because Gammy had...

Her chest hitched, and she choked on a sob. Hot tears splashed her cheeks, blurring her vision.

Gammy was gone. The woman who'd raised her after her parents' tragic car accident, who'd tended to boo-boos and broken hearts from stupid boys, was gone. She wasn't supposed to die, either. Especially not without Rebecca by her side, holding her hand.

Yet, they'd buried her today just the same.

Last time Rebecca had been home was Christmas. A few short months ago. Gammy had been fine. Fit as a fiddle. She'd cooked a sugar ham, sweet potato casserole, fried okra, and gingerbread cookies thick with icing because that was Rebecca's favorite. Didn't matter that it had been just the two of them or that they'd eaten leftovers for two days. That was all they'd needed was each other, full bellies, and a roof over their heads.

The fact she'd never get to eat Gammy's cookies again was enough to slice agony through her midsection. Mortality was such a fragile thing. Rebecca had taken it for granted.

The house wasn't in the best part of town, but in Vallantine, Georgia, they never had the need to lock their doors. A tiny two-bedroom ranch with a postage stamp yard. Cookie-cutter, like all the others on the block, with white vinyl and blue shutters fading more by the year. There were at least twenty casserole dishes on the front stoop, a product of townsfolk offering comfort. That's what people did in the south when someone died. They cooked. En masse. More than any one person could consume. She'd almost forgotten that since moving north.

She vaguely wondered if that made her a Yankee now. She'd left their small, picturesque town to go to college in Boston straight out of high school, then had secured a job at a newspaper right after graduating. Big hopes and bigger stars in her eyes. She was gonna be somebody. Do great things and change the world. How foolish. Ten years since she'd called Vallantine home. She'd been unsuccessful at all of it, including fulfilling her life-long dream of becoming an award-winning journalist.

Perhaps she didn't belong anywhere.

A loud pop, followed by the chaotic rev of a dying exhaust jarred her from her thoughts. It took mere seconds for the noise to click her memory. Shaking her head, she dropped her chin and sighed.

Good ole Harold. Dear Lord, how was he still alive? He had to have been a hundred years old when she'd started grammar school. The only thing that might be passably older than him was dirt. Or his pickup truck.

She turned her head, watching the blue rust bucket chug up the street, pausing to deposit mail in the boxes by the curb. He waved to the kids playing a few houses down. Nostalgia smacked her upside the head as he stopped by her box and stuck his face out the window. His white strands ruffled in the breeze and sunlight made the deep grooves of his wrinkles seem like caverns.

"Miss Rebecca, as I live and breathe."

Yeah, the *live and breathe* part was hard for her to believe, too. "Great to see you, Harold. How are you, sir?"

"Gettin' along, gettin' along fine. Sorry to hear about Mavis passing."

Her, also. She'd had to hear it from bestie number one, Scarlett, via phone. "Thank you, sir."

He held his arm out the window, offering a stack of envelopes. "How long you stayin'?"

She took the mail from him. "Indefinitely." No sense in stirring the rumor mill by elaborating. Small towns were synonymous with gossip, and Vallantine was the crowned victor.

"The Bookish Belles together again."

"Yes, sir." That wouldn't be a hardship. Rebecca and her two best friends had been inseparable since in-utero. Their mothers had started the first bookclub in town and named each of them after great southern literary heroines. The town had dubbed them the Bookish Belles in kindergarten, a nickname that stuck through the years. "It's good to be home."

A truth wrapped around a lie.

"Bet it is, darlin'." His eyes narrowed. "You ain't gonna be actin' like no Yankee, are ya?"

Strange she'd had the same thought. "I wouldn't dream of it, sir."

She swore, a good part of the south behaved as if the Civil War was still kicking. Or that they hadn't lost.

"Glad to hear it. Have a blessed day."

"You, too."

The screen door slammed shut with a clack on the house beside Gammy's, and a man stood on the stoop, hands on his hips. Oddly, he was wearing a gray suit, even in the late day spring warmth. Most people wore casual dress in these parts. He had longish black hair on top, but cropped close on the sides, and appeared to be around her age. A shadow of a beard dusted his jaw. She couldn't make out his eyes from her spot, but tension knotted his shoulders as he stood motionless, stance wide, posture rigid. She'd not seen him before, but in a town with twenty-five hundred residents and constant tourists, it wasn't like she knew everybody.

8

Harold drove right past the neighbor's box, tossing mail onto the grass, and kept going.

Rebecca tried and failed to suppress a laugh.

"Damn it!" The man flew off his stoop, vaulting the three steps, and marched toward the curb. "What in the hell are you doing? I'm getting real tired of..."

Harold turned the corner, and with a wave out the window, disappeared from view.

"...talking to myself." The man dropped his arms, hands slapping his thighs.

Rebecca rolled her lips over her teeth. "Sweets."

He turned, brows raised as if surprised to find her there. "Hi."

Green. His eyes were a shocking shade of green. Wicked Irish hellion, this one. Great athletic body to boot. Taller than her by a head, putting him at about six feet, with wide shoulders, and a lean waist. His accent wasn't from this side of the Mason-Dixie line. Midwest, maybe?

She smiled, still firmly amused. "Hello."

He scratched his jaw. "Sweets?"

"Yep." She pointed to his mail littering the ground. "Harold has an affinity for sweets and an aversion to newcomers. Put cookies in your mailbox with the door open. He'll see it as a sign of respect and warm up to you in no time."

He stared at her, unblinking, like she'd gotten hit one too many times by the stupid stick. "Cookies," he replied, deadpan.

"Make sure they're homemade. Don't want to add insult to injury."

"Homemade cookies." More staring. After a moment, he swiped his hand down his face. "What kind of fresh hell is this?"

"Not from around here, are you?"

"No. Where I come from, carriers actually put mail in the boxes and don't require sweets by way of a bribe. I should call the post office and file a complaint."

Someone was ornery.

"Harold *is* the post office. The *whole* post office."

He crossed his arms, brows wrenched in disbelief. "What?"

She shrugged. "There's a few people who sort packages or answer phones, others who deliver mail to the shops and businesses, but it's pretty much just him running the joint."

He huffed a dry laugh devoid of humor. "Of course, he is. Why would I expect any different in this hillbilly backwater town?"

Now he was just showing his ass. Irritation tapped her temples. He was a handsome devil with an angular face and wide jaw, thick lashes and full lips, but he was so stuck up, he'd drown in a rainstorm. "We might be simple folk to you, but you'd catch more flies with honey. Best remember that if you intend to hang around."

Done with him, she strode toward the house. She got up the stoop and was digging for the keys in her purse when he shouted behind her.

"You bought the house?"

She turned, glaring at him, not bothering to reply. His nose didn't belong in her business.

"They haven't cleared out Mavis's things yet."

Tilting her head, she debated how to respond. If he had an ill word for her Gammy, she might fillet him where he stood. "I'm aware. You knew her?" Gammy hadn't mentioned him in their weekly phone chats.

"I did." He took a few steps closer and stopped, crossing his arms. "She lived next door, after all. She was one of the few redeeming qualities of Vallantine, thus far. I cut her grass every Sunday and she baked me a peach pie."

Well, butter her biscuit. Maybe he had a heart under all that brass. "That was kind of you."

"Not really. Decent thing to do. She was getting up there in age and didn't need to be out here with a mower. Besides, I'd kill for her pies. Ever try one? Nothing like it."

Grief, so profound, so sharp, consumed her until she couldn't breathe. Gammy *did* make the best peach pie. And Rebecca would never get to enjoy one ever again. Chest tight, eyes hot, she closed her lids for a beat to compose herself.

"I didn't realize they'd sold the house."

"They didn't." She cleared her throat, drawing in a calming breath. "I'm her granddaughter."

She didn't wait for his response. Today had been horrible and overwhelming. The past week, actually. And her pain was bordering on crippling at the moment. All she wanted was the comfort of Gammy's and to be left alone. Unlocking the door, she stepped inside and promptly shut it behind her.

Pressing her forehead to the door, she inhaled hard, fighting tears. But that didn't help much because all she could breathe was the familiar scents of home. Lemon dusting spray and fabric softener. Gammy's gardenia perfume and, oddly, tissues. That cottony soft smell tissues embodied. Familiar and typically reassuring. All they did was remind her of what she'd lost. Guilt clawed at her ribcage.

She spun and leaned against the door, tossing her shoes on the mat. The small living room, consisting of a gold and white plaid couch, two yellow wingback chairs, a flatscreen on a small stand, and a couple light oak tables with lamps, was exactly as Gammy had left it. Family pictures in mismatched frames covered the ivory walls, and crystal bowls or vases occupied tables. Rebecca had paid to have the carpet replaced with hardwood some five years ago when she'd received a sign-on bonus for joining the newspaper. Gammy had retired as a hairdresser many moons before and hadn't had much money.

Since arriving in Vallantine, Rebecca hadn't spent much time in the rest of the house, having clung mostly to her old bedroom. It had just been too difficult. Even now, she half expected Gammy to waltz in from another room, wrap Rebecca in a hug, and offer her something to eat, claiming she was too skinny. If Rebecca was going to keep from going insane, she'd have to get over her avoidance.

But first, comfy clothes.

Shoving off the door, she strode down the hallway to the right, bypassing Gammy's room and the bathroom to head to her bedroom. Which had remained unchanged since she'd departed for college. A full-sized bed with a purple flowered comforter sat between two windows on the back wall. A tall white dresser rested beside a tiny desk on the left, the closet on the right. Bookshelves lined the same wall as the door, and she recalled without looking that they held everything from classics to mysteries to young-adult romances. Books, her forever escape. Books never let her down or demanded things of her.

After closing the drapes, she dug in her dresser for a pair of sweats and a tee, then tossed her dress in the hamper in the closet. She pulled her hair up in a ponytail on her way to the bathroom. The gray tile was cold and reminded her to throw on socks when she was finished. A mint green mat in front of the tub matched the plain shower curtain, which she'd left open in her haste this morning to get ready for the funeral.

Gammy's products stared back at Rebecca as if taunting her to do something. Throw them away or let them collect dust in memory. They weren't brands she used, but she couldn't junk them just yet. She closed the curtain in avoidance, washed the makeup off her face, and found socks in her room.

Backtracking down the hall and through the living room, she went into the kitchen to start a pot of coffee. Distressed dark blue cabinets and white tile. Formica counters. The kitchen was dated, but like every other room in the house, it was spick and span. Not a crumb or spot of dust. A two-seater white wood table was in the corner, an empty fruit bowl in the middle. She swallowed hard, caught up in flashes of memory.

She'd sat at that very table when Gammy had told Rebecca's devastated eight-year-old self that her parents had died in a car wreck on their way home from dinner. Date night. Her folks used to have one every month, and Rebecca got to sleep over at Gammy's. The rain had been terrible that evening, torrents leftover from a hurricane that had brushed near their town. Even now, storms made her uneasy. Lord, how she'd sobbed and wailed and carried on. At that age, she'd been too blinded by her own pain to wonder how her grandmother had felt or how hard on her the situation had to have been. She'd buried her only son and his wife, something no parent should ever have to do. Not once had Rebecca been afraid, though. Gammy had taken care of her, had taken care of everything. Like she always did.

She'd died alone. Just fell asleep and never woke. Rebecca couldn't imagine a more peaceful way, but guilt for not being here churned in her belly. Her friends Scarlett and Dorothy had been the ones to find her, as they used to pop by a couple times a week to check on Gammy.

There was no one left to take care of things. Her whole family was gone. Mama's folks had lived in South Carolina, and had passed when Rebecca was too young to remember. Her grandfather on Daddy's side, Gammy's ex-husband, had divorced her when Daddy had been just a boy. Simply got sick of married life and walked, never to return. She'd raised her son all on her own, on a hairdresser's salary, in a time and in a town where that sort of thing was frowned upon. People didn't get divorced back then. Gammy was still the strongest person Rebecca knew. She might be an adult, but she was far from having her crap together. In the back of her mind, she'd always figured Gammy would be here to pick up the pieces, offer wise advice, or hold her when she fell apart.

A brisk knock, and the creak of the front door snapped Rebecca's gaze from the table to the doorway. Her pulse tripped.

"Rebecca? Where you at, girl?"

A sigh, and she smiled. It was only Scarlett. Rebecca had been in the big city too long if she was freaking out about who'd opened her door in Vallantine.

"We brought reinforcements." And Dorothy, too.

Gawd, how she'd missed her besties.

"In here," she called, stepping into the living room. What a sight for sore eyes. She'd told them at the funeral she'd be okay, not to stop by. They obviously knew her too well.

Dorothy held a brown paper bag to her chest, and sported a pair of plain blue and white PJs. Her naturally reddish hair was cropped just below her shoulders, a new addition since Rebecca had last seen her at Christmas. The video chats they did every week just didn't hold a candle to being with them in person.

She almost laughed. Then there was Scarlett. Rocking red sparkly pajamas, she held a plastic grocery bag and flipped her long, sleek cocoa locks over her shoulder with the other hand. Only she could wear makeup with jammies and pull it off.

"What did you bring?" Rebecca took the bag from Dorothy and peered inside. *Yes,* alcohol. Gammy had none in the house. "Bless you."

Scarlett held up her bag. "And snacks, but uh…" She jerked a thumb at the door. "Do you know you have a whole restaurant on the stoop?"

"Crap. I forgot." Rebecca set the bag on an end table. "Help me bring them in, would you? I was in such a rush to get away from the new neighbor that it slipped my mind."

Scarlett cocked a hip. "Why are you trying to get away from the new neighbor?"

"Because he's a Yankee asshole."

Hand at her bosom, Scarlett gasped. "How judgy of you. I love it."

Opening the door, Dorothy picked up two dishes and headed toward the kitchen. Scarlett and Rebecca did the same until all the items were in the fridge. Afterward, they found respective seats in the living room.

"So, what's with the neighbor? Name, age, deets. For you to drop *Yankee* in a sentence considering you've been a northerner for a decade is saying something." Scarlett waved her manicured hand. "Out with it."

"This convo requires cocktails." And probably chocolate.

"I'll get it." Dorothy rose and sorted through the bags. Grabbing glasses from Gammy's China cabinet, she mixed peach schnapps, brandy, grenadine, and lemon-lime soda for their customary Georgia Sunset cocktails. Good thing because Scarlett, per Dorothy, was too heavy-handed with the booze portion. "There we go."

Rebecca took a sip. "Damn, that's good." She folded her legs under her and leaned back in her chair. "I don't know the new guy's name, but he's about our age. Midwestern accent. He referred to Vallantine as hillbilly backwater."

Dorothy twisted her lips in a frown. "Not cool."

"Definitely not." Scarlett tilted her head. "From a newcomer standpoint, I can see the reference. How long's he been here?"

"Don't know. He was having a duck fit because Harold was tossing his mail on the curb and not in the box."

"Ah, so not long enough to know he needs to feed Harold's sugar fix." Scarlett nodded in understanding. "He could maybe be forgiven. Is he good-looking?"

Dorothy gave her the hairy eyeball. "Because that matters."

Rebecca laughed. How she missed this, missed them. They were three very different women with three very different personalities, yet they fit. Completed one another. Supported and encouraged. She always felt like she was waiting for a punchline in their presence.

*A blonde, a brunette, and a redhead walk into a bar...*

"Well? Is he?" Scarlett demanded.

Rebecca sighed. "Oh, yeah. He's handsome, all right." And he also thought the sun came up just to hear him crow. No, thank you.

# Chapter Two

Inside a popular tavern in the tourist district, Graham Roberts stared at his beer from a corner table. The Tipsy Turtle. No lie, that was the name of the joint. It was sandwiched between What A Pickle Deli and Guac On Mexican Restaurant in what passed as historic downtown. Or Main Square, as the townsfolk called it, which was shaped like an 'I'.

An old library, beaten down and falling to shambles, was at the tip of said I, flanked by park grounds and a cemetery. Down a ways was a giant one hundred and fifty year old peach tree that no longer produced fruit. Locals called it 'Miss Katie,' after the town founder's wife. She and the tree were pretty legend in these parts. There was a wrought-iron fence around the trunk's base and benches to sit and bask in its glory. First time he'd heard that tidbit, his eyeballs thunked the back of his skull, he'd rolled them so hard. The library had once been owned by the Vallantine descendants, but someone else had possession of the place now. In the two months he'd been here, they'd done nothing with it. Apparently, the building was haunted by the same woman the tree was named after, but not in a *boo* sort of way. Another eye roll.

The center of the I, all the way to the end and down both directions, had independent shops and restaurants with colorful awnings. Cobblestone streets, cast-iron old-world lampposts, and even flower boxes at the curb. Cherry blossom trees were finishing their spring blooms and drifting pink petals everywhere. Idealistic small town. He'd give Vallantine this, it was pretty, and the patrons were friendly. Hell of a lot better weather than Minnesota, for sure.

"You're not drinking."

He glanced at Forest, sitting beside him, then back at his untouched ale. They'd gone to college together and stayed close after Forest had moved back here and Graham had stayed in Minneapolis. If not for Forest, in fact, Graham would've been shit out of luck after the scandal.

"Sorry. My mind was elsewhere." He took a sip, glancing around.

Polished dark wood floors, tables, and bar. The walls were a rich navy color, but the ceiling was aqua with white swirls, bubbles, and a giant sea turtle painted in a mural. Metal lanterns on the tables and blue neon overhead lighting. It was a neat place. More like what he was used to in the city than the bars on the outskirts catered to locals.

The clientele was mostly not from around here, best he could tell and judging by the t-shirts.

"You okay, buddy?"

Glancing at Forest, Graham took in his friend's short, wavy brown hair and overgrowth on his wide jaw. Concern radiated in his deep brown, almost black, eyes, causing remorse to shift yet again in Graham's gut. He was trying to start his life over and a good chunk of his career, and Forest was coming fresh off a nasty divorce to the Wicked Bitch of the West. What a sad pair they made.

"Yeah, man. Sorry again." He was always sorry, and a sorry excuse for a human. "How's work treating you?"

Forest had gone to his father's alma mater for college on his dad's request, all so he could take over the bank one day. He currently was in charge of the loan department until his father retired. He rarely, if ever, talked about it, giving Graham the impression he wasn't all that happy.

"Eh." Forest shrugged. "Same ole, same ole. Nothing exciting. I'll be going over the library renovations for the historical society, though. Looking forward to that."

"Renovations?" Graham had heard whispering around town, but nothing he could connect the dots on. The building had been closed since he'd moved. "What are they doing?"

"Not sure yet. I have a meeting with the Belles on Monday."

The Belles? Was that some kind of garden club for debutants?

Forest took a sip of beer and did a double-take at Graham's expression. "I forget sometimes you don't know all the inner workings of Vallantine." He chuckled, shifting in his seat, and leaned back. "So, the Vallantine Library was built by the original town founder, William Vallantine, for his wife, Katherine, who loved books. It was on the estate until a hurricane took out the mansion in 1898 and killed some of the family. That's where the park is now. The library survived. About six months ago, the last living descendant, Sheldon Brown, decided he couldn't handle it anymore. He and his wife, Rosemary, bequeathed it to the Bookish Belles."

Part of that Graham knew from chatter around town or his employees, but... "Bookish Belles?" Only in the south. It was like another country sometimes, he was learning.

"Yep. Rosemary Fillmore, or Brown now, was our eighth grade teacher. The Belles were her favorite students, and in my graduating class. They love all things literature. In fact, their mothers started a bookclub way back. Don't know if it's still running. I'd have to ask Mama."

Ah, okay. Probably the right people to leave a historical library to, then, if that was the case.

"Speak of the devils." Forest bumped his chin toward the bar. "That's them."

There were quite a few patrons at the bar, but only three females together. And wearing pajamas, no less. "A blonde, a brunette, and a redhead. There's a joke in there somewhere."

Forest huffed a laugh. "The redhead is Dorothy, named from *The Wizard of Oz*. She's an accountant. The brunette who looks like she's photoshopped? That's Scarlett, *Gone With the Wind*, obviously, and funny enough, she owns a plantation where she has an event business. The blonde's Rebecca from—"

"*Huckleberry Finn*. Tom Sawyer's feisty girl." It was Graham's favorite book. He couldn't see her face, she had her back to him, but it looked an awful lot like Mavis's granddaughter from next door. He'd been a jerk to her this afternoon. Not on purpose, but nonetheless, a jerk.

"That's the one. She just moved back home after her grandmother died." An ah-ha expression lit Forest's features. "Your old neighbor."

Graham grunted. Guess it was her. "I owe her an apology. I stuck my foot in it earlier."

"Oh yeah? What did you do?"

"Nothing I can't fix." He *did* need to fix it, though. He'd made assumptions and said crap while in a pissed off mood instead of biting his tongue. And after she'd tried to give him advice. Word got out about that, and the town would have another reason to shun him, besides being a new guy from up north.

Finally, she turned from the bar, passing to-go bags of food to her companions. She looked like a different woman than the one by the curb outside their homes. Gone was the coifed champagne-colored hairstyle, perfect cosmetics, and elegant black dress. Instead, she wore a pair of gray sweats, a pink tee, no war paint, and her hair was up in a messy knot. Most notable was the dull etchings of grief her in features from before had been replaced with a carefree smile. The kind that lit her eyes.

Amazing eyes. Baby blues, and too big for her face. They were a focal point and had stolen the wind from his sails this afternoon.

But her, like this? Damn. Nothing sexier than a natural woman, minus the polish.

She spotted him from across the room, their gazes locking. For a moment, time sucked through a vacuum as his gut heated. Stirrings of attraction nudged from behind his ribcage.

Her smile flatlined, indicating she hadn't felt the same magnetic pull. Bummer. She tilted her head to say something to her friends, then began making her way over. The two others followed in her wake. It reminded him of a high school drama clique.

Her walk bordered on sauntering. Hip sway, hip sway. Great body. Full breasts playing cat and mouse with the V of her shirt. Legs that went into the next zip code. She was slender to the point of breakable, but instinct told him her backbone was pure titanium and she wouldn't easily snap.

Strong women were sexy.

She set her hand on the table—no ring, he noted—and leaned into it. "Forest, good to see you. It's been a hot minute." Her gaze shifted to Graham. "You should be mindful of the company you keep."

"Wheeeew-weee." A chuckle, and Forest leaned back in his seat, lacing his fingers behind his head. "Done made her mad, my friend."

Mercy, she was hot as hell. Fiery, indeed, proving her namesake correct. She'd had a slight twang to her accent in their first encounter, barely detectable, but it was currently sliding toward a drawl as if preparing for battle. The heat in his gut shifted south.

The last thing he needed was to get tangled in a woman or relationship, but she was fascinating. Not that she appeared interested in him or anything.

"That I did." Graham studied her a moment. Fair complexion. Thin, angular face. High cheekbones that were flushed. He suddenly wanted to make her blush everywhere, and vaguely realized he was in trouble. Somehow, he didn't give a damn. "I deserve whatever punishment is deemed fit."

Well, look at him. He hadn't been a part of the human race or interested in rejoining for going on six months. Also, lust at first sight could be a dangerous game that he rarely won. Yet, here he was, flirting with a gorgeous blonde in a bar.

The brunette—Scarlett?—waved her hand in front of her face. "Y'all be hotter than blue blazes."

Southerners and their expressions. Sometime in the realm of never, he'd get used to it.

"I don't think we've been properly introduced." He leaned his elbows on the table, still eyeing Rebecca. "Graham Roberts. And you are?"

"Fit to be tied," Forest mumbled under his breath.

Her eyes narrowed to slits, ignoring everyone else. "Rebecca Moore. What are you doing out in our hillbilly backwater? Aren't you worried stupidity is contagious?"

The redhead's brows shot to her hairline as she gazed heavenward, shaking her head.

"I deserve that, too." He nodded. "I apologize for what I said when angry."

That seemed to stump her. She straightened, expression dialed to contemplative.

"You said what, now?" Forest darted his gaze between them.

"I insulted Vallantine and its residents." Before his buddy could lay into him, Graham held up his hand, gaze still on Rebecca. "And I apologized. It was wrong of me." If he wanted to make it here and truly start over, he needed to acclimate.

"I do declare. A man who can admit when he's wrong. I thought they were a dyin' breed." The brunette held out her hand. "I'm Scarlett."

"Pleasure," he returned, shaking her hand. It took effort, but he glanced away from Rebecca to her friend. She was a looker, but didn't do it for him. High-maintenance radiated from her in waves.

"Dorothy." The redhead nodded politely, not offering a handshake. "Welcome to Vallantine."

"Thank you." She was pretty, also, but tongue-in-cheek quiet. Not his thing, either.

And why, exactly, that mattered, he hadn't a clue. He wasn't hunting for a relationship.

Undeterred, Rebecca pointed a finger at him. "You might look like a tall drink of water, but—"

He quickly glanced at Forest. "Is that a compliment?"

"Yessir."

Graham grinned at her. "Thank you, then."

No such luck, however. She wasn't done.

"*But* you're lower than a snake's belly in a wagon rut."

Again, he turned to Forest. "Was that an insult?"

"Yessir."

"Damn." Graham swiped his phone off the table and swiftly activated a search engine. "I think you're fine as frog hair split four ways," he read from the screen. He lifted his head, frowning. "That doesn't sound much like a compliment. Alas, Google says it is."

Forest dropped his head in his hand, laughing.

"Thank you." Her expression indicated that had been difficult to say, but manners bred deep required the acknowledgement. "We best be getting home before the food gets cold."

About that. "Didn't you have an abundance of offerings at your front door?" He'd thought about putting the dishes in his fridge so they wouldn't go bad until someone claimed them, but she'd shown up minutes after him. There had been enough to feed an army.

"Yes, but when a girl has a day like the one I did, then comfort food is in order. There's nothing better than Tipsy Turtle's onion stacks."

Shredded onion rings. He'd seen 'em on the menu and thought about getting some. "Enjoy."

"We will." She turned back around while her friends continued toward the door. "You should order them. They go well with beer."

She got two steps before he called her name.

"I really am sorry about Mavis. She talked about you all the time."

Guilt and grief twisted her expression, similar to how he'd first encountered her outside their homes, and he almost regretted the endearment until a ghost of a smile curved her lips.

"Thank you."

Once they were gone, Forest sighed. "Made quite the first impression on her, didn't you?"

Graham nodded. Yeah, he had, but hopefully she'd accept his apology and he'd try to do better. He'd always been a bit of a hothead and sullen with his moods. She was right. Their ways might be different than what he was used to, but it didn't mean they were bad. Taking his sour attitude out on the town wasn't going to help him adjust or fix his past.

"Got a favor, since we're on the subject." Forest wiped the condensation from his glass with his thumb. "I'm not for certain, but if she comes into the Gazette looking for a job, I'd appreciate it if you could find her one."

The Vallantine Gazette was the town's small newspaper, owned by the mayor, Gunner Davis. He'd hired Graham as editor in chief, leaving him responsible for staff and content. Didn't mean he'd hire just anyone. Odd that Forest would ask Graham for this particular favor.

"She have any experience?"

Forest nodded. "She went to college somewhere in the northeast. New York or Jersey or Boston. I forget, but she was on staff at a paper up there when her grandmother died. I assumed she was back to get affairs in order until Dorothy told me the other day that Rebecca was staying."

Okay, that already gave her more education and experience than his current employees. "I'll see what I can do."

"Like I said, I don't know if she will or not, but thanks."

They ordered an onion stack, finished off their beers while munching, and parted ways.

Since he'd met Forest for drinks right after his encounter with Rebecca, Graham had walked to the tavern because it wasn't far, and he'd wanted to clear his head. Breathing in the scents of spring, he headed down Main Street, passing the office storefront where the Gazette was located, several other shops, and turned for his street, lampposts dimly lighting the way. Crickets chirped and leaves crackled, but other than that, it was quiet. No horns. No sirens. Stars unmasked by smog or buildings.

There wasn't much in Vallantine he couldn't visit on foot, unless he went the other direction toward the plantations, beyond the park and cemetery, or toward the riverfront. It was such a change of pace from the big city life, and he found he liked it. More laid back, friendly faces, and milder climate. Back in Minnesota, there might still be snow on the ground and a bitter nip to the air. Grass would be dormant, trees bare, and nothing in bloom yet. Here, the temperature was hovering near the mid-sixties with a warm, humid breeze.

Every day, sometimes more than once, he'd acknowledge the little things, pleasantries, as he spotted them or as they arose because he found he was less grouchy. Glass half full. He'd made the choice to apply for the position at the Gazette on Forest's suggestion, accepted Gunner Davis's offer of employment, and moved a thousand miles away from where he'd grown up, all to begin anew. Part of that hadn't been choice, but he'd owned up to his mistakes. They'd landed him here. He either rolled with it or wound up miserable.

Damn, but he was trying. The fish out of water scenario was proving true more times than not.

He passed Rebecca's house and stopped outside his own before realizing he'd walked the four blocks home. Lights were on inside her place, but the curtains were closed over the front bay window.

He wondered what had drawn her back besides her grandmother's funeral. If she had been a transplanted southerner in the north, had she not liked it? Missed home? There were a few people he'd met who'd moved to Vallantine due to jobs or family, but the majority had been from here, spanning many generations.

She seemed like neither, actually. There were traces of an accent when she spoke, at least when she wasn't angry, but that had appeared more for show than breeding. Her dialect was a mix of upper east coast and deep south. Heck, had he met her anywhere else, he'd have no clue where she was from. Urban polish and sophistication warred with chill pleasantries and down-home mannerisms. Such an interesting contradiction.

Letting himself in the house, he called for his dog, Twain, and thought about how he'd like to know more about what made Rebecca tick. Attraction aside, she was...interesting. She had the same regret in her eyes that he'd been living with for too long.

Pitter-patter of nails hit the wooden floors, and his rescued mutt came around the corner to greet him. Part hound, part shepherd, parts unknown, Twain had found Graham his first night in the house by creating a ruckus with the garbage cans out back. He'd offered the dog his other half of a cheeseburger, which had been readily accepted, and they'd been buddies since. After a vet visit and flea bath.

Graham adored the doofus to no end. He rubbed the soft, longish brown, black, and white fur, telling his excited companion how he, in fact, did miss him while away. Soul mates. Twain behaved as if he'd been born to be Graham's dog, sticking close on walks or snuggling beside him on the couch when he was in a crappy mood, gaze adoring. It had ebbed the loneliness that had taken up residence in Graham's chest.

The house wasn't half bad, especially compared to his old shoebox apartment in Minneapolis. A small two-bedroom, but he didn't need much. It had been flipped by the previous owners and move-in ready, which had been a bonus. Light gray birch hardwood throughout, except the bedrooms, which were carpeted. Navy blue drapes matched his two couches. The white walls were bare. He should hang pictures or something. There weren't any personal touches on the gray tables to make the place homey, either. Every time he walked in, he thought the same thing. He needed to make the place his, but a needling niggling sensation in the back of his head had kept him from doing so.

He sighed. Chances were, he wouldn't get comfy in the house until he was settled in town or his job. Everything felt fluid or temporary. Like it could all be taken away from him.

Just like it had in Minnesota.

He headed to the kitchen, also remodeled with black cabinets and gray speckled granite countertops, and fed the dog while talking about his day. Habit. The mutt seemed to understand, too, tilting his head, barking to add his two cents.

"Met the new neighbor. She's pretty. I think you'll like her. She's quick on the take with a smart mouth."

*Bark.*

"You're probably right. She'll like you better than me. I apologized, but I don't think I've won her over yet. Too soon to tell."

*Bark.*

"Correct. I'll keep at it."

A laugh, and Graham threw the ball out back for Twain, then changed out of his work clothes and into sweats. Remote in hand, he parked his butt on the sofa and turned on the Braves game in time to catch the ninth inning, dog beside him, head in his lap.

He couldn't focus on the TV, however. Rebecca kept playing through his mind in a loop, their banter, the interactions.

"Hey." He glanced at the dog. "You don't know how to make chocolate chip cookies, do you?"

*Bark.*

"Yeah, me either."

28

# Chapter Three

Outside the library, Rebecca stood with Dorothy, waiting on Scarlett and Forest for their meeting on renovations. Warm sunshine and a slight breeze bathed her skin, and she tilted her face to stare at a cloudless sky. Gorgeous day. Even better, they got to begin phase one of their project.

A handful of months ago, Rebecca and her besties had been blown over by inheriting the library. In nearly one hundred and fifty years, the building had never left Vallantine heirs. And then, *boom*. Dorothy had met with Mayor Davis on his request for reasons unbeknownst to them, and learned Sheldon and Rosemary Brown had bequeathed it to them. They'd also left them a sizeable check, which Scarlett had put into a new checking account in their names.

Rebecca shook her head. They'd dreamed as girls to one day own the library. Had discussed fantasies of opening a bookstore and all the things they'd do. Never in a million years had Rebecca thought they'd ever come to fruition. Yet, here they were.

By Zoom, while she'd still lived in Boston, they'd made tentative plans for the place and had thrown ideas around. Dorothy had gathered contractors, plumbers, and electricians to get estimates on repairs. Costs of those were astronomical, and wouldn't leave much wiggle room.

Dorothy sighed, gaze on the library. "I can't believe we're here."

"Me, either." Rebecca looped her arm with Dorothy's and leaned closer. "I can't tell if I'm excited or nervous." After all, they could fail in their attempt.

"Same."

The library was a severely dilapidated two-story old colonial-style building with a tiny parking lot out front, large enough to hold maybe five cars. Six if they got creative. The white exterior had been repainted many times, but it had been years, and it was flaking off in chunks. The shutters were gone. A small concrete porch held no furniture or coziness, and only a few holly bushes lined the stairs, overgrown and gnarled. Two Greek support columns flanked the front overhang on either side of the door, and another two at the corners of the porch. A gabled roof, rectangular shape, and symmetrical windows were classic staples of the architecture, but it also had trace design elements like dental moldings along the eaves and pedimented dormers.

It was really a Vallantine focal point, due in part to the history, and because it rested at the tip of Main Square, overlooking the shops as if protecting them. Behind it were the roads that led to older areas of town like the cemetery and plantations.

Memories swamped her, filled her with happiness she hadn't known in too long. She hadn't realized it until she'd come home, but for years she'd merely survived and settled for getting by. It hadn't been living. "Remember how we'd come here every Saturday and sit on that old smelly couch in the back? We'd read and gossip about boys."

Dorothy tucked a stray strand of her red hair behind her ear, cherubic face lit in amusement. "And drive poor Mr. Brown nuts."

Rebecca laughed. "Yeah. The man was a saint for putting up with us." She hoped he and Mrs. Brown were living their best life traveling in their RV.

"Well, we were about the only people who graced the library back then. Plus, we did play matchmaker for them."

"True story." It was because they'd helped two introverted bookworms find their ever-after that the three of them had been gifted the library. At least, that's what the letter had said. That, and they were the only ones who'd respect its walls or do it justice. "Gosh, how we'd talk about all the things we'd do when we grew up, how we were going to take the world by storm."

So long ago, it seemed. Young girls with stars in their eyes and hope in their hearts. And then they actually had grown up. Life and circumstances and reality had chimed the final say.

"You and Scarlett wanted to take the world by storm. I just wanted a house and kids."

Rebecca smiled at her. "One out of two goals ain't bad. You have plenty of time for the rest."

"Maybe." Dorothy tilted her head. "You got your journalism degree and on staff at a huge newspaper. Scarlett got the plantation and started her own business. Seems you two got everything you wanted."

Not everything. "I'm still here, though, back where I started."

"Could be worse places than here, Rebecca." Dorothy looked at her, understanding in her depths. "I don't know what happened to bring you home for good. Perhaps you'll tell us the whole story someday. You didn't seem happy in Boston, though. Not for a long, long time. So, yeah. There could be worse places than here."

She was right. So very right. There was nothing wrong with Vallantine. It was a quiet, charming town with a lovely backdrop. All the people and places were familiar, and in this chunk of time, it was what Rebecca needed. Familiarity. Comfort. Plus, her besties were here.

Dorothy had not strived for grand adventures as a girl. All she'd ever mentioned was an accounting degree, a house, husband, and kids. The simple things most took for granted. She did the books for more than half the shops in town.

Scarlett had craved activity and social circles. Perhaps a hot lover on hotter nights who didn't try to trap or own her. She'd utilized her decorative talents and people skills to create a thriving event business on her family's old plantation. Lovers were still coming and going.

Rebecca was the only one of the three of them who'd wanted out of Vallantine. Not because she'd been unhappy, but because all the news and stories were elsewhere. Action was not within these city limits. Unless one counted rumors. She'd achieved two of her three goals, and should be proud of herself. Yet, all she could feel was failure. She'd done nothing of consequence, per her own high standards.

"You're so wise." Rebecca batted her eyelashes, shoving disappointment back into its hidey hole.

"That's me. The grounded, smart one of the bunch." Dorothy's dry tone implied both boredom and displeasure with the personality moniker.

"And just what is wrong with that?"

Before Dorothy could respond, a red pickup truck pulled into the lot and parked.

Forest Truman. Former high school star quarterback and all-around great guy. Until the other night in the bar, Rebecca hadn't seen him in ages. He'd been a cutie as a teen, but he'd filled out quite nicely as a man.

Which reminded her... "You still have a crush on him?"

Dorothy pinned her with a glare. "Must you? That was a long time ago."

Hmm. Rebecca narrowed her eyes, watching Dorothy watch Forest as he exited the truck. She ducked her head, avoiding his gaze, and cleared her throat like she often did when nervous.

Yup. Still had a thing for him.

"Ladies. How are y'all on this fine day?" His grin should be on a billboard for selling wholesomeness as he flashed a row of straight white teeth. He'd shaved the whiskers since Saturday and finger-combed his longish light brown strands. A pair of khakis and a blue polo indicated he was probably heading back to work at the bank after their meeting. "Amazing weather."

"Yes, it is." Dorothy smiled politely, glancing toward the road. "Scarlett is late."

He huffed a laugh. "Nothing new there. Would you like to start without her?"

Dorothy handled the financial end of things. Rebecca was good at marketing and product. Scarlett was the one with the eye for design and really should be present. Before Rebecca could point that out, Dorothy pulled a folder from her handbag and opened it.

"Scarlett has the key to the library, but we can go over a few things out here."

Forest glanced at the packet Dorothy held, nodding as she summarized original structural features.

"So, the roof will need a total replacement. The crawl space is solid with no issues, as is the porch. All windows will need to be upgraded, though. As for the wood siding, many boards are rotted. The plan is to pull those off and swap 'em out with new ones. Painters suggested sanding the many layers of paint, treating the wood, repainting, and then sealing it. I'll go over plumbing and electrical inside."

He grunted a sound of understanding. "Thus far, everything sounds good. The roof will have to maintain the original shape and materials, such as black shingles. Same for the siding, keeping it white. The windows might be an issue if you intend to change the one in the upstairs loft."

Rebecca recalled a large stained-glass window depicting a book lying in the grass under a peach tree that allowed filtered light upstairs, and consumed nearly an entire wall. So pretty. It had been designed by William Vallantine himself when the library had been erected for his wife Katherine.

"Oh, no. That one's in amazing shape and we wouldn't dream of changing it. It's a focal point, as Scarlett would say." Dorothy flipped a page. "Back to the porch. There're four steps, and it's not wheelchair accessible. We would like to add a ramp beside the stairs."

Forest glanced at the library, squinting. "I don't foresee that being an issue."

"Great." Dorothy pointed to the right of the building where there was a large grassy field. "We would like to add a concrete lot over there for cars and make these five spots here handicap parking. Not the whole acre, but about half. Per the contractor, it would allow for approximately ten to twenty vehicles."

Rebecca's gut tightened in anxiety as she proverbially crossed her fingers.

Forest slowly nodded, gazing in that direction. "Terrific idea. Currently, parking is minimal. You wouldn't be taking out any structures, elements, or trees in the process. Not to mention, it'll free up parking on the street for the shops. I'll sign off on that."

Okay, good. That was one of three things that they'd been worried about with regards to their plans. Relief filled Rebecca, her shoulders relaxing, and she winked at Dorothy as they exchanged a brief thank-the-Lord glance. Any major changes that weren't basic design features had to be approved by the Historical Society because the building and estate were landmarks. A parking lot was a huge change.

"Let's go around back." Dorothy tilted her head in that direction. "We can run through those plans."

They made their way around the side of the library, Rebecca's sneakers sinking into soft, plush green grass. Once behind the building, she crossed her arms and glanced around.

As girls, they'd not ventured into the backyard. If not for Scarlett and Dorothy sending her pictures before she'd moved home, Rebecca wouldn't have the foggiest idea what the grounds looked like. There was at least half an acre of knee-high grass and weeds between the library and the tree line at the very back of the estate. Lots of potential usable space, as Scarlett had noted in one of their Zooms.

Dorothy exchanged a worried glance with Rebecca. This part of their plans was concern two out of three with regards to changes they wanted to make. And it all hinged on what the Historical Society allowed.

"What we'd like to do back here," Dorothy hedged, "is add an addition to the building. The library itself is rather small. We have ideas on how to better use the space inside. However, it doesn't really account for tables, computer kiosks, or a sitting area. Which isn't helpful. People need a place to research or set their books, to sit and read."

Forest pressed his lips into a thin line. "Not sure that's gonna fly. What do you have in mind?"

Dorothy pulled out the plans. "So, the addition would be one-story, cover three-quarters of the grounds in back, and only be as wide as the current building. Ergo, you wouldn't see it from the road. We'd slant the roof to look like a natural element or wing, because some Colonials had those, plus the siding and shingles would match. Part of the current back wall would need to be knocked out to accommodate double doors into the wing."

Rebecca chewed the inside of her cheek and held her breath. Without approval for the addition, a good chunk of their plans would have to get refocused. They'd intended to put in tables with chairs on one side toward the front of the new wing, a casual sitting area with couches in back, and a kids' area in the remaining portion. They didn't have the funds for that part of the project, but Scarlett was going to front the money and just have the wing dedicated in the Taylor family name. She could afford it. She came from old money and her event business was booming.

"Sounds like it wouldn't detract from the original floorplan or architecture." Forest frowned and rubbed his jaw. "I'll have to take this to the Society and vote on it."

Rebecca let out an exhale. That wasn't an outright no.

"I thought you might say that." Dorothy smiled. "You can keep that copy for the Society. The backside of the blueprint has what materials we intend to use, right down to flooring, lighting, and wall color."

He nodded. "That'll help."

"I'm sorry. So sorry I'm late, y'all." Scarlett rushed toward them, red cocktail dress the same shade as her lipstick and heels. She had her sleek cocoa locks in a high ponytail that swung with her frantic baby steps as she maneuvered across the grass. Somehow, she made even that seem elegant. "Betty Lou Jorgensen has done changed her color scheme for her bridal shower this weekend three times in as many days. I swear, between her and her future mother-in-law, they have put me half in the grave. Bless their hearts. What did I miss?"

Forest huffed a laugh.

Dorothy sighed. "We went over the outside plans. I'll fill you in later."

"Perfect." Scarlett grinned, her excitement obvious as she was busting at the seams. She held up a key. "We ready to go in?"

"Yes, ma'am. After you."

"Now, Forest. Surely, I'm not old enough to be a ma'am." Head tilted, Scarlett's eyelashes created a wake.

He scratched the back of his head, expression contrite. "My mistake."

"Lordy." Rebecca rolled her eyes and steered Scarlett along the side of the building toward the front. "You know damn well it was ingrained respect, not an insult." Rebecca lowered her tone. "And why are you flirting with Forest Truman, of all people?" No matter how long ago, Dorothy had a thing for him. Or used to. Perhaps still did. Whatever. Besties didn't go after forbidden fruit.

Scarlett gasped. "I did not flirt with him."

Maybe not. She was social and outgoing to a fault. It was hard to tell with her.

Rebecca eyed her as they walked. "If you say so." She glanced over her shoulder, noting Forest and Dorothy were lagging a few steps behind and chatting amongst themselves. "The parking lot, porch ramp, roof, and siding are a go. He has to have the Society vote on the possible addition."

A wrinkle of her nose, and Scarlett all but skipped in place. "That's awesome."

"Word. Hopefully, the vote will go in our favor. Now, behave yourself."

"I am always on my best behavior."

Rebecca let out a sound of disbelief. "You don't have a best behavior."

"You love me anyway." Scarlett made a kissy face and climbed the porch steps, unlocking the library door.

Following her inside, Rebecca glanced around as Dorothy and Forest spread out paperwork on the ivory marble counter in the center of the room, where Mr. Brown used to sit.

It had been eons since Rebecca had seen the place, but fondness squeezed her throat. This wonderful, wonderful building had been their refuge as girls. They'd sit and read, gossip, and make plans for the future. It's where she'd daydreamed about working for a newspaper, all the stories she'd report. The boys who'd captured and broken their hearts. The library was worse off than she'd recalled, yet they'd fix it. Restore it to its former glory and do right by it. She closed her eyes a brief beat, smiling. Gosh, it smelled the same, though. Aged paper, old wood, and a trace of dust.

Square footage on the main level was roughly twenty-five hundred square feet, and about half that for the second story loft. Wide-open floor plan. A wrought iron set of curved stairs led to the upper area with a matching railing. The top portion of the large stained-glass window could be spotted below. The loft otherwise was empty. Had been for a long time. The ceiling was coffered with copper plating. The floorboards were original cherry. Wall-to-wall, floor-to-ceiling bookcases lined the left, right, and part of the back wall. Empty now, which made her sad. Dorothy said many of the books were in a storage room in back. Mr. and Mrs. Brown had only taken the family volumes with them. Still, there was nothing more heartbreaking than a vacant bookshelf.

There was an errant scent of dust and mildew that stung her sinuses. A testament to time marching on and taking no prisoners. They'd freshen that up, too.

"Alright," Dorothy said through a sigh. "The floorboards needed refinishing two decades ago. That's on the docket." She glanced up. An enormous lead-glass chandelier overhead had cobwebs forming their own cobwebs. "The chandelier is original, and we intend to keep it, just have it cleaned. Same for the copper plating. Plumbing and electrical haven't been updated since the turn of the twentieth century. Electricians are going to switch the fuse box with a circuit breaker and add more outlets. We also have cable providers coming in to hardwire ethernet cables for internet. Plumbers plan to replace several pipes, plus the bathroom is getting remodeled. We'll keep the original tile."

Forest surveyed the papers. "Sounds fine by me."

"Here's where things get tricky. To add heat and AC, they'll have to run ductwork in the crawl space, then cut out spaces in the floor for vents." Dorothy eyed him, worry creasing her brow.

It would suck if they couldn't upgrade. The library had never had heating or AC. Rebecca watched him closely as he scanned the blueprints on where vents would go per the contractor.

"Honestly," he said at length, "I don't see this being a prob-lem, either. Visitors are going to be more comfortable, and the vent placements aren't looking like they'll screw with anything. If I may offer a suggestion? I'd consider old-fashioned vent cov-ers to fit with the period."

Scarlett set her hands on her hips, nodding approval. "I like it. Good idea."

Dorothy shuffled some papers. "Chunks of plaster are miss-ing from many areas in the walls upstairs. The contractor said he can fix that, or at least fit drywall to blend. However, the Greek support columns for the loft are possibly unstable."

Yeah. One of them slanted precariously to the left. Rebecca gave it a look since she'd only seen photos. There were two columns holding up the overhang of the loft that resembled the ones on the porch. Beyond them was the back wall shelving, where the couch they used to hang out on as teenagers had been removed. She always thought of it as a cozy nook.

Forest frowned in thought. "What are you thinking?"

"Complete replacement." Dorothy crossed her arms. "We can try to match what's currently there, but it won't be exact."

"Okay, just so long as you don't use metal poles or something that'll throw off the design. I mean, the place has to be structurally sound, so go ahead."

Rebecca shuffled her feet. "Sheldon Brown's great-grandmother carved her name on one of the columns when she was a girl. It's been painted over, but you can still see traces of the knife indentations. We were thinking of cutting that out and framing it somewhere."

"Didn't know that." He rubbed his jaw. "If I'm on the Historical Society and wasn't aware, I'll bet others don't. Regardless, I like the idea of framing that part of the library's past."

That was a huge relief. Rebecca shared a look with Scarlett, who appeared just as grateful the columns wouldn't be a problem. All issues had been addressed but one, and it was a biggie.

"Last but not least." Dorothy cleared her throat. "Lighting is sparce. As it stands, the chandelier is the only source, minus the storeroom and bathroom. We'd like to add recessed lighting here, here, here, and here." On the blueprints, she pointed to the four areas they'd discussed by Zoom, which were under the loft overhang, two in the loft itself, and two along both the right and left walls by the built-in shelves. "Recessed lighting doesn't fit with the architecture, but it would be the least invasive, offer the most light, and is cost-effective for us."

"Eesh." His nostrils flared as he inhaled. "Not sure on that one." He tapped his fingers on the counter. "I'll bring it to the Society for a vote. Could go either way. On the one hand, you don't want it too dark in here, but on the other, it has to fit the style."

Scarlett snapped her fingers, an aha expression lifting her brows. "What if we add a ceiling medallion design plate around each light? It'll give the period appearance, yet still allow for the fixtures. It would mesh well with the copper plating, too."

Rebecca metaphorically patted Scarlett on the back. The idea was brilliant. They could get medallions at any home improvement store for little money. Plus, it was a win-win for them and the Society.

"Okay, that might sway the vote." He jotted what she assumed were some notes on his copy of the packet. "That should do it. I have one question, though, not related to your plans." He grinned, carefree and child-like. "Is the library really haunted?"

Scarlett threw her head back and laughed.

Rebecca shook her head, amused. Legend was, Katherine Vallantine loved books. It was why her beloved husband had built the library for her in the first place. Somehow, through the years, word got around she haunted the place after she'd died, that she assisted all who entered seeking knowledge. Rebecca and her besties had never encountered such a spirit, but Mrs. Brown had mentioned once that Katherine's journal had appeared out of nowhere to her and Mr. Brown before they'd married. Anything was possible.

"I doubt it." Dorothy slid paperwork back into a folder.

"Oh, come now." Scarlett placed a hand on her chest, laughter residing. "You never know."

They saw Forest out and locked the door. Dorothy and Scarlett had to get back to work, which reminded Rebecca of her next task. She had to bite the bullet.

Once everyone had gone, she glanced at her reflection in her car window. She'd worn light makeup, her hair down, and a lavender blouse with khaki capris. Casual but nice. It would have to do.

A sigh, and she grabbed her portfolio from the passenger seat, then headed down Main Street on foot. Gammy's house didn't have a mortgage, but there were bills piling up. It was time she got herself a job.

# Chapter Four

Graham leaned back in the chair in his office, gaze on the computer screen in front of him displaying a spreadsheet with numbers. It wasn't looking any better than it had the last twenty times he'd glared at them, but something had to be done. Perhaps an idea would light a bulb over his head if he stared long enough. He was just desperate enough to try anything.

Six months. That's how long Gunner Davis, town mayor and owner of the Vallantine Gazette, had given Graham to turn things around for the paper. Subscriptions were down, advertising near zilch, and the newspaper could barely eke out one page of material a day. His whopping two-person staff team consisted of Joan Hornady and Jefferson McCraw. The former did a gossip or opinion column and pulled the Atlanta weather report. She was a baby boomer who spent most of the day at her desk scrolling Facebook. The latter handled sports and sometimes local news if there was anything noteworthy. Which wasn't often. He was in his seventies and often napped the entire afternoon. Both were part-timers.

Graham had no idea what he was paying them for, but firing the entire staff after two months on the job wasn't going to earn him any friends.

A sigh, and he glared at the ceiling. He wasn't good at this kind of crap. Managing? Sure. Writing a good story? Yep. Editing? Absolutely. Marketing, building subscribers, and fixing what he feared was a permanently damaged system in a small southern town of twenty-five hundred residents? Not so much.

Acid ate away at the lining of his stomach. If he failed, he had nowhere else to go. There wasn't a newspaper or blog in the fifty states that would hire him after the scandal that got him canned in Minneapolis.

A jingle indicated someone had opened the outside door to Main Street. Probably Joan heading out for a smoke break. Again. He didn't bother checking.

But then a newly familiar voice lilted from the front of the room toward him instead of silence.

The wall in his office in back facing the newsroom was glass. On the other side were six desks, two of them occupied by Joan and Jefferson. Rebecca Moore stood in the aisle between them, chatting with both people.

Honestly, until she walked in, Graham would've sworn on his mother's life that Jefferson was incapable of cracking a smile. The elder black man showed up for work three days a week in pressed slacks and a button-down short-sleeved shirt, nodded hello, then parked it in his chair. He was straight-up old school. Alas, he was not only grinning, but engaged readily in conversation. Most Graham had gotten out of him were one word replies.

Joan, who arrived for work in tracksuits of varying colors, warpaint resembling a clown, and bottle brunette hair teased like 1980's Texas, often wouldn't quit yammering once he got her going. Anything from nail polish color to her grandkids' names or hobbies. Thus, he tried hard not to start anything he couldn't or wouldn't finish. Whatever she was telling Rebecca had her animated, hands flailing, and a polite smile from her avid listener.

His heart did some kind of shift. Perhaps started beating again, he didn't know, but Rebecca was lovely. The classic kind that didn't require artificial help. Sunlight from the big bay window storefront lit her blonde strands and created a halo around her form. The term *angel* came to mind, but her feisty attitude toward him didn't fit the adage. That, or he was finally losing his gourd if he thought seraphs were coming down from On High.

She shifted the strap for a portfolio bag on her shoulder, patting Jefferson's arm as she passed to walk Graham's way.

Her stride resembled her personality. Strong. With purpose. Confident. About halfway to his office, she lifted her gaze to his, and her steps faltered. Confusion wrinkled her forehead as she moved slower. Once she reached the doorway, she looked at the nameplate beside the door, then at him, then at the plate again. A close of her eyes, and she dropped her chin, sighing.

He wanted to laugh. Badly. Guess she'd been unaware he was the new editor. "Hello, Rebecca."

"Mr. Roberts." She stared at him, deadpan.

He smiled. Not a difficult feat, yet it still felt foreign to his cheeks. "You can call me Graham. We're neighbors, after all."

"I suppose we are. Graham, then. Do you have a moment?"

For her? He had all day. "Of course. Come in. Have a seat."

She claimed one of the black leather chairs across from his desk and set the bag in her lap, looking around. Her gaze traveled over the diplomas and framed articles on the brick wall behind him, then at the tall black shelving units on the walls beside him where he had books and trinkets of his life.

"What can I do for you today?" After his conversation with Forest the other night, Graham figured he knew what had spurred the visit, but he'd learned not to assume.

"I'm looking for a job." She opened her portfolio and passed him a folder. "That's my résumé, references, and letters of recommendation."

Her accent had shifted from the drawl in the bar when she'd been pissed off at him to barely a trace of her southern lilt. And her tone was coolly polite. Pity. He preferred the sass.

"Let's have a look." He'd been itching to know more about her, if he was being honest.

He glanced briefly at her deets. She'd been a reporter at her college paper for three years. Graduated in the top tenth percentile of her class with a journalism degree. She'd gone right from school to the Boston newspaper, where it appeared she'd remained until a few weeks ago. Again, he had to wonder why she wanted to shift from a huge print syndicate in a large city to a small press in an even smaller town. His position required him to be careful in asking.

"Why did you leave your previous position?" There. A common inquiry.

"It wasn't a good fit for me, and I was looking for a change."

A very practiced reply and proved she knew her way around professionalism. Most people around these parts interviewed like they were dining with kin and discussing the grapevine. "You were there almost seven years. Why wasn't it a good fit?"

A swallow worked her delicate throat as she glanced at her lap. A few beats passed before she inhaled and met his gaze with her blue one as if shoring her reserve. Like a cobalt sky in fall, her eyes. "There was really no room for advancement."

Another practiced reply.

Frustrated, because he wanted candidness, he looked at her file again. "What was your position in Boston?" Her résumé only stated the dates employed.

She offered a slow blink, and when she looked at him, it was through him instead. Defeat turned the corners of her lips downward. "Obituaries. Sometimes, they had me play with ad space if someone was on vacation."

Oh. That seemed almost insulting to her skill set. No wonder she was upset and wanting a change. Everyone had to start somewhere, but after six years, she should've been promoted.

"Do you have examples of your writing?" Maybe she wasn't very good. He doubted that, though.

She extracted another file and passed it to him.

The articles from her college years were everything from political commentary to security issues on campus to protest movements she'd covered. He scanned one article just to get a gist for her style, and liked it. A lot. She was to the point, backed up her words, but it read like a conversation over whiskey by a fire. Very inviting. She'd obviously found and knew her voice. Some journalists took half a decade to figure out theirs. Her example at the Boston paper was one article on a prominent art gallery owner who'd passed away. The other was a copy image of the obituary section.

"I assume you didn't care for your role and level in Boston? Did you try to submit other stories?"

"My first few years, yes. After that, it was apparent they preferred me where I was, and I got overlooked for other positions I applied to."

He wasn't sure what to make of that. She had talent and a good eye. If he got to know her better, perhaps she'd share more details, but for now, he moved on.

Resting his forearms on the desk, he leaned forward. "What are you hoping to work on here if we employ you? Are you seeking full, part time, or consignment?"

Her gaze darted to his desk, expression flat. "I prefer full time, but will accept whatever you have available, including any positions that are open."

Damn, but he despised this version of her. Someone, probably former employees or bosses, had beaten the spunk out of her and left her professionally dejected. Brimming under the surface was talent and, he hoped, some of that resolve she'd left Vallantine to pursue. No one exited small town America for a huge city seeking mediocrity. He searched for a way to bring out that backbone he'd witnessed in their previous encounters.

"And what if the only position available is a receptionist?"

Again, she closed her eyes in a leisure blink, the thick fan of her lashes creating shadows on her cheeks, as she appeared to gain control of her emotions. The quiver of her lower lip indicated she was wrangling the urge to cry. "Whatever openings you have are fine."

He didn't know whether to weep himself or take her by the shoulders and shake her. He'd be damned if he was going to be another person on a long list to stomp on her, though, so he leaned back in his seat and tried brutal honesty.

"The Gazette is failing."

Her gaze whipped to his, wide, but she said nothing.

He nodded, rising to close the door, then reclaimed his chair. "Gunner Davis hired me to fix it, or he was going to stop print for good. Apparently, it hasn't been in the black for a decade. Only reason he hasn't quit before is because the paper's been a long-standing staple for seventy-five years. I have six months, four now, to bring it back to life." Exhaling, he scrubbed his hands over his face and looked at her. "I inherited those two out there," he pointed to Joan and Jefferson, "but they have little more interest than what they're doing, and offered no suggestions. You're the first person to walk through that door at all, never mind with experience. I'm a journalist turned editor, not a marketing guru."

Chewing her lower lip, she stared at him, contemplation in her eyes. "I can't imagine Vallantine without the Gazette."

Gunner Davis had mentioned something along the same lines.

"You have more to say." It was obvious by the way she'd scooted to the edge of her seat. "What's on your mind?"

Her pretty, perfect, pouty mouth opened and closed several times before she shook her head and dug in her bag. She set a copy of today's paper on his desk. "It's only two pages."

"Yep."

"It's mostly filler content."

"Yep."

Her eyes narrowed. "Can I speak frankly?"

Finally, they were getting somewhere. "Yep."

"Running a small town paper is different than a metropolis. Especially in the south. It has to be a mix of personal and informative, catering to the clientele. All the info here," she tapped the paper, "is something anyone with a phone can Google, so why pay for the news? Times are tough right now, also, between the economy and hits from the pandemic. The Gazette needs better stories, better access, and better reach. Not to mention revenue."

Heck yeah. There she was, the woman he'd met outside their homes and in the bar. The feisty, speak her mind, hot as hell blonde who didn't back down.

She snapped upright. "Why are you smiling at me?"

Despite better judgement, he chuckled and scratched his jaw. "I like this version of Rebecca better. Plus, you're right. Any ideas on how to go about what you suggested?"

She gave him a speculative glare. "First and foremost, the tourism market should be considered when doing content. Strategic marketing and placement of the paper, to boot. The Gazette doesn't have social media accounts, nor does it have an e-print version."

Steepling his fingers, he grinned. "What else?"

Deadpan stare. "Am I hired?"

She had the job before she'd walked into his office. "I can't offer the salary you were making in Boston."

"Okay."

"Nor can I assure job security with the state of the paper now."

"Okay."

"You might be doing work you don't like some of the time instead of the hard-hitting journalism you prefer."

"Okay."

Yeah, he figured she knew all of that, but it needed to be said. "What are your terms?"

"Full time, two weeks paid vacation a year, five sick days, salary versus hourly pay, access to the archives, and permission to work on what stories I want, within reason."

She'd come prepared. His grin widened to the point his cheeks ached. "Done."

"If you hire me, I will help you get this paper back to something great again, but it'll require you trusting me. Some methods may seem unorthodox."

"Done."

Fifteen minutes in the same room with her talking shop, and he had zero doubt she'd deliver. She had her pulse on the community and knew her way around a newsroom. It appeared her particular skill set was marketing, which was his weakest point. They'd be a good counterbalance.

"To make money, you might have to spend money."

He jutted his chin. Gunner had given Graham an allowance, of which he had yet to use. Frankly, he'd had no clue how to go about utilizing funds in order to help the Gazette thrive. He hadn't even written half the articles or implemented the changes he'd contrived because they had no reader base.

"I'll agree, if you stick to a budget."

"Okay." She cleared her throat. "I would suggest switching Joan and Jefferson from part time to consignment. It'll save money. There's no reason the two of us can't handle things. Consignment would be a happy median as opposed to laying them off. You also might want to get more specific in what stories you want from them to justify the expense, make sure you're getting solid articles that are worth it and not fluff filler."

He hadn't officially hired her yet, and they were already on the same track. "What would you recommend? Story-wise?"

She set her gaze on the ceiling, lips pursed in thought. "Joan does mostly opinion pieces. I'd perhaps have her do a restaurant or product critique twice a week. It would spotlight businesses and shops while serving our purpose."

His brows rose. "Damn good idea."

"Thanks. As for Jefferson, he solely writes about sports, but all he really does is a condensed version of a game wrap up. We can add a section to the paper for professional Georgia team scores that'll take zero time, eliminating his position. However, why not highlight the local middle and high school sports? Possibly a few state colleges. It'll tie in with the community and give him something unique to write about while engaging the town."

Nodding, he wondered where she'd been the past couple months while he'd been floundering. She'd just added two to four new sections to the paper without hiring fresh staff, ones that would engage or interest the town. Not to mention... Brains were sexy. "Excellent idea again. I'll discuss it with both of them this afternoon. They can finish out the week, and I'll move them to consignment."

She politely nodded, but in her eyes, hope bloomed.

"What else?" he prompted.

"Lots of things, but they're fluid ideas."

Evasive little minx. "Such as?"

She studied his features as if searching for a chink in his personality. "Am I hired?"

God save him. "Absolutely. When can you start?"

She grinned slowly, and it nearly leveled his kingdom in three seconds flat. "Yesterday."

A laugh, and he swiveled in his chair to a file cabinet. He passed her a packet of new hire paperwork. "Go ahead and fill this out, please. I'll get a laptop set up for you while you're working on it."

Clicking her pen, she used the edge of his desk to write.

He went to the closet in the newsroom, grabbing one of three laptops left, and reclaimed the chair in his office. When Gunner had hired him, it was one of the few requests Graham had made of his boss was to supply new equipment. Four of the six desks up front had new computers. The other two were empty. Seemed an awful waste of space in his opinion.

"With just the two of us in the office most days, what do you think about the newsroom?"

She didn't look up from her task. "I have ideas."

Of course, she did. He'd bet her mind kept clacking even while asleep. They'd get into it later.

He focused on making sure programs were installed for her, created an email address under the Gazette's account, and passed her the laptop to plug in a password.

"I'll need access to the website server." She gave him back the laptop. "It needs updating. I'll ask permission before doing anything."

She just jumped right in, didn't she? What a relief. "You got it. Installing now."

Setting her paperwork aside, she leaned back in her seat. "Do we have a list of emails for current and former subscribers?"

"Yes." He'd planned on doing an e-print version of the Gazette before she'd suggested it, but with content as it stood, it hadn't been worth it yet. "It's in a csv file. I'll put it on your desktop." He tapped a few keys, then inserted a thumb drive. "Done. What else?"

"Where are the physical archives?"

"Upstairs." There was a small storage space above the newsroom. He hadn't been up there since his interview. "Why?"

She looked over her shoulder at the newsroom. "Why wait? Gunner gave you six months, and if you're down to four, we should get going."

It would kind of help to know what she had in mind, but at this point, whatever ideas she had floating around couldn't be worse than how things currently stood.

A nod, and he rose. He stuck his head out his office door, sending Joan and Jefferson home for the day. He'd discuss consignment with them tomorrow instead.

Once they'd left, he crossed his arms. "Okay, Obi-Wan. I'm all yours." Newspaper run files for tomorrow were already at the printers, so he had nothing else pressing.

She smiled at the nickname and stood, setting her bag on the chair, then strolled into the newsroom. She locked the door, flipped the sign to Closed, and eyed the room once again.

He followed, waiting on her. Sadly, this was the most exciting day he'd had in the office since he'd moved to Vallantine.

The room was divided into two sides, three desks on each. There were two empty chairs up front. That was about it, besides a small closet and the unisex half bathroom. The walls were old brick, which he found neat, but they were bare, and the floor was a solid ivory tile pattern. Overall, it was roughly a thousand square feet. The big bay front window had a large sill and room for displays, but nothing was there. Just as it had been when he'd started the job.

After an excruciatingly long pause, she made a humming noise in her throat. "Can we look upstairs?"

He huffed a laugh. "Sure."

The door to the second floor was in his office, so they back-tracked. He pulled the keys from his desk, unlocked the door, and flipped on a light.

He gestured for her to go first. "After you."

The staircase was narrow and steep with dull lighting, making it seem grungy.

Once at the top, she set her hands on her hips, eyes wide. "Holy crap."

Following her gaze, he grunted, using the switch on the wall to turn on the fluorescent overheads. "Yeah."

One large open space. Wooden floorboards. Unfinished walls. Low seven-foot ceilings. Rafter beams. A thousand years of dust. Boxes were stacked in haphazard piles along the street-facing wall, and mismatched furniture pieces toward the back.

She made her way to the boxes, crouching to examine them. "These go back to 1948? The first year in print?"

"Yes, and I don't know what you're thinking, but they're more organized than they look. There are dates written on the boxes, and from what Gunner says, there's one copy of each paper since first run. He had someone come in ages ago to sort them. I have a box in my office that has copies since I was hired."

"So much history," she whispered. "This is amazing. The library didn't keep files of the Vallantine Gazette. Which can work to our favor."

He didn't see how.

She shifted to the other side of the room, looking at the furniture. A few desks, one of them a tall podium counter. A couple wingback chairs. A bureau. There was a glass display case and a few bookshelves. At one point, the newsroom must've been set up with cubicles because there were divider walls in varying heights, folded and leaning against several large empty poster frames.

The weird thing? There was a huge birdcage, which she paused in front of, smiling.

"When I was a little girl, Mr. Forester, the old editor, had a yellow canary he'd keep in this cage in the display window. His name was Plucky, and everyone loved him. He became this strange sort of staple to the town. Even tourists would stop by the window to say hello." She laughed. "He'd chirp when the door opened."

Interesting. "We should do that again. Get another bird." They were noisy and he didn't care for them, but if ole Plucky had been that memorable, why not?

She set her gaze on him, and there it was again. That click between them, like time had narrowed through a vacuum. Nostalgia softened her otherwise determined features, a gentle smile curving her lips. If he wasn't mistaken, respect shone in her eyes as if he'd done something worthy to warrant it.

"I love that." She looked at the cage again, rapidly blinking. "We should get another Plucky."

He nodded, unable to do much else. These rare moments where she exposed her tender underbelly were enough to punch the wind from his lungs.

A sigh, and she brushed her hands together. "Ready to hear my ideas?"

# Chapter Five

A few hours later, Rebecca was amped to start the changes. They'd brought down the birdcage, sections of cubicles, a podium desk, two bookshelves, and very precariously, the glass display cabinet. Her body was protesting the physical activity, causing her neck and shoulders to become more than her typical achy. While Graham had been distracted with cleaning the podium, she'd popped a couple over the counter pain relievers and did a quick stretch. She'd take a hot bath tonight.

The amp in stiffness was worth it. Not only had Graham been good with all of her ideas, but he'd given her high praise every chance he could.

For years, she'd gone to work at the Boston paper, at a tiny corner station, doing little more than taking up space. Half the journalists thought she'd been an assistant and had asked her to fetch coffee if she hadn't been at her desk. No name for herself. No one who'd considered her story ideas. No one who'd given her a chance.

Thirty minutes in Graham's office, while applying for a job, *any* job, and he'd not only listened to her suggestions, but had blindly allowed them. It seemed like he'd simply needed fresh concepts and a set of eyes to get out of his rut. His success in revamping the Gazette would be hers, too.

He glanced around at the furniture they'd brought down from the storeroom. "Where do we start?"

Bless the man, he could take direction.

"Let's get the reporter sections up first. We'll know how much room we'll have to work with once that's done."

"You got it."

Together, they moved stuff out of the way. The plan had been to set up two desks along the glass wall to Graham's office, one on each side, facing front, and separate them from the rest of the newsroom with the four-foot cubicle sections. A desk for her, and one for Joan and Jefferson to share if they ever came into the office, which wouldn't be often if they were switching to consignment.

After playing around with design, they opted for a bookshelf along the brick wall per each cubicle flanking Graham's office door, a desk beside them. That way the reporters had a place to put materials. While she moved Joan and Jefferson's things from their old desks to their bookshelf, Graham attached their nameplates to the outer corner of their cubicle wall.

"I'll get a nameplate made up for you tomorrow."

"I have one, but thank you." She hauled a computer monitor from Joan's old desk to the new one. "I'll bring my things in the morning."

"Okay. I'll get you a key, too." Following her lead, he began connecting the tower cables to complete their setup. "You've got a laptop, but we'll put Jefferson's computer on your side so you can work from that while here. We'll move files and programs tomorrow."

Fine by her. She rolled her head to stretch her neck. Damn, but she hurt.

"You okay?"

She hadn't realized he'd been watching her. Though her condition wasn't serious, he should probably know about it as her boss. She wasn't ready to get into it, though.

"I'm fine, thanks."

While he was preoccupied setting up, she tried to formulate a plan for their next step, but wound up pausing on him to admire the view. He was good-looking, for sure. He'd shed his suitcoat and tie when they'd begun moving furniture, and had rolled up the sleeves of his white dress shirt. Great arms. All sinew and coiled tendons. Veins. Tanned, olive-colored skin. Huge hands. She'd bet her right leg he knew how to use those hands. Since he was hunched under the desk, the dark gray suit pants were stretched taut over his very nice backside. Lean waist. Wide shoulders.

*Quit, girl. Now.*

Suppressing a sigh, she fanned her face, suddenly hot. And not from her fibromyalgia. Attraction shifted as if by warning in her belly. Not good. He was her new boss and next door neighbor. If there was ever a need for caution, this was it.

She'd not had a very good impression of him after their first couple of encounters, but she was warming up to him. After all, he'd apologized and had not only given her a job, but had been open to suggestions for change. It took a man comfortable in his own skin to do both. He had yet to call the Boss Card or make her feel like a subordinate. He didn't throw his power around, either.

Didn't mean she should ogle him like candy.

"What do you think?"

She shook her head to clear it. She hadn't realized he'd finished hooking up the computer, or that he'd been talking.

"I was lost in thought." Or naughty daydreams. "Sorry. Could you repeat?"

He flashed a grin, darn him. "I do that, too. Go off in my head. Must be a writer thing."

Uh huh. It was, but there was no need to embarrass herself farther by telling him that hadn't been the situation just now.

"I was saying, I think the glass display case would look good in front of the high podium desk over there." He pointed to the wall to the left of the bay window.

It was a good corner for it, yes.

"Agree." The plan was to put older newspapers in the display case in plastic to preserve them and show off the Gazette's history to visitors. A mini-museum. He'd loved the idea. A cash register would go on the podium to check out customers. "Instead of buying a register, though, we can just get a program for one of the existing computers. It'll save money."

"Good thinking. I'll look into it tomorrow." He eyed the cluster of desks in the middle of the room. "How do you want to arrange the prints? I'm not understanding your vision."

Now that they'd set up the reporter cubicles, her tentative fengshui needed refocusing. The space was slightly smaller than she'd envisioned. Upstairs earlier, she'd had the idea to copy older newspaper articles and sell them as page prints to visitors. They could go as-is in scrapbooks or be matted and framed. Souvenirs for tourists or memorabilia for townsfolk. It wouldn't rake in a lot of dough for the Gazette, but it would be additional income and bring people inside. Get them interested.

She frowned. "Not sure."

"Let's move the podium and display case. Go from there."

They did what he suggested, engaging in small talk.

Furniture in place, he straightened. "So, you were raised by your grandmother?"

It was the first instance he'd asked something personal, and after a brief pause, she realized she didn't mind. He wasn't from Vallantine, but it was a small town. There was no need to keep up her defensive walls. She was home. Easier said than done, though. She'd been in a big city too long if that sort of question tripped her meter.

"Forget I asked." He waved his hand. "It's none of my business."

"No, no. It's okay." She stretched her arms over her head to loosen her back. The display case was heavy. "Yes, my grandmother raised me after my folks passed away. She's my dad's mom." She blinked, her throat suddenly tight. "Was, I mean. She *was* Dad's mother." It felt so wrong using Gammy in past tense.

Genuine sympathy turned the edges of his eyes down and tightened his lips. "Damn, that sucks. I'm sorry. How old were you when they died?"

Since his question and tone were non-abrasive nor intrusive, she didn't hesitate in answering. "I was eight. It was a car wreck."

A slight shake of his head. "That must've been horrible."

"It was, but I had Gammy." Not anymore. She was gone. Tears burned her eyes, and she glanced away, focusing on something else. Anything else.

"Do you have any other family?" His rough timbre skated across her skin from several feet away, but his irrevocably kind tone wrapped her in a hug.

She almost lost it, but then she processed his question and swallowed the hurt. "No, but I have my besties."

His green eyes lit with a smile, crinkling the corners. A dimple appeared through the scruff on his cheek. "The Bookish Belles."

She laughed. How, she hadn't a clue. "Yeah. Known them since birth."

He nodded, running a hand through his midnight strands. "Friends make the best family because you get to pick them yourselves."

What a lovely sentiment. "Exactly."

"Forest and I met the first day of college. We got paired as roommates. Been close ever since." Fondness laced his tone and radiated in his eyes.

"He's a good guy. Is that how you wound up in Vallantine?"

All good humor drained from his features. "For the most part." He puffed his cheeks and blew out his breath, glancing elsewhere. "What next, Obi-Wan?"

Not sure what caused the shift, she looked at the remaining furniture. She'd maybe ask him later. "I think we should put the wingback chairs from upstairs in the corner." She pointed to the opposite end from the display case, to the right of the front door. The chairs were a pretty navy pattern and in good shape. They'd just need a fabric refresher spray and dusting. "It'll balance the room and give people a place to sit. We can put the end table from upstairs between them."

He offered a thumbs-up. "I'll go get 'em."

While he was gone, she thought about space and how to display the prints. Considering the history and how far back the paper went, they'd need a lot of shelves, which seemed a waste of money. Plus, shelves would offer no support. They had four remaining desks, though. There had to be something they could do, aside from framing the print copies.

Graham came back with a chair, a box of newspapers on the seat.

And it hit her... "Comic boxes."

"Huh?" He set the chair down, moving the box to a desk.

"I had a boyfriend in college who collected comic books. He put them in plastic sleeves to protect them, then into comic boxes. They're like filing boxes, sort of, and you can put dividers in them. What if we arranged the desks, two on each side, and put the prints in sleeves in comic boxes on the desks?"

He straightened, hands on his hips. "That'll work. We can label the outside of the boxes with specific years, and put dividers in for easy access to find prints. It leaves the center of the room pretty open, however."

"True." They'd need something short that they could show-case prints, yet not be imposing to the space. Perhaps put a few copies in frames already. "The library used to have a couple of those magazine rack stands. About five feet high. I wonder if they're still there. We could put them back to back, right in the middle of the room."

He mumbled something to the tune of "good idea" as she pulled her phone from her pocket. She thumbed a text in her group chat with Scarlett and Dorothy.

*Do we still have those magazine rack stands in library stor-age? If so, can I steal them? BTW, I got a job at The Vallantine Gazette!!!*

Scarlett: *OMG! Grats! Yes. There are 2 shelves. IDC if you steal them. Thief.*

Dorothy's text came a second later. *Congratulations. They're lucky to have you. Go ahead and take the shelves. Don't think we were gonna use them. We can always buy more if we want later. No biggie.*

Rebecca shot them a *thank-you*, then looked at Graham. "Yep, two shelves. They won't fit in my car, though."

"Lemme try Forest. They probably won't fit in my car, either. He has a truck."

While waiting for a reply, they moved the remaining four desks to the outer walls, two on each side. They'd need table-cloths to look nice, but that was simple and inexpensive to fix.

His phone chimed, and while he texted back, she eyed the vacant brick walls. There were a lot of poster-size black frames upstairs. Gears started turning in her mind.

"Forest said he can meet you at the library at 5:15." He glanced at his watch. "Which is in an hour."

63

"Okay, I'll go run errands for stuff here and meet up with him. Can you do a couple things to save time while I'm gone?"

"I gotta run home to feed the dog, but that won't take long. Sure. Whatcha got?"

He had two industrial copy printers in his office. "Do your printers go larger than standard page? And is there paper that size?"

"Yes and yes."

She rolled through the contents of upstairs in her mind. "Maybe bring down the frames and a few of the oldest archive boxes? Find a few papers that have good front pages and print them to poster size to fit the frames. We can hang them on the walls. Would that be all right?"

He reared, then turned to glance behind him. "You're just full of great ideas. I'll start on it as soon as I get back."

"Thanks." She headed toward his office to grab her things when something dawned on her. "We can pick this up tomorrow if you prefer? I hate to keep you from plans." Just because she didn't have anything going on didn't mean he didn't. Not to mention, they'd be staying way past business hours.

"I'm good. Do you like dogs and pizza?"

Confusion had her freezing in place. "At the same time?"

Rubbing his eyes, he laughed. "I can pick up a pizza for dinner, and do you mind if I bring my dog with me?"

"Oh." She laughed, suddenly nervous. Which was stupid. They'd spent the afternoon working in harmony. "Both are fine."

He removed a wallet from his back pocket and held out a credit card. "For expenses on your errands. If it's for work, charge it. What do you like on your pizza?"

"Anything but dead fish."

Another laugh. Rich and from the gut. She was beginning to like the sound. Warm, hearty.

"No anchovies. Got it."

She walked back to the library to fetch her car, then drove to Scarlett's to grab the library key from her.

Once back in town, Rebecca stopped at the small hardware store to copy the key for her and Dorothy, and buy a few hooks, nails, and a hammer.

There was a thrift shop next door she hadn't been to since she'd been in college. Why not? She might find something useful.

Shrugging, she set the hardware store bag in her car and popped into Twice But Nice thrift shop. The owner, an elder woman Rebecca recognized, but couldn't recall her name, was busy at the register, so Rebecca just waved.

The scents of dust and time immediately hit her as she took in shelves of mismatched items. A lot seemed like junk, but to each their own. They did have quite a few eight-by-ten photo frames that would serve to house the Gazette's prints they would try to sell. She kept going, around the other side of the second aisle, and there was an old typewriter. Teal in color with pop keys. It was awesome.

"That doesn't work, dear."

"Oh." Rebecca whirled toward the owner. The woman only came to Rebecca's shoulders, but she'd managed to sneak up on her. "I didn't see you there."

"Sorry for the startle. I've had that typewriter here for years. No one uses them anymore. It's all about phones and computers and gadgets. Crying shame, if you ask me. Listen to me, carrying on. Anywho, it doesn't work."

Rebecca glanced at the typewriter again. It was a lovely old piece, and she didn't need it to function for what she had planned. The price sticker said five bucks.

"Sold."

The owner tilted her head, short white strands not shifting the slightest. "You certain, dear?"

"Yes, ma'am. I'd also like to take a lot of those photo frames off your hands."

"Alrighty."

Rebecca brought the typewriter to the counter, then went back for an armful of the frames. They were only a dollar and they'd be very useful.

The owner rang up the purchases and offered Rebecca a box. "Thank you, kindly. Have a blessed day. Please come back soon."

"I certainly will." She turned to leave. "Oh." She whirled around. "Is that pet shop still over by the café'?"

"Bark & Beyond? Yessiree. Clive's grandson runs the place now."

"Thank you again."

Rebecca put the thrift shop box in her car and headed down Main, turning onto a side street and parking. Uncommon Comics had odd hours since most of their sales were online, but she'd caught them while open. She didn't know the clerk and he didn't appear interested in her. She bought six plain white comic boxes, and two packs each of what they called bags and boards. Essentially, white carboard inserts for support and sleeves for the pages.

From there, she met Forest at the library, helped him get the magazine racks in the truck, and thanked him profusely.

The pet store was closed by the time she got back that way, which was disappointing, but she'd pop in tomorrow morning before going to the office. The little party supply store next door was still open for another thirty minutes, however, so she stopped to buy tablecloths in a navy color that would closely match the wingback chairs.

Satisfied, and giddy, she drove back to the Gazette, parking in the alley behind the building. It had been so very long since she'd had purpose or felt like she'd been useful that she almost didn't recognize the bubbles in her belly. The Gazette had been a noteworthy addition to Vallantine since long before she'd been born. She'd watched its decline slowly through the years, and it had broken her heart. Utilizing newsroom space for a shop and bringing alive its history would hopefully return the newspaper to its former glory, and get townsfolk interested again. That, and the changes to the print itself.

Between remodeling the library, a dream of hers, and getting onboard at the Gazette, her mind was whirling with possibilities. Mostly, if she were being honest with herself, it was the fact she was no longer invisible that had hope blooming in her chest. For years, she'd been an unrecognizable face among the fray. Idle. Stagnant. Just one woman in a city of thousands. Vallantine may not be where she'd envisioned herself as a girl, but she'd adapt. There was more than one way to leave an imprint on the world.

Forest and Graham had brought in the magazine racks by the time she got inside. She found them eating pizza in Graham's office, feet kicked up on the desk.

At the close of the back door, a dog lying by Graham's shelf jumped to attention, rushing to examine Rebecca. She bent to pet his soft fur, talking gibberish. He was quite cute. Adoring, trusting eyes. Brown, black, and white, he looked like a mixed breed.

"Aren't you a sweetheart? What's your name?"

"Twain." Graham set his feet on the floor, nudging a pizza box toward the edge of the desk. "Have a slice."

"Great name." Cheesy Italian goodness wafted from the box, and yeah. She was starving. "Thanks." Straightening, she took a slice of pepperoni. My, how she'd missed Pizza My Heart. She spoke around her food. "I got stuff in the car when we're done eating."

Graham's brows rose. "What did you get?"

Digging in her purse, she gave him the receipts, letting him know the purchases. "I bought this kickass old typewriter for the front window display."

"Never would've thought of that," he mumbled, frowning at the receipts. "This can't be right. You spent under a hundred bucks?"

Nerves clenched her throat. "Too much? I can pay it off if you—"

"No. I just expected the tab to be way more, considering all you bought." He set the receipts aside. "Not to mention, everything we're doing up front is refurbishing crap we already had, for the most part. Gotta admit, I was a little nervous handing over a credit card."

Forest threw his head back and laughed. "How sexist of you."

She grinned. "More like stereotyping."

"True, dat." Forest saluted her with a can of cola. "I love what you're doing to the place, by the way. Very clever."

Her face grew hot at the compliment. Which was silly, but it had been too long since she'd heard them that she feared she didn't know how to accept them anymore. "Thanks. I hope it helps."

"Time will tell, but I think it will." He winked.

Graham, eyes narrowed as if annoyed, watched them.

Not sure what that was about, she changed the subject. "Were you able to print some of the posters?"

"Yep." Graham rose, tossing his crust to the dog, who caught it midair. "There are seven poster frames. If you plan to hang them on both sides of the room, it's an odd number. To appease my OCD, I printed six random front pages."

She nodded. "You have OCD, too?"

Forest laughed.

Graham gave him the hairy eyeball. "A little."

"I do, as well. I can use the last frame for something else or set it aside."

"Forest here offered to help." Graham closed the pizza box and stretched. "Figured it couldn't hurt."

"That would be great." They had a lot to do, going through all the boxes, copying, bagging the prints. "We won't get all this done tonight. We should close shop tomorrow with a basic issue run for Thursday. Then maybe on Friday, incorporate the big changes and make an announcement."

"Works for me." He glanced at the newsroom outside his office. "You think we'll get it finished by then?"

Perhaps, depending on how fast they worked. "I could call for reinforcements tomorrow." If Scarlett and Dorothy weren't too busy, they could scan and copy. It would give Rebecca and Graham breathing room to work on the paper, website, and emailing.

"Sure." He shrugged, strolling into the newsroom.

Forest followed. "I can come by after work again tomorrow."

"Thanks!" She texted her besties and set her hands on her hips, looking at the chaos. "Let's get the stuff from my car."

For the next few hours, while Forest and Graham put the posters into frames and hung them, Rebecca put tablecloths on the desks that would hold the comic boxes, cleaned out the birdcage, hung it in the front window display, and set the typewriter on the sill. It still seemed a little too sparse for her liking, so tomorrow she'd figure out how to fill the space.

It felt so good to be a part of something again. Building up instead of maintaining. Between trying to save the Gazette and restoring the library, her plate was full. And she loved it.

As they were getting ready to call it a night, she checked her phone. "Dorothy says she can come all day, and Scarlett says she'll be available after her morning appointment, probably about noon."

"Fine by me." Graham sighed. "Good work, Obi-Wan. I'm beat."

So was Rebecca. An odd mix of excited and dead tired. She'd take a hot bath when she got home and crawl into bed.

Except, halfway to Gammy's house, she got an epiphany on what to do with the last poster frame, and spent half the night on her laptop working on it.

# Chapter Six

Flipping his keys in his hand, Graham strode to the front door of the Gazette. For once, he actually looked forward to work, which hadn't been the case since further back than he could recall. Small newspaper, no hard-hitting headliners, spending most of the hours alone at his desk while his stomach ate itself in worry over the paper tanking.

Rebecca had changed all that with one interview. He hadn't minded getting out of bed today. There was no telling if her ideas would be fruitful, but at least they were trying.

Wait...

He paused, backtracked, and stood on the sidewalk in front of the display window. Birds chirped and a fresh, humid breeze blew across his skin, smelling faintly of the river on the outskirts of town, while he stared stupidly at the window.

When had she done this? Last night, the only things Rebecca had out were the typewriter and the birdcage. An empty birdcage, that now had a yellow canary inside it, swinging merrily. It hung from the center of the display window. A little laminated nameplate on the bottom of the cage said, "Plucky II." To the left, on the sill, was a child's wooden chair, and on the seat, an old fedora hat with a "Press" tag on the band. Two small planters with something leafy flanked the chair. She'd placed the typewriter under the birdcage with a pair of folded reading glasses. And to the right? Well, she'd found a use for the seventh poster frame. The top of the image had the Gazette's logo with the year of establishment and website. Below that, a picture of Gunner with the title of owner, Graham's photo as editor, her picture as journalist, and just Joan and Jefferson's titles with no pictures. She'd also included all of their work email addresses and the newspaper's general inquiry email. The frame sat in one of the many individual book stands that had been in the office closet, the poster easily seen and read from the sidewalk.

Damn, but it looked great. It drew the eye, was well balanced, and fit a newspaper theme. He had a feeling townsfolk and tourists would no longer stroll by, uninterested in the store-front. All because of a few bucks and a crafty woman.

Shaking his head, he let himself inside, and the scent of freshly brewed coffee lofted throughout the room.

But they didn't have a coffee maker.

Check that. They did now.

Next to where they'd put the wingback chairs last night was a small table where she'd set one of those machines that brewed by the cup. Styrofoam cups were stacked beside it, and a wire rack of pods, as well as a bottle of powdered creamer and a bowl of sugar packets.

The light was on in his office.

He opened his mouth to call for Rebecca, but magazine stands in the center of the room caught his attention before he could. She'd arranged them back to back. All the frames she'd bought yesterday were exhibited with various copies of newspaper clippings inside. A laminated sign on top of the rack showed the price of the framed prints.

So, she'd not only set up the front window, a coffee counter, and the racks, but she'd copied and printed old headlines and framed them. Just when, exactly, had she shown up for work this morning? Hell, he was thirty minutes early.

He glanced around, wondering what else she'd done, and could only laugh. The glass display counter. She'd finished that, too. Walking closer, he found several more of the individual book stands from the closet holding old newspapers in clear protection plastic. She even had a small notebook and pencil next to each with the original year of print. Their own showcase of the Gazette's history.

Feet shuffled the floor.

He turned around.

Rebecca entered the newsroom from his office carrying two boxes, and did a double-take. "Oh good, you're here."

"Yep. Looks like you haven't left." He hurried to take the boxes off her hands, setting them by a stack she'd obviously been accumulating in his absence. "When the hell did you get all this done?"

"I came in early. It didn't take long." She waved her hand like she hadn't single-handedly revamped the whole office. In a day. "Dorothy said she'd be here at nine. Figured I'd bring these down for her to start copying."

"Uh huh." Lookie there. Someone had whooped him with the dumbass bat. "I like the front display window."

"Thanks."

"And the coffee station."

"Thanks. I bought that for Gammy two Christmases ago, but she never took it out of the box. She preferred a regular coffeemaker. You can't have a legit newsroom without coffee."

"Word. The magazine rack with frames is cool."

"Thanks."

"And the display counter. Very creative."

"Thanks. Once I got going, I couldn't quit." She huffed a laugh. "Thought up a lot of ideas after we left and I—"

"How much caffeine have you consumed?" Should he be concerned? She looked fine. Blonde strands in a high ponytail, light cosmetics, a green top with black leggings. Better than fine, really. She was gorgeous. Huge blue eyes alight with determination, pouty pink mouth smiling, cheeks flushed in excitement...

"Last night or this morning?"

"What?" He really, really wanted to kiss her. The sensation came out of nowhere and struck him square between the eyes. She smelled like honeysuckle right off the vine. Her perfume or bath product or whatever. It was both lightly refreshing and erringly intoxicating. He hadn't noticed it before now, but damn if he never wanted to breathe anything else.

"Never mind." She laughed. "I'm only on my second cup."

Cup? That's right. They'd been discussing caffeine. He needed way more of it.

"Well, it looks great. I'm speechless." For more reasons than redecorating.

"I appreciate that. Thank you. If you don't like something, just let me know."

He doubted that would happen. "I sure will." She'd knocked out quite a few things on their list for today. "What's the plan, Obi-Wan?"

The canary chirped quietly in the background.

"Well," she said through a sigh, "I figured we'd let Dorothy and Scarlett copy the headlines or various parts of the newspapers. They can bag and board them for the boxes to list for sale. I was going to work on the website and building an email list."

He nodded. "I need to get tomorrow's paper ready to go to print, but if we're announcing the changes in Friday's edition, we should work on that."

"Sounds good. Have you talked to Joan and Jefferson?"

Damn. "No. I'll call them now."

"See if Joan can do a quick product review and ask Jefferson if he can write up an article on the high school's upcoming baseball season. We can add it to Friday's edition."

She was quite brilliant. "Good thinking." He glanced at the boxes. "Let me help you bring down the rest of these for your friends, and then we can get to work."

By the time they'd lugged all the old print boxes down, his office looked like an episode of Hoarders. Dorothy was working on copying, utilizing both printers until Scarlett was able to join in. Rebecca was at her desk on the other side of the glass wall, doing whatever juju she deemed fit to save the Gazette.

There was a constant flurry of motion. Humming and page shuffling and beeping and clacking of keys. The canary chirping a tune. Though he'd worked in a newsroom his whole career to date, it had been a long while since he'd been a part of it. A strange sense of melancholy washed over him that he'd never be a true journalist again. Not in the way he'd envisioned.

A sigh, and he picked up his desk phone to call Joan, then Jefferson.

To his utter amazement, both parties seemed almost relieved to be shifted from part-time to consignment, and to be working on something specific. Graham should've thought of that sooner, should've been a true editor and doled assignments instead of wallowing in self-pity. Though he was grateful, it shouldn't have taken Rebecca to light a fire under him.

He'd do better. Be better.

Pulling up his program for the printing press, he uploaded the info he had ready to go, shifted a few things for space, and sent it off. Sad. Two pages of meaningless filler. Just like it had been the past two months.

Come Friday, that would change. Thanks to Rebecca. He wondered if his attraction to her was based on gratitude, but shook his head. He'd been drawn to her before she'd interviewed.

Leaning back in his seat, he stared through the glass barrier between them. Despite the fragile appearance of her frame, she seemed like one tough cookie. To lose her parents at such a young age, even if she'd had a doting grandmother, had to have been immensely difficult. Probably lonely. And to leave a small town, where there was certainty and comfort and a shield from the outside world, to venture out into the great unknown? Hopes and dreams as companions? Titanium spine, this one. She didn't seem to take crap from anyone, himself included. Smart and creative. Tenacious and more than a little stubborn.

He didn't know how he got so lucky at this point in his deadend career to have her as an employee, but he'd take it, for however long it lasted. When he'd accepted the job, he'd assumed it'd be a breeze compared to the hustle of a huge city. Following leads, generating stories, forever climbing to stay above competitors. Deadlines and zero sleep and meals from a paper bag on the go. More than one relationship had gone down in flames as a result of that pace.

How wrong he'd been. Running the Vallantine Gazette was harder. Much harder. Rebecca had been right. Small town papers were a whole different class and speed. The sections often found in other prints would have no bearing here. Some remained, but he hadn't had his thumb on the pulse of the community long enough to know what to attempt. Not to mention, his staff didn't have the experience.

So, he'd done nothing.

That changed now.

Mercy, she was lovely. Elegant, regal neck. Blonde strands bordering on caramel. Lean, lithe frame. She had her back to him, so he couldn't see her facial features, but her eyes could stop time. And that mouth. It begged to be kissed.

He dragged in a ragged breath. Office romances were not a good idea on a great day. She'd given no indication she had any sexual interest in him. He'd be wise to remember both.

The chirping of the canary made him blink, pulling him from his thoughts.

The quietness of the room intruded the fringes of his consciousness, and he swiftly glanced at Dorothy. Who'd obviously caught him staring at Rebecca, if her faint smile and raised brows were an indictor. A subtle nod, and she resumed copying, paying him no mind, leaving him to wonder if her reaction had been acknowledgement or approval.

She was a gentle one. Calm. A presence in itself. Natural red hair, curvy shape. He hadn't known her long, if merely in passing, but he liked her so far. Intelligent and honest. Sincere and intuitive.

Why couldn't he be attracted to her? No complications there. She was pretty.

But there was no gut punch, wind from his sails, or rug out from under him holy-shit sensation like with Rebecca. He couldn't explain the phenomenon if he had a week and ten writers. He'd met the woman all of a few days prior. They'd barely grazed the surface of conquering personalities. The pull didn't make a lick of sense.

Later. He'd analyze it later. There was work to be done.

Rising, he left his office and yanked an extra chair beside her desk. "Whatcha got?" By the look of it, she had a thousand tabs open.

"First, there's the website." She moved her mouse and pulled up the server program. "The only thing on it is an About page and the Home page." More clicking. "I added a Contact tab, which has our images and emails, like the sign up front. Is that okay?"

"Absolutely. It looks good." It did, too. She'd changed the plain blue background to off-white and framed it to make it look like a newspaper with Vallantine Gazette as the header on all pages. Clever. "I'd maybe add a picture of the front window, magazine racks, and the glass display cabinet to the About page."

"Good idea." She paused, staring at the screen. "I created a Facebook page and a Twitter account. Links to those are replicated on all pages. I'm thinking every time we send out or print an issue, we post highlights on both accounts. For instance," she brought up the Twitter account, "this is what I just posted."

*Weather is looking great in Vallantine today. See if that's going to change in the coming week...*

"Hmm. Smart." She'd linked the Tweet back to the Gazette's site. Teasing, and making the reader go check out what's in store.

"So, we'd do that for all print sections. A partial headline with an open-ended cliffhanger to get them to click."

"Brilliant. Can I get the login info?"

"Already emailed it to you. My message to Joan and Jefferson just had the links for them to follow." She switched pages. "I updated the Home page. Nothing major there. I added an Advertise page where businesses can email you to pay to advertise with us. I put a rate for quarter and half pages, with two different options for print or e-print. Here's where things get fun." A blank page opened. "If we're going to do an e-print version, we're going to want readers to have links to back issues. I think we should start doing those with Friday's print run. Thus, this page will be links with issue dates."

He scratched his chin, staring in thought. "How would you suggest we do an e-print?" He'd never been on the tech side of distribution before. They didn't have the funds to hire a service.

And her honeysuckle scent was distracting as hell.

"Oddly, that's the easy part." She backed out and went to what looked like an administration page. "Our web server has email marketing as an option. It's tiered for pricing. Considering there's about twenty-five hundred residents in Vallantine, we won't go above tier two. Thus, we'd only be paying fifty bucks a year." She went to yet another page. "In essence, we'd be doing a newsletter. Either one of us can put it out. It's as simple as copying and pasting what you send to the printers, just in one long column with a hyperlinked table of contents."

What she was doing was making him feel stupid for not checking into this sooner. "How do they subscribe and how do we collect payment?" Gunner's people were in charge of physical copies and payment. Graham never had to deal with it.

"There're two signup forms I created. One for print, which is automatically drafted monthly, and is a higher fee at this rate." She pointed to the screen. "That number is at the low end of the national average. It has them plug in their address for delivery and payment info. I added a PayPal option besides just a credit card." She switched screens. "This form is for e-print email delivery at this rate." She pointed. "Again, drafted monthly, and if they unsubscribe, the program will remove them from the newsletter at the top of the month and quit auto-drafting funds. The site updates will go live at one a.m. Friday. I'll need you to get banking deets from Gunner for money to get dumped."

He shot off a quick text to Gunner to do just what she requested. Leaning back in his seat, he cracked his knuckles. "You're one impressive woman. Hard part will be getting subscribers."

"I have a plan."

Rubbing his eyes, he laughed. "Of course, you do."

Yet another screen. "The town's website for tourism has all the shops and restaurants listed with addresses, websites, and contact emails. I plugged the latter into a CSV file. I've scheduled an email to go out Friday morning to all local businesses announcing a facelift for the Gazette and our advertising rates. Links to social media and how to sign up for subscriptions, too. I also mentioned requests for product reviews or food critiques go to your email so you can assign Joan accordingly."

He'd be damned. "Wow. Great idea."

She then spewed something about the second email list being small, but it, too, would go out Friday morning to the elementary, middle, and high school administrators with Graham's info for them to forward school announcements or athletic games for the Gazette to post. How she thought up this stuff was beyond him. The local shops and schools alone would bring in enough revenue to get them in the black with advertising and subscribers. The third list was residents who were already print subscriptions or had signed up through email before. Two-hundred eighty-seven people. Not a lot when compared to census, but hopefully it would climb. Especially if her idea of sending out a free issue of Friday's paper to all three email lists would show the Gazette's changes to townsfolk and get them to register.

He rubbed his jaw. "Friday's issue is going to need to be fantastic."

"Yes, sir." She opened her mouth to say something else, but a knock on the front door had her snapping it closed again.

Dorothy came out of his office. "That's Scarlett. I'll let her in. As you were."

Once the commotion of Hurricane Scarlett subsided, Graham asked Rebecca to open a spreadsheet. "Let's start a list of content. I think we should put in specific roles on the website and in the newspaper every issue based on content, so people know who to email with tips."

She nodded, her fingers a blur over the keyboard. "Divide and conquer."

"Yep." He ticked his first point off on a finger. "Weather is obvious. Why don't we pull Atlanta and Savannah's forecasts daily."

"I can do that. Can also report on any upcoming storms or hurricanes we'd be affected by."

"Perfect." He scrolled through notes in his head. "We need a catchy title for Joan's content."

Her lips pursed adorably in thought. "Word on the Street? Since she's doing reviews or critiques."

"Nice. Let's go with it."

She plugged that into the spreadsheet, along with Jefferson's content under Sports. "I think we should put horoscopes back in the issues. It won't fill much space, but I know lots of people who read those. We can correlate with one of the spiritual bloggers in Georgia to send us one daily and, in turn, put their website below it for free advertisement as payment. No cost out of pocket."

Why not? "Okay. Know anyone?"

"I'll look into it right away." She added it to the list. "Word-search puzzles? They used to be a big hit. Gammy did them all the time. There's a free site that'll generate one if you put in the words we want to use. Some of the reporters in Boston used it for baby and wedding showers. We could do a different theme daily."

He bumped his chin toward the screen. "Add it. Good one."

Feet shuffled behind them.

"Hate to interrupt." Scarlett batted her eyelashes. "We couldn't help but overhear." She and Dorothy came around to the side of the cubicle. "Are you up for suggestions?"

"Absolutely." Crossing his arms, he rocked in his chair. "Help is appreciated."

Dorothy tucked her auburn strands behind her ears. "When we were kids, the Gazette used to have an Artist of the Day thing. Students from the school would submit and get chosen to be featured."

"Oh, that's right!" Rebecca typed it into the list. "I'll add this to the email to the administrators and the townsfolk. Hopefully that'll engage more people again."

That triggered something for him. "In Minneapolis, the local TV station had a weather picture of the day sent in by viewers."

Rebecca nodded. "Added. Will also put a shout-out for Pets of the Day. Plucky II can go in our first Friday issue."

Scarlett's thumbs were going to work on her cell. "I'll send you a pic for the weather one to use Friday. I took a great shot at sunset from home the other day."

Rebecca's cell pinged. "Thanks."

"I think you guys should introduce yourselves in the issue." Dorothy darted her gaze between him and Rebecca. "We didn't know you were editor. The town can get to know you better."

Without hesitation, Rebecca typed it on the list. "Good. What else?"

"Know what y'all really need?" Scarlett cocked a hip. "Book reviews. With the library getting remodeled, it'll boost interest for us when we open. I can send an email out to Mama's book-club that we're reinstating it. We can get together at the plantation until the library is finished, then meet monthly there."

He grinned. "Belles Bookclub."

"Yes!" Scarlett beamed, excitedly clapping. "I'll send the email tonight. First meeting Friday night at seven. Can you put a call-out in the paper?"

"You bet," Rebecca muttered as she typed. "Any way you can pick a book to start with so I can add it to the article?"

"I'll text you one in a bit."

Which reminded him... "You should do a weekly exposé on the library renovations." He looked at Rebecca, fiercely typing to keep up. "The town will be up to date, and they won't feel so in the dark. Perhaps write a bit about the history."

"Love it. I'll try to get a story written for Friday."

Dorothy wrung her fingers. "What about the garden club? Maybe tips for planting?"

Scarlett was right on her heels. "Take pictures of the changes inside the Gazette. Let people know the stuff we're copying is for sale."

He shook his head. How he missed this. Bouncing ideas and interaction. Being a part of something again. Rebecca's friends had come up with wonderful ideas. "You three are a force to be reckoned with."

Scarlett tsked. "And don't you forget it."

"Not even if I tried." He slapped his hands on his thighs and rose. "I'll tackle Joan and Jefferson's articles for edit, and call someone from the garden club for a tip." He pointed to Rebecca. "Send me the link for the wordsearch and I'll do that, as well. You want to reach out to someone about horoscopes and get the various notifications ready?"

"Will do, boss. I'll write a brief intro for me. Don't forget yours."

A sigh, and he turned for his office. "Yes, ma'am."

He could all but hear her grin. "Now you're learning."

# Chapter Seven

They'd spent the entire following day writing articles, organizing the Friday edition, and coordinating efforts. Emails were scheduled. Files were off to the printers. All the comic boxes were filled with prints of old editions to sell, thanks to Scarlett and Dorothy, who'd copied endlessly and put them into sleeves. The podium counter behind the glass display case now had one of the spare computers with an accounting program so they could ring up purchases, and a cash drawer, all courtesy of Forest's help. The Gazette was ready for the big reveal tomorrow morning.

Rebecca was stupid excited.

Forest, the night before, had broached the idea to Graham to begin restocking the sidewalk newspaper boxes around town again. Rebecca had no idea when they'd stopped, but Forest thought it had been at least five years. It had taken Graham an hour of finagling to get the ten boxes reset on price and another hour to figure out who'd fill them each morning from the printing press. Funniest part had been discovering a little over thirty-five dollars in quarters still sitting in the machines.

It was a great idea, however, Scarlett had pointed out most people may not notice with as long as they'd been empty. Thus,

Graham had printed signs in bold colors and laminated them to affix to the outside of the boxes. Currently, they were sitting on his desk between him and Rebecca because they hadn't wanted to put them out too early.

Graham had also suggested adding a slot box up front for townsfolk to drop their pet or weather pics and kid art for the folks who didn't email them. After a run to the store, said box was attached to the building beside the door under the awning.

She slouched in the seat across from his desk, staring blankly at the ceiling. "I don't know about you, but I'm exhausted." And sore. Dark had descended sometime an hour ago.

"Ditto. I can't feel my fingers."

She laughed. "I like your idea for a Healthy Report section. It's smart, getting tips from the medical clinic every day." The nearest hospital was in Savannah, but Vallantine did have an urgent care and physician's office. A good chunk of citizens didn't get a yearly check-up. His first article for tomorrow was signs of a heart attack and what to do.

"Appreciate it. All the concepts we knocked around, and it seemed fitting." He paused. "I like your ideas for a Recipe addition. We might get subscribers for that alone."

After calling and emailing this morning, she'd run home during a break to get Gammy's recipe for peach pie. "We did good, boss."

"Thanks to you. We make a good team."

"That we do." She sighed. "It wasn't just me."

"No, it wasn't. Your friends were very helpful. I like them."

She smiled, and even that took effort. "Me, too. But I mean that we used your ideas as well as everyone's. It was a coordinated effort."

"Again, thanks to you."

Biting the inside of her cheek, she rolled his answer around, and didn't like the way it sat heavy in her head. "I was raised in Vallantine, so I know the town and what they'd be looking for, but you were handed a broken system. Fixing it wasn't as simple as adding filler or more articles. Yes, I helped, but don't underestimate yourself. A good editor listens to suggestions, delegates appropriately, seeks guidance when necessary, and supports their staff. The past few days, you've done all those things and more, not accounting for your own ideas to add to the mix. You haven't run things like a dictatorship when you really could have, and you showed gratitude." She drew a deep breath and exhaled. "Coordinated effort, Graham."

He was silent so long, she wondered if he'd fallen asleep from an adrenaline crash. She lifted her head, and found him staring at her.

She couldn't read his expression, other than he appeared contemplative. Emerald eyes searched hers for an extended breadth. His jaw ticked. Otherwise, he remained motionless, and it was beginning to unnerve her if not for the uncanny, strange sensation he was burrowing in her head. Dissecting. Infiltrating.

They'd spent immeasurable time together the past few days. He'd proven her first impression false and that he was a decent person. Honestly, he just seemed like a fish out of water. She hadn't an inkling what had brought him to their tiny little town, but she found she really wanted the answer. Get to know him. Understand what made him tick. His motives and desires. Her friends liked him. If he had Forest's stamp of approval, Graham had to be solid.

Not for the first time, his scent invaded her space. Bergamot or something akin to it. Citrus and spice. Clean, refreshing. Masculine without being overpowering. Like him, really. Or what she'd gathered thus far. Stirrings of attraction rose again, just as they'd done periodically since they'd met, but she let it settle this time. Analyzed.

Oh, he was a looker. Midnight hair and scruff dusting his jaw. Lashes that were an unlawful waste on a male. Firm lips that could decimate when he grinned. Which wasn't often. Angular face. Wide shoulders. His hands, though. A weakness of hers, a man's hands. There was something erringly sexy about them. The size, the strength, whether they could be gentle or commanding. She'd bet he knew how to use his for pleasure.

It had been way too long since she'd had a lover.

The last thing she needed to be doing was lusting after her boss. Some emotions couldn't be helped, though. Like attraction. For the sake of sanity, she'd try. They had caution written all over them.

And he was still staring.

Plucky began chirping another song quietly from the newsroom. She'd already grown used to him because his singing had become white noise today.

She cleared her throat. "Something wrong?"

A slow shake of his head, yet Graham said squat.

Struggling, she tried to conjure something, *anything* to say to fill the silence. It was becoming its own entity. "We have some of those large black wire basket stands upstairs." She didn't know what they were previously used for, but they had legs and were about three feet high. "Since we're only doing Monday through Friday editions, we can line the baskets on the floor inside the window, one for each day of the week, and put the unsold previous week's edition in them for half off. In case someone missed an issue and wants to catch up."

"Mmm hmm." His gaze searched hers. Again. Or still. "Your brain never stops, does it?"

Was that an insult? She couldn't tell. "Rarely."

"Figured as much." He finally looked away, and she was oddly disappointed. "Another great idea. I'll bring them down tomorrow." He rubbed his jaw, creating a scratching sound of skin against whiskers, and she realized how quiet the office had become. "I should get these posted on the sidewalk boxes." He jerked a chin at the signs on his desk.

Once again, she wished she knew him better because she couldn't translate if that was a cue for her to leave or him attempting to work up the energy.

"Trying to get rid of me?" She smiled, hoping humor might draw out more from him.

His gaze stealthy narrowed on her. "Why in the hell would I do that?"

Well, okay then. "Got a burr in your saddle, boss?"

Up went his brows. "You should write a book on southernisms. It's like a whole different language at times."

Stretching her neck, she laughed. "Same could be said for anywhere in the States. Soda versus pop. Bubbler versus water fountain. You Minnesota and Wisconsinites have a specific dialect all your own. *Errr, noo?*" she teased in her best Fargo accent.

He did the damnedest thing. He threw his head back and laughed. Unbidden, coarse, and spanning ten seconds. Her belly heated, lighting a zing through her whole midsection. He really should do that more often.

"Touché." He sighed, amusement subsiding. "How did you not pick up the craggy Boston accent after living there ten years? How often did you drive your *cah* in the city?"

Slapping a hand over her mouth, she bent over with a fit of hysterics. It was true. Bostoners replaced all "r" sounds with "ah" or "aw." It wasn't a half-bad impression. It had taken her forever to get used to it.

Fanning her face, she blew out a breath. "Just lucky, I guess."

He made a grunt of agreement. "In all seriousness, you do have an odd accent. Southern drawl when you're mad, northern when you're focused, and a mix of both the rest of the time. When amused, it's a light Georgia lilt."

Interesting observation. Most wouldn't have noticed. Must be the reporter in him to be that detailed.

"Keen ear." Crossing her arms, she resettled in the chair. "I tried hard to drop the southern accent, especially after college. My immediate supervisor and co-workers looked at me funny every time I opened my mouth to speak. I found they were focusing more on my dialect than my words. There's a common stigma throughout the country that a southern accent equaled ignorant or uneducated. It pisses me off. Like all we do down here is roast pigs behind our trailers, play the banjo, make moonshine, and pick our tooth." She raised a finger for emphasis. "Tooth, not teeth." She shook her head. "One time, this snobby bitch from the fashion column patted me on the head and told me to go back to the plantation to fluff my hair."

"Whoa." Leaning forward, he set his elbows on the desk. "Is she still breathing?"

Bless him. "Yes. She was a lead columnist and I was a no one. Going to HR wouldn't have done any good. Anyway, that's why I have a blended accent, I suppose."

Nodding slowly, he studied her. "Not all of us Yankees are condescending." He grinned slowly, reminding her of the Cheshire Cat. "I'm rather fond of your angry drawl."

Was he flirting? Kinda seemed like flirting. "Are you sayin' you like it when I'm madder than a wet hen at you?"

Nostril flared, he inhaled. Hard. "Gonna plead the fifth." Quickly, as if to dispel the mood, he rose. "For the record, you're not a no one. How do you feel about Mexican?"

She was getting whiplash. "The country or in a general sense?"

"Smartass." He collected the laminated signs. "Let me buy you dinner. What's a southern term for you worked your ass off and have been busier than hell?"

Standing, she lifted fingers to punctuate points. "Running all over hell's half acre. Busy as a one-legged cat in a sandbox. Busier than a moth in a mitten."

He raised his palm, chuckling. "Yeah, that. I'd like to thank you. Dinner?"

"Yes to dinner. I appreciate the thank-you, but a reward is not necessary. It's my job and we all worked hard." The giddy little girl still buried inside her relished the praise, as it had been difficult to come by in her career, but the professional side scoffed at the attention. She was just grateful he'd noticed.

He strode toward the doorway, waiting for her to exit before cutting the light. "I just have to put these up first."

"I'll help." Outside, while he locked the office door, she faced him. "What about the dog? Don't you have to head home?"

"Forest took care of it for me after I realized how late we'd be working."

She nodded, walking beside him on the cobblestone sidewalk. "You should bring Twain with you to work."

"You think?" He paused outside the first box by the curb. "It seems unprofessional."

"Not at all." She held the laminated sign while he taped. "I mean, if you worked at the bank or courthouse, maybe, but not at the Gazette. Besides, Twain is super sweet and mild-mannered. He could be another unofficial mascot, like Plucky."

They continued toward the next box, and she rolled her head to stretch her neck. Her fibro was getting overly achy again and fatigue was threatening to put her under. Most of the excitement from the day had wound to a close.

"Yeah, okay. I could try to bring Twain for a few days and see. He'd probably love tagging along."

There were a few stragglers out and about, but most of the shops had closed for the night. All except the bars and restaurants. Vallantine liked to roll its sidewalks up after dark, or so the expression went. She'd have to get used to that again now that she was home. Boston never seemed to sleep.

A cool breeze blew, tinged with scents from the river and spring blooms. Cherry blossom trees lining the curb were at their peak, as pink petals floated in the air, coating the street. Soon, leaf buds would replace them. Cast-iron old-world lampposts lit the way with a yellowish glow while purple and white pansies danced in the curbside flower boxes. Stars winked overhead, too vast to count, and she'd missed it. More than she'd remembered. Missed this. Being able to see this many stars and stroll in early spring without five layers of clothes or watching over her shoulder to be sure she wasn't followed. Colorful awnings and turn-of-the-century buildings. Window displays and people who waved.

Distracted, she turned to look at him, and found him staring at her. Again. He'd paused by the next news box, stoically watching her. A silent smile crinkled the edges of his eyes, even if his lips hadn't caught up yet.

"Sorry." She shrugged. "I was reminiscing."

"Nothing wrong with that. Do you know you wrinkle your nose when you're embarrassed?"

Shoot. Did she? No one had told her that before. She brought her hand up to cover the traitorous body part, but he gently grabbed her wrist, lowering her arm.

"Don't. It's an adorable trait. Besides, I need all the leverage I can get when it comes to you."

His timbre had dropped a note. Seductively lower. The motion of touching her had shifted him closer, so that they were nearly toe-to-toe, and he had yet to release her wrist. Warm hands. Calloused fingers. Thoughtful eyes. So darn green. More like moss in the low light. And Lord help her, his scent was alluring.

One of them needed to speak, so she said the first thing that came to mind. Which was dumb. She hadn't done that since she was a kid. Plus, she couldn't comprehend what had come out of her mouth because she was distracted staring at his.

"He was a stray."

What? Blinking back into focus, she raised her gaze to his. His answer still didn't compute. Probably because she didn't know what she'd said.

"You asked where I'd gotten Twain." One corner of his mouth curved in a half smile like he'd known her thoughts had plummeted south into naughty territory. "One of my first nights in the new house, I caught him digging through the trash cans. I had a dog growing up, but not when I'd lived on my own. Not sure why I decided to keep him. Had a connection, I guess. I love the doofus."

Aww. "Meant to find one another."

Grunting, he pivoted to continue walking. "Don't tell me you're one of those that believe in fate and destiny."

Keeping pace beside him, she thought it over. "Not sure. Maybe. There are certain situations where I have to wonder if more is at play. A higher power or planets aligning."

Huffing a laugh, he crouched by the next box. "Or it's just a coincidence. The choices we make steer us on one path versus another."

"True." So, he wasn't spiritual. More a black and white sort of guy. She wondered how many shades of gray he allowed in with that mentality. "Some things can't be explained."

Shaking his head, he grinned, continuing their trek. "Most things can."

They approached the corner of Main Square where a small courtyard held the town's infamous peach tree, and it gave her an idea.

"How do you explain this, then?"

Up went those brows. "A tree?"

She smiled, glancing at the current topic in question. A black fence surrounded its base with a brick walking path. Smaller lampposts and benches decorated the grassy part of the courtyard around the tree, which had been planted by the town founder William Vallantine for his wife Katherine. Thus, its name, Miss Katie. It had telltale characteristics of Belle of Georgia peach trees with a rounded crown shape on top, upward reaching branches, and dark green deciduous leaves. Currently, like Belles did each spring, brilliant bright red flowers adorned its foliage. Very pretty.

That's where the similarities ended. Miss Katie was a modern marvel.

Tilting her head, Rebecca glanced at Graham. "The tree was planted in 1875, making it almost one hundred and fifty years old."

"Uh huh." He narrowed his eyes, obviously unimpressed. "And?"

"*And*, Belle of Georgia's have a lifespan of fifteen to twenty years."

Crossing his arms, laminated signs still in hand, he widened his stance as if preparing for an intellectual throw-down. "It's made of good stock." He shrugged.

"They typically grow to a maximum height of fifteen to twenty-five feet with a span of twenty feet at maturity. They rarely even get that big."

A slight rear, like she'd finally surprised him, and he redirected his attention to Miss Katie. "That's got to be, what, thirty feet tall and twenty-five around? It must really have liked this location."

Stubborn man. "The 1898 hurricane that killed William and Katherine, plus took out their mansion, left this tree and the library intact. Both have withstood countless tropical storms and hurricanes since."

He nodded. "Weather can be fickle, especially storms in what damage they cause. It's a phenomenon in itself." A sigh. "I'll admit, that's a lot of coincidences, but the town obvious took great care with the tree. They built a damn shrine to the thing."

"That we did. History is important, even if embellished with legend. The garden club fertilizes her every spring. All of these shops were built around her, in fact." She looked at Miss Katie, gorgeous blooms and strength in her branches. "She's known to grant wishes, you know."

Shaking his head, he barked a laugh. "Don't tell me you believe that."

"Maybe once, long ago." Wistfully, she exhaled, recalling the instances as a young girl where she'd run to Miss Katie with whatever ailed her. Wishing for her parents to still be alive, for a certain boy to like her, to get accepted into her college of choice, to become a somebody in her career field. None of it had happened. "You never know." Perhaps they hadn't been the right wishes.

Or perhaps she'd just been unworthy.

"Alrighty." Turning, he began walking anew. "I'll meet you halfway and agree we'll never know for certain." A mischievous grin lit his eyes, curved his lips. "Are you superstitious, too? Seven years back luck for breaking a mirror, that kind of thing?"

"Not particularly." She thought it through for the sake of being truthful. "It begs the argument for crowd mentality, doesn't it? Do superstitions exist because they actually happen or because enough people believe they do, giving credence to nothing at all?"

A jut of his chin as if impressed by her answer. "Good point."

They posted signs on the box by the curb outside the library, and he paused to stare at the building. She tried to look at it from an outsider's perspective.

It wasn't large compared to most colonials, but it had been built with love and was meant to be a private library collection. The place did need quite a lot of help. Or maybe it just needed to be loved again. Rebecca had gotten the impression Mr. Brown had a like/loathe relationship with the library. He hadn't had a lot of aid from the town or funding to keep it afloat. She wondered if his father and grandfather before him had felt the same way. All the Vallantine heirs. Perhaps, between resentments and time, the library knew those facts. Had simply given up, too.

"Do you think buildings have a soul?" She could feel Graham's gaze on her, but she kept hers ahead. The library resembled, in a way, old courthouses from back in the day. Peaked roof. Pedimented gables. Greek support columns. Rectangular shape. It stood alone, against a navy sky littered with stars, trees to the rear, and surrounded by grassy fields. It seemed rather lonely. "That places can absorb the energy around it or the people who once lived there?"

"Eh." He issued a sound of contemplation. "Honestly? No. Buildings are nothing more than framework. Lumber and glass and drywall. I think they definitely develop personalities over time, in the broad sense of the meaning, based on architecture, design, and what the occupants have done. Actual feelings? Nope."

Humming, she smiled. "So, you don't believe in ghosts?"

"Ha." He strode to the opposite side of the road, her following, toward the other half of the sidewalk boxes. "I don't believe in spirits, no. Nor tarot cards or any pseudoscience."

"A lot of experiences back up the claims. Who knows what happens to us when we die."

"Agree on that front. In my opinion, ghosts are another mass hysteria based on circumstances and inspired by a sense of dread or fear. The recent boom in paranormal programs only adds to the mindset."

Yup. Black and white, this guy.

She was enjoying this immensely, the vast conversation and genuine meeting of the minds. "Hauntings and lore have been around longer than television or film."

"Fables meant to prove a point, tell a tale, or scare children into obedience."

Interesting take. "Which simply means, you've never had a paranormal experience."

Dropping his chin, he shook his head. "And you have?"

"Nope." She winked. "But I'm young."

"You threw a *but* in there." He pointed like she'd just made his case for him. "Meaning, you're open to suggestion. Take your library, for example. You spent a lot of time there growing up, but you've not witnessed the supposed ghost of Katherine Vallantine. You'd think she would have appeared to you by now if she existed."

Maybe. Maybe not. "She assists all who enter seeking knowledge. Guess I wasn't asking the correct questions."

He sighed, but it was on the undercurrent of a smile. "Agree to disagree."

She couldn't help but think the world might be a better place if more people did that. Beliefs on their proper sides of the aisle, calmly making their case, listening to opposition, and agreeing to disagree. No name-calling or insults. Simply a differing of opinions.

They crossed the street, heading back to the Gazette. A check of her watch revealed an hour had passed without her realizing, and they'd finished the laminated signs. It seemed like they'd just left.

And they hadn't even gotten to dinner yet.

# Chapter Eight

Graham waited for the hostess to walk away before glancing around. Guac On was located almost directly across the street from the Gazette. It was on the smaller side, like the other storefronts, but they utilized space to their advantage. The bar to the left of the door only seated eight, hightop tables filled the center, and booths on the right. Yellow walls with painted murals of iguanas. Dark hardwood floors.

"Never seen it this empty in here." There were only a few other patrons. He scratched his jaw. "I get takeout from here a couple times a week."

"Past the dinner rush." She glanced at her watch. "It's almost eight. They close in an hour. It's a weeknight, too. They're packed to the gills during lunch and dinner."

Yeah, he could attest to that. He'd learned to call in his meal ahead of time.

Maria, one of the owners who often took Graham's orders, came over with a pad and pencil, her salt and pepper hair in a loose bun. "Rebecca Moore. When did you get back in Vallantine?" Her grin indicated friendliness in the inquiry.

Rebecca returned the affection. "Not long ago. I'm so glad you and Juan still own the place. How's Veronica? I haven't seen her in ages."

"Oh," Maria waved her hand, "so busy these days. She's in Charlotte now with a husband and a bambino on the way. We're excited."

"I bet. Send her my regards."

"I will." Maria eyed Graham. "Nice to see you eating with company tonight." Wink. "You make a good couple."

Rebecca laughed. "It's a working dinner, Miss Maria."

"Mmhmm. What would you lovebirds like to drink?"

Rubbing her forehead, Rebecca chuckled through a sigh. "Strawberry daquiri, please."

"I'll have a margarita on the rocks."

After Maria left, Rebecca studied the menu. "They used to have the best enchiladas. I went to school with their daughter. We weren't close, but she was cool."

"I get the enchiladas often." He pushed his menu aside, already knowing what he wanted, and trying to imagine a younger version of her. "I suspect you were one of the cool girls in high school."

She eyed him over the menu. "We didn't have a lot of cliques or tiers of popularity here. Small graduating class."

He doubted that. The popular part, not the size of her class, but he let it slide. "I don't know about you, but I could eat my own hand right now." They'd skipped lunch.

"And my left leg."

She had the quickest comebacks that either amused or flustered the hell out of him. "Just your left?"

"For now." Setting the menu down, she leaned forward. "Know what we should do? Write a weekly differing opinion article. Any given topic. Our discussion earlier about ghosts and houses got me thinking."

He questioned if she ever quit thinking. Though their chats proved how polar opposite they were, he found her mind fascinating. She was always respectful of his opinion and in her counter replies. "You're a sleep-walker, aren't you? I bet you talk in your sleep, too."

She straightened. "Are you saying I talk too much?"

"Not even implied." They could be arguing about the color blue, and he'd gladly listen. She'd probably conjure ten bullet points he'd never heard of to back her side. He'd only have one...and it would pertain to her eyes.

"Well, I don't sleepwalk and, that I'm aware, don't talk in my sleep, either." Idly, she tapped her fingers on the table. "Haven't slept with anyone in a hot minute, so I can't verify."

Just how long, precisely, was a "hot minute?"

Maria returned with their drinks, then took their order. Rebecca got a steak fajita salad with cornbread and him a taco platter with rice. He couldn't wait. His stomach was rumbling now that there was no work to focus on.

Distraction was needed, but she jumped the gun on him before he could ask her anything.

"You grew up in Minnesota? Is your family still there?"

"I did and they are. My parents are in a suburb near Minneapolis. Dad's folks are gone, but Mom's live close to them. I have a few aunts and uncles on both sides, and a scattering of cousins."

She smiled. "Big family. Bet holidays were fun."

"Oh, yeah." And loud. It dawned on him again she didn't have any family left. He didn't know what he'd do without his, even though he didn't get to see them often. "Was it difficult for you moving so far away from your grandmother for school or work?"

"At first." Her face scrunched in an adorable wishy-washy thought process he'd caught in a few instances before. "I always had chores and she taught me how to cook, so I was self-reliant, but the absence of her being in the next room was tough. I came home often as I could and we talked nearly every day by phone." The edges of her eyes cast downward as her expression fell. "There's been many times since she's passed that I open my mouth to call for her, to ask a question, to tell her about my day, only to remember she's gone."

She offered an absent shake of her head, yet the anguish in her baby blues remained.

"I'm sorry." And he was. Immensely. Sentiments and general condolence offers rarely made those left behind feel better, but he was at a loss for words on a proper reply. He could only generally sympathize with her situation, as he'd not lost anyone he loved that much, but he could imagine how he'd take the news if his parents died. Even then, he had other family to lighten the burden and grieve with him.

Maybe he and Rebecca were getting closer or a bond was forming after working side-by-side. There was no other explanation for the tightness in his windpipe or the absurd urge to hold her.

A delicate clearing of her throat, and she politely smiled. "What are your parents like?"

"Pretty awesome, actually." Grateful for the topic change, he took a sip of his margarita. Damn, it was good. The right mix of tequila and sour lime. Most bars mucked it up. "Mom's an estate attorney and Dad kind of does a bit of everything. He stayed home with me growing up, taking odd jobs here and there."

"A jack of all trades."

"Yes." Thankfully, the light was back in her eyes. He took the win. "You got something broken, he can probably fix it. Or install it."

She smiled around her straw as she took a sip. "Unusual for our generation to have the stereotypical gender role reversal. That's awesome."

"I never thought about it as a kid, but yeah. Mom worked, Dad stayed home, and that was my normal. He cooked, helped me with homework, threw the ball around in the yard, packed my lunches. They're both immensely supportive."

"That's amazing."

It was, and something he'd not take for granted again. He couldn't fathom what it was like for her, having her folks taken from her, and at an age when she was old enough to realize what was gone.

"I bet they're very proud of you."

They were, even if he wasn't. "I think so."

Maria dropped off their meals, and neither wasted any time digging in.

They ate in silence for a short while, a comfortable one. Most people felt the need to fill quiet with inane chatter or mundane conversation. Not Rebecca. She seemed to appreciate the solitude when it came instead of being awkward. And when they did talk, if not about the Gazette, they had interesting discussions or debates.

She speared a bite of her salad, pointing the fork at him. "What made you move all the way down here if your family is up there? I know you're college buddies with Forest, but still."

How about that? He almost lost his appetite. Her inquiry wasn't meant to be intrusive. Even if he didn't know her well yet, it was a common question.

Forcing himself to swallow, he wiped his mouth with a napkin. "Long story."

Her brows shot up, but she remained mute.

Sighing, he stared at his plate, contemplating. If she dug deep enough on Google, she might find out anyway. He just hadn't talked about it with many people. The short version with his family, a slightly longer one with Forest, glossing over it with Gunner Davis during the hiring process. Buying time, he took another sip of margarita.

"You don't have to tell me."

"It's okay." He raised his palm. "It's not my proudest moment." It had all but killed his career, in fact. Where to start, though? Backstory would help her relate. "Since I was a kid, I've wanted to be a journalist. I watched the news with my mom, and I'd think to myself, that's what I want to do when I grow up. I'd get to be with people, travel, and write about interesting things. But I never saw a lot of personal stories in the news, or when I did, they were brief and only in relation to a catastrophic event. Earthquakes, tornados, fires, war, and all I wanted to learn about was the people it affected."

She smiled, and something in her expression made him realize she understood, even before she tried to comment. "Like interviewing Edgar Allen Poe, but instead of asking about his literary works, you delve into his military or love life to see when and how he became so macabre."

"Yes! Exactly." She did get it.

"Sounds like you're a biography nut. More *how* and less *why*."

"Yeah." No truer words. "Anyway, in college, professors helped me hone my craft, and I developed a niche for really getting to the heart of a matter. Afterward, I was hired as one of the lead columnists at a newspaper. Unfortunately, due to my skill set, I wound up writing mostly political commentary. Not what I wanted, yet I could dredge secrets, and find a spin on a situation most couldn't. I often did the best I could to steer toward topics that dealt with the community in interviews and ask the questions common reporters missed."

Encouraging him, she nodded, focusing on him, their food forgotten.

"Over time, I had built quite the reputation as taking no punches. Politicians, their staff? They'd take my calls and talk, all the way down to city council. Had quite a few informants and back door entrances to get a scoop." His gut clenched even now, thinking how far he'd fallen.

"There was a small county upstate, and a mayor some say the attorney general was grooming to replace him upon retirement. Elected position, but it may run uncontested or a plug would get the job done. There was also a secretary of state and a few commissioner bids up for reelection soon, and many lower positions. High political climate. All over the news. Speculation. Accusations on all sides. I'd been covering it periodically over the span of six months."

He rubbed his jaw, thinking how to explain. "Something wasn't right with the upstate situation, though. I could feel it in my gut. Because of other crap going on, that story was moot as far as everyone was concerned. I mentioned it to my editor, and she gave me the clearance to go."

Exhaling, he leaned back in his seat. "The mayor came from a rags to riches family. Hush-hush on how they accumulated millions. Seedy business transactions. No trail on why the attorney general might be interested in this guy." He shrugged. "I wormed my way into the mayor's office, doing a series of interviews over the following weeks. He thought the attention would help his career down the road, so he complied. Meanwhile, my informant in his office was feeding me intel to blow the whole thing wide open. I slowly trickle these into my column three days a week. Drunk driving charge at age twenty-one that paralyzed his passenger? Swept under the rug."

"If it bleeds, it leads."

"Yep. Started with that story for that very reason to begin opening his web of lies." He stared at his half-eaten food, hating himself. "Everything the informant told me panned out. An extramarital affair where he forced an abortion on his mistress. Racism slurs. Five articles total. Meanwhile, the community was in an uproar and my stories were getting national attention."

A humming noise, and she offered a sympathetic pout. "This day and age, the public almost doesn't care anymore with the way sides are divided."

True story. "Either way, this guy was shady as shit." He shook his head. "My man on the inside had proven to be a confidential reliable source. Even though I looked into everything he fed me, he'd been right."

Graham paused as his stomach rolled. "I was such an idiot. Things had gone cold for a few days. One night, I'm packing my suitcase in the hotel, ready to head home, thinking I'm done, when the informant called. He told me our guy had made his millions in a drug ring with legit businesses as a front. I'd dug into his financials prior, and they were off, but could never put my finger on why. I took the deets to my editor, who told me to go with it."

"Oh, no," she breathed, eyes wide. "The source had bad info?"

"The source had his own agenda, using me as a pawn. I wrote the story."

Hand trembling, she covered her mouth. "Oh, wow."

He slammed the rest of his margarita, wishing it was bourbon. "He gained my trust. I wrote. All facts. Until they weren't." Graham rubbed his eyes, nauseous. "They were in on it the entire time. All of them. Informant, mayor, and I suspect, the attorney general."

Her jaw dropped. "They figured some of his past would come out if he obtained higher political office." She slowly shook her head in awe. "Why not use you to do it, then discredit one story, rendering all your articles suspicious."

"Yep." And Graham fell for it. Hook, line, and sinker.

"That's horrible, but you didn't know. You had a source telling you otherwise."

"Didn't matter. Extremely high-profile case, because I made it so, and then I reported bad intel. They filed a slander suit against my newspaper. I was fired in dramatic fashion. And my informant? He announced his run for city council two weeks later."

Her hand slapped the table. "Holy crap."

"Yeah. The paper redacted all the articles and issued a public apology. The lawsuit was settled in under a week with a payout. My reputation was ruined." He rolled his head to stretch his neck. "I laid low for six months." He'd had to use all his money in savings and part of his 401K to stay afloat. "Figured I'd apply elsewhere when things died down." But they didn't die. Every place he'd applied had said he was a liability.

Abject sympathy he didn't deserve stared back at him. "I'm so sorry."

"My fault." That was life. His life.

Her expression said she disagreed. "Journalism has been listed as one of the worst careers in America for three years in a row because of environment, low salary, stress, and long hours. You went to your editor with the story. You wrote the facts as you knew them. You had a source for information. You did your job."

Yet, here he was, in Small Town, Nowhere, America, editing a newspaper where his sole reporter had better concepts and execution in her pinkie than he did in his whole body.

Regardless, he appreciated her reaction. To be honest, he was more than a little concerned she'd hate him. "Thanks."

She took a sip of her daquiri. "Your editor should've had your back instead of throwing you under the bus."

Maybe, but with a lawsuit and all the negative media, he couldn't blame her. "She did what she had to."

Staring awfully hard into her drink, she tilted her head. "You applied for the Gazette position, then? After waiting for things to blow over?"

"Eh, for the most part." Nowhere else would hire him. "Forest had just gotten his divorce and came up for a long weekend to visit. I told him what happened, and he mentioned your mayor was looking into filling an editor position. I had Gunner call me, and we did some interviews via video chat. He knew about the scandal, but didn't seem to care. He just wanted to get the Gazette overhauled."

"I'm glad he knows, just so it doesn't come back to bite you."

Irritation tapped his temples. "I'm an honest person. I would've told him if Forest hadn't mentioned it first. I did address the situation in one of our calls, regardless."

Her wide, surprised gaze jerked to his. "I didn't mean it that way."

He realized that too late for him to retract his response.

"My bad." After watching her reaction and reminding himself of all she'd done for him, the paper, and how she'd responded to what had happened to him, he believed her. She didn't appear to blame him, even if he did. "Touchy subject."

Actually, to date, she was the sole person he'd told the entirety of the scandal. He didn't know why, nor understood, but maybe it had to do with her not having been happy in the same field of work as him and also winding up here. She'd comprehend the logistics, too, being a journalist.

"I just meant that you were screwed over once, and I'd hate to see it happen again."

Unsure what to say, like a handful of encounters before, he just stared. She'd thrown him for a loop in the office when she'd defended him. To himself. Bolstered and encouraged instead of taking all the credit. The damn lil spitfire had actually sat across from his desk, and ticked off merits of why she'd thought he was a good boss.

Maria came by, collected their plates, and offered refills.

Without realizing it, they'd been sitting in the booth for over an hour, so Graham asked for the bill and paid it. Guac On was past its closing time.

Outside, he took a healthy gulp of air, not spotting her car. "Where are you parked?"

"Usually, I pull in the alley behind the building, but I walked today."

So had he. "Walk you home?"

"Sure." She smiled, turning, tugging her purse strap higher on her shoulder.

They strolled in silence a beat, and again he was struck by the sleepiness of after-hours. All the storefronts were closed. Street-lamps created a mystic yellow glow on the cobblestones. Very few pedestrians. No noise but crickets and a whoosh through the leaves from a breeze.

Perhaps one day, he'd get used to it.

"You know," he offered a side-glance, "good thing I was here to walk you home. Really dangerous around these parts."

She emitted the most sensual, gut-clenching laugh. Like smoke under a doorjamb. He had to exert effort to not groan aloud.

"Come now. Don't be making fun of our precious Vallantine. We do have our share of crime from time to time."

Ha. "Like gossip? One of the gals at the salon get a bad perm? A gentleman get screwed in a game of golf? Terrible tippers at Tipsy Turtle?"

"Aw, you're stereotyping again." Amusement lit her expression as she stared ahead. And that delightful southern drawl he was beginning to adore made a reappearance. "High crimes, indeed. But, no. Petty stuff, mostly. Some tourism-related vandals or theft. I don't think we've had a murder here since the twenties."

"As in, 2020?"

"*1920*, dear sir. A brawl between brothers over a woman, if I recall."

"Huh." That was quite surprising, all joking aside. "Regardless, I'm glad you're not walking alone."

"Big, strong man protect me," she mocked in a low grunt.

He laughed. She was something else. "That's right."

Digging in her purse, she extracted a small pink cylinder. "Pepper spray. Also had self defense classes in college. I can protect myself."

"Never had a doubt." He shoved his hands in his pockets. "You'll have to show me some of those skills sometime."

Abruptly, she halted, hands on her hips. "Are you flirting with me?"

Criminy, he was, wasn't he?

"Gonna plead the fifth." Since she seemed more amused than affronted, he started their trek anew. "I will say this, Ms. Moore. You're a smart cookie." A delicious looking one, at that.

"Thank you."

"You're welcome." He debated, then said the hell with it. "Pretty, too."

"Thank you. Not so bad yourself."

It had been a while since he'd done this dance, but he could've sworn she was... "Are you flirting with me?"

"Gonna plead the fifth," she mocked.

The little minx.

They rounded a corner, leaving Main Square behind, heading toward their subdivision. Cobblestones changed over to regular concrete sidewalks and old-world lampposts became LED streetlights. Full magnolia trees created a canopy along the curb.

The longer their pause in conversation hung, the more his fingers itched to touch. Her petal soft fair skin. Her blonde locks that created loose waves down her spine. Plush lips that begged to be kissed. Since the first instance he'd laid eyes on her, he'd found her attractive. Getting to know her better only amplified his interest.

And she was giving off vibes that implied he wasn't alone. He could all but see, feel, and hear the crackle between them.

He just didn't know what in the hell to do about it. Not only was he her boss and neighbor, but he wasn't exactly in a great place to...

She'd quit walking.

Turning, he looked at her. Moonlight cast her in ethereal tones. So lovely. Starlight, actual starlight, reflected in her eyes as she stood on the sidewalk, apparently waiting for something.

He shook his head, because words failed him, and he didn't know what she wanted.

Crickets chirped. An owl hooted.

A crinkle of her nose, and she pointed to her left.

Well, shit. Alrighty. They were home, and he hadn't noticed.

Smile. "Goodnight, Graham. See you tomorrow."

Sighing heavily, he watched her walk into her house and out of sight.

# Chapter Nine

It was insane. Chaotically insane.

Rebecca closed and locked the Gazette door just after noon, flipping the sign for lunch. Between emails, call-outs, articles in the paper, and word of mouth, it had been a zoo all morning. Townsfolk had cleared the shelves of framed prints. Many of the single sleeves in boxes had been purchased, too. It seemed their efforts had paid off. At least, with foot traffic, anyway. She'd no sooner opened the door at nine, and a steady stream had filtered in all morning.

The two of them barely had a chance to breathe. She'd had no chance to check numbers online or get her materials ready for Monday's edition. Graham, an hour in, had chucked his tie and suitcoat in the vicinity of her desk and rolled up his sleeves. Even Plucky had been vocal in singing all morning, though he seemed to be napping on his perch now.

"Holy cow." She strolled to Graham's office, where Twain lifted his head from his spot on the floor beside the desk. "That was nuts."

"You think that's crazy, look at this." He bumped his chin at the computer screen.

He laced his fingers behind his head and rocked in his chair. The position stretched his white button-down dress shirt snugly across his torso. She tried and failed not to stare. Wide chest. Ripples of abs beneath the fabric. She'd bet the small amount in her bank account that he worked out. Or had extremely good genetics.

*Focus.* She dragged a chair around to his side and plopped.

And there was his bergamot scent again, filling her with images, distractions, and fantasies. She'd lain awake half the night, thinking of him and their dinner. Not once, in all her years, had she been this affected by a man's cologne.

Then again, she supposed it could be Graham and not whatever product he used. They had chemistry, banter, and intellectual conversations. He was handsome, kind, and had just enough of a dark edge to render him interesting without being problematic. Her pulse thrummed a tripping rhythm and her chest heated. Would he be the type of guy to shove everything off the surface and take her right here on his desk? Or more traditional and drive her home to stumble toward a bed? Up against the wall frenzy or slow and meticulous?

"I can see you're also in awe." His low, deep timbre was laced with amusement, yet it infiltrated her senses and slithered into her bloodstream.

She blinked and glanced at his monitor, drawing in a measured breath for clarity. She really needed to knock it off every time they were within the same room. He had his emails pulled up, but none of them were open. Quickly, she zeroed in on what he'd referenced.

Two hundred emails. As she stared, the number climbed.

"Jeez. I wonder how many are sitting in my inbox. I haven't had a free moment to look." Best she'd done was boot up her computer when she'd gotten to the office.

"Since you set it up for certain subject matters on who gets emailed for what, I'm betting yours is just as whack."

"Probably." This was a really, really good sign that the towns-folk were interested in the Gazette again. Or still. "Can you pull up the web domain? Let's see how subscriber statistics are panning."

His large, deft fingers danced over the keyboard, and she did her level best to look at the screen instead.

He grunted. "Not sure what I'm looking for or where to go."

"May I?" She pointed to his mouse and keyboard.

A shrug, and he waved as if to say *have at it.*

She showed him the various tabs on how to get to the newsletter and lists. "Holy crap."

Narrowing his gaze, he leaned forward. "That can't be right. We had a little less than three hundred subscribers yesterday."

"For print. We're up to almost six hundred now." And it was only noon. Hopefully, that would hike. Word of mouth in Vallantine went a long way. Small town and all. "E-print subscribers are trickling in, too. These are new as of today. Remember, we had zero because we'd not had an electronic edition."

"Almost up to one hundred." He shook his head as if in awe. "That's not accounting for the sidewalk boxes, either."

His low chuckle filled the room, and he swiveled in his chair to face her. A glance in her direction, and his laugh gained momentum until he grabbed his side and bent over.

Unsure what was so hilarious, she stared at his thick black hair, curled slightly at the ends, mere inches from her lap, and she wanted to thread her fingers through the strands. Just once, to see if they were as soft as they looked. See if he would encourage more or politely ease out of her grasp. If he enjoyed the contact or preferred different forms of touch.

They'd flirted up to this point. Had there been anything more from his standpoint? She'd never been a great judge when it came to the opposite sex. Put her in a room full of people, and she could figure things out. Based on body language, facial expressions, or demeanor, she could read said room. It was a gift and skill she'd learned. Yet, when it involved someone she was interested in, or the flip side, that ability took a backseat. In most aspects of her life, she took charge. Dominated. Conquered. At least, when it came to things she could control. Relationships, though? She'd followed their lead.

Frankly, she'd just not been very good at...dating. Proven by her longest relationship lasting a mere year.

Attraction was one thing, but she was inching past interest and speeding toward lust with Graham. Not a first, except way more intense than anything she'd experienced to date. She wanted to know him. In a biblical sense. It had seemingly come out of nowhere and had grabbed her by the trachea.

"Mercy, Rebecca." He raised his head, and the distance between them shrank. Golden flecks were immersed in his emerald irises, unnoticeable if they hadn't been in each other's orbit. Warm hands framed her face. "You saved the paper."

She...what?

He gave her a little shake. "No telling how long it'll last, but you saved the Gazette."

A denial was on the tip of her tongue, that they'd worked together to fix the newspaper, but he brought her to him. Or he'd moved even closer. Something. What little thought remained in her head vanished. Millimeters. That was the meager space between his lips and hers. *Millimeters*. They were sharing air, and she got dizzy from the rush.

"Shit." His gorgeous, mesmerizing eyes widened. Up went his hands, and he straightened. "I apologize. That was uncalled for. I'm your boss. We work together. I'm sincerely sorry."

Somehow, she'd grown short of breath without moving a muscle. He looked genuinely horrified and contrite. Eyes round and beseeching. Lips rolled over his teeth. Meanwhile, her heart was just trying to resuscitate.

Silence, heady silence ensued, until she muttered the first thing that came to mind. "I'm not."

A speculative glare. "Not what?"

"Sorry." Not sorry he'd touched her or that he'd almost kissed her. But because he hadn't been wrong, they did work together and he was her superior, she scooted her chair back and rose. Rejection lanced her belly. "I'm going to work on my end for Monday's edition while it's quiet."

At a snail's pace, he lowered his arms and gripped the chair like he was trying to refrain from moving. His gaze darted back and forth between hers, imploring, studying. Eventually, he nodded, though the wrench of his brows indicated his confusion remained.

He could join the club.

Resetting her chair on the other side of his desk, she went to her own. Twain followed, resting his chin on her leg while she got her PC out of sleep mode. Smiling, she absently petted the sweet dog. And nearly fell out of her chair.

One hundred and five emails. She would've swallowed her tongue if it were anatomically possible.

She took the rest of her lunch break skimming through messages, answering a couple questions, and deleting spam while munching on a granola bar. More than once, she could feel Graham's gaze on her, and a twisted sense of giddy empowerment washed over her.

The afternoon proved less busy up front than the morning, though stragglers had moseyed in. To keep sane, Rebecca created folders for Artist of the Day, Weather of the Day, and recipe submissions, numbering them in the folders to coordinate with details for attribution. She also made a list of Announcements that had dropped in her inbox from the schools and a few townsfolk to send to Graham. Once the emails were off to him for the Monday edition, she popped over to the social media accounts and scheduled posts to run all weekend with open-ended teasers like they'd discussed. They had virtually five hundred new followers on Twitter and Facebook.

Without turning around, she called updates over her shoulder to Graham.

"Nice! Great work."

Pleased with herself, she smiled, and opened a blank Word document.

Typing clacked behind her. "Hey, I've got the Wordsearch, Garden, and Health Tips ready."

"Awesome. I'm writing a quick book review now. Once the bookclub gets going, the reviews can be more of a collective response."

"Nifty. Joan and Jefferson's stuff is in. I need the Weather Report for all weekend, along with the Horoscopes."

"On it." She minimized the document and pulled up her browser instead, copying deets. "Done. Emailed."

"Thanks!"

She stroked the dog's soft multi-colored fur and whispered, "Nice to be appreciated for a change." And it truly was. Spending seven years in the corner of a busy newsroom, hardly recognized, underutilizing her talents, and feeling utterly alone had left her with a great appreciation for the contrary.

Twain sighed as if he understood, dark brown gaze adoring.

"You're a sweetheart, aren't you? Yes, you are."

Tail wag.

Graham's typing paused. "What?"

"Nothing. I'm talking to your dog."

Chuckle. "Is he talking back? If so, I'm working you too hard."

"No comment."

Another laugh.

Based on a women's fiction book by a Georgia author she'd just finished reading last week, she typed a quick review and emailed it off to Graham.

Done with everything on her docket for today, she opened another blank page and inserted a table for future Wordsearch topics. It would hopefully help him on those days he was inundated. She plugged the months with coordinating holidays and seasons into the headers, along with a random section, then Googled ideas for each one. Not completely satisfied, she color-coded it. After emailing it to him, she sent it to print and stood.

Twain followed her into Graham's office.

"Who's a good boy? You are."

Behind her, Graham laughed while typing. "He likes you better than me. I think I'm jealous."

"Naw. I just smell better," she joked, her back to him, waiting on the printer to finish.

"That you do." Type, type. "Honeysuckle straight off the vine," he muttered in an irritated tone, seemingly to himself.

He knew what her perfume smelled like?

A glance at Twain proved he would offer no more insight for that remark than the man who'd spoken it.

She peeked over her shoulder. He was paying her no mind. "Should I switch to something with rose or gardenia undertones instead?"

Gaze on the screen, he paused, but didn't look up. "Nope."

She'd bought the brand a few years ago because it reminded her of home, and it wasn't overpowering. "But you don't like it."

"Never said that." Type, type. More refusal to look her way.

"Sounds as if you don't like it."

"I do."

"You sure?"

"Yep."

Grinning, she pulled pages from the printer and attached them to the blank corkboard on the wall with push pins.

"What's that?"

So, he *was* paying attention. "Wordsearch topics."

"Huh. Thanks."

"You're welcome." Thoroughly amused by the interaction, she went back to her desk.

Twain followed.

She sent a bunch of copies of the archive articles they'd sold in frames to the printer to replace stock, then glanced at the clock. It was only three. "Do you mind if I take off at four? We have the bookclub meeting at Scarlett's tonight and I'm in charge of snacks. I can buy more frames for the magazine racks while I'm at it."

"Not a problem."

"Thank you."

A grunt came by way of acknowledgement.

Shaking her head at the dog, she sighed. "Ornery men."

A few more stragglers came in, looked around, and bought some prints in sleeves. While she was up front, she made sure the plants in the bay window were hydrated, Plucky II had enough food and water for the weekend, and changed the pan liner on the bottom of his cage.

Back at her desk, she checked social media again, and read a couple blogs. Which gave her an idea. "Do you mind if I send you a piece for Monday?"

"No. Just get it to me by five."

She'd have it to him by four since that's when she was leaving, but okay.

If they were trying to keep the Gazette thriving and townsfolk from getting bored, they'd need to incorporate various topics by way of trends. One of the articles she'd read was how to refurbish old clothes into usable things, and which fads were making a comeback.

Using the blog as a source, she got ideas and put her own spin on it, then did a search for other items in that category and added it to her piece. Not a long editorial, but it was something fresh. A quick skim for edits, and she emailed it to Graham.

Shutting down the computer, she grabbed her laptop bag, manilla folder with copied archives, and rose. "I sent you the piece. Need me to do anything else before I go?"

"Nope. I'm good. Thanks for everything. Have a good weekend."

"You, too." She frowned, petting the dog one last time.

Graham still hadn't looked at her, and she wondered if it had to do with their almost kiss. Was he mad at himself? Her? Embarrassed?

Not certain how to address the climate change between them, she left, her stomach in knots.

She hit the thrift store and cleaned them out of photo frames, then dialed Scarlett on her way home. "Hey, how many people are we expecting tonight?"

"Not a clue, girl." Voices muffled in the background. "Aden Abner, you could piss off the Pope. Git outta here." A beat passed, and Scarlett sighed. "Ugh, that man makes my ass itch."

Rebecca laughed as she pulled up to her house. Aden's family had worked for Scarlett's since before they were born. He was in their graduating class, where he'd gotten a degree in annoying the hell out of her. Sometimes friends, usually frenemies, they had an odd push/pull no one but them seemed to understand.

With her blessing and support, he'd started his own business on her family's estate doing horse drawn carriage rides for tourists and events.

"Anyway," Scarlett said on a dramatic sigh. "Mama's original bookclub had forty-three members. Not accounting for the two that have passed away, I emailed the rest. Only a handful responded, Dorothy's mother included. No tellin' how many will show based on your notice in the Gazette."

Rebecca's mom being one of the two who'd died. She wondered who the other was, but let it go. "What snacks do you think I should get? Fruit and vegie platter? Maybe chips and salsa?"

"Fine by me. I'd grab a few packages of cookies from the bakery."

"You got it." Rebecca climbed out of the car and unlocked the front door. "I just have to change and hit the market. Be there soon."

Thirty minutes later, she drove past Peach Park and wove through the historical district of town. Vallantine Cemetery was on the right, huge plantations on the left. Brick-laid curvy roads, large sprawling acres, ornate gardens, and hundred year old oak trees teeming with Spanish moss. Some townsfolk called it black or long moss, but the very older generation, like Gammy, referred to it as horsehair. Probably due to its resemblance. Rebecca supposed it did look like a greenish-gray version of a horse mane.

She'd done a project on it in high school, and it gave her an idea now for an upcoming article. Most tourists and a bunch of residents didn't know squat about it, other than it was pretty. Funny thing? Spanish moss wasn't actually from Spain, nor was it moss. It's actually a bromeliad, a tiny flowering air plant that clung to itself as it dangled from tree limbs, gulping moisture or nutrients from the surrounding atmosphere and rain.

She chuckled to herself, surprised she'd remembered. Gammy used to say Rebecca was a plethora for useless knowledge and her mind was a sponge.

Lord, how she missed Gammy. An ache that would never abate, Rebecca feared. She rubbed the hollow sensation in her chest, glancing at headstones in the cemetery. Gammy was there, in the newer section. So were Rebecca's Mom and Dad. Countless others, dating all the way back to William and Katherine Vallantine. Some tombstones were large, baroque, and darkly weathered by time. Others were simple markers with flowers.

She sighed, glancing ahead. This area of Vallantine was gorgeous, and she'd almost forgotten. As girls, Rebecca and her besties often hung out at her house or the library. Not all the time, but usually. Dorothy's folks had been dubbed boring by their teenage selves because bedtime had been eleven and it was strictly enforced. Scarlett's parents were on the pretentious side and treated sleepovers as if they were a royal circus. Plus, her house was like a museum. Gammy hadn't cared how late they'd stayed up, so long as they didn't wake her, and always had a batch of homemade cookies waiting. Thus, the go-to location.

It had been some years since Rebecca had ventured this way. During daylight, the wispy hanging moss that clung to the trees was reminiscent of romantic days gone by. Old south and its hidden gems. Sitting on the front porch drinking sweet tea and waving to passersby. Not a care in the world, except if it would rain. But, at night, moss played tricks on the mind or added a dreary, creepy sensation. Fingers crawling up the spine. Snarled dangling limbs that forever reached. A reminder that shadows hid dangers. True murky fantasies gallivanted at night.

Honestly, Rebecca just thought it made the oaks seem sad.

Scarlett's plantation was the first estate on the corner, which was convenient since she'd turned hers into an event business.

Several others on the lane had been converted to B&Bs or inns, but the ones farther from town remained private residences.

Rebecca pulled into the brick-laid driveway, long and winding, and lined with massive oaks that made it appear like the gnarled boughs were hugging the path. Welcoming. Waving hello. Once she finally got to the mansion, she parked on the far end of the circular drive beside the fountain instead of the parking lot Scarlett had put in a number of years ago for event guests. Easier access to leave later.

She stood by her car, shaking her head, as a floral-scented breeze teased her strands.

Dang, but the place was huge. And gorgeous. It had been built pre-Civil War and impeccably maintained. Two-stories, white siding, and black shutters. Boxy and symmetrical. A true Antebellum southern home with neoclassical Greek-revival architecture, twenty Corinthian columns, and ten Doric ones. There was a cast-iron balcony that wrapped around the mansion's upper level, and the front portico centered the covered front porch spanning the width of the house. Triangular pediments and detailed dormers. Inside, there were thirteen furnished rooms, five of them for events.

The Taylors had been cotton farmers, and like most southern plantations, they'd had slaves. All of the fields had been turned into landscaped gardens with gazebos and vast sitting areas for entertaining by Scarlett's grandmother. The former slave quarters had been torn down and the barns had new added additions. When Scarlett had inherited the estate, she'd dedicated a room to black history for her guests and customers. Many other places offering guided tours of southern plantations glossed over the atrocities of slavery, instead focusing on romanticizing the lives of the slave owners who'd run the plantations. Scarlett refused to do that. She'd dug up as many old photos and farming tools as she could for display.

Honestly, looking at the place gave Rebecca an overwhelming sense of sorrow. She couldn't put her finger on why, other than specks of childhood memories where she and her besties had fantasized about their future weddings. Unlike Scarlett, Dorothy and Rebecca had come from middle-class families, and all this was but a dream, never to be a gleam in their eyes. Not to mention, lovely and breathtakingly beautiful as the estate was, Scarlett had done exactly what she'd envisioned. She'd turned a chunk of her family history into something amazing. Not just a private mansion to stare at from a distance, but a part of Vallantine where everyone was welcome. It made Rebecca feel like she'd settled or never reached her potential.

Stupid, being jealous of her best friend. Sighing, she hit the fob to open her trunk, where she'd set the snacks for bookclub.

Someone called her name. Turning, she shielded her face with her hand to block the sun.

Aden Abner, having rounded the driveway from the direction of the barns, strode toward her. His strut was exactly the same. Long, labored, and at his own leisurely pace. He'd get there when he felt like getting there. No need to rush. He had on a worn pair of jeans and a blue tee that fit snug against his contoured torso. Biceps bulged, straining his cuffs. A product of physical labor and tending to his horses. Wildly cut sandy blond hair was disheveled and his grin could still melt panties.

"Damn, that *is* you." He jogged the rest of the way to her, opening his arms. He swept her in a hug, spinning her around. "Still pretty as a picture."

She laughed as he set her down. "Aww, well thank you. You're still a charming good ole southern boy, I see."

"Why change perfection?" He shrugged, expression affable. "How's the Gazette treating you? I hear you and the Yankee got a romance blooming."

Hmm. Small towns and their gossip. "It's going well, and where did you hear that?"

"Around." Ah, that mischievous smirk. Now she recalled why he gave Scarlett such fits. The blue eyes were merely an exclamation point. "It true?"

"No, and don't you be spreading rumors."

"Hard to do that when word's already out, darlin'."

Whatever. "Wanna help me carry these inside?" She pointed to the trunk. "We got bookclub tonight."

"I heard it's been resurrected. I done signed up."

Laughing, she glanced at the house. Scarlett was on the porch, leaning against a pillar with her arms crossed, her brows raised, and her lips pursed.

"You didn't happen to join our bookclub to irritate a certain Belle, now, did you?"

Leaning over, he hefted a tray and winked. "It's my favorite pastime."

# Chapter Ten

Graham had just finished loading the files for Monday when a knock on the front door startled him. He glanced at Twain's perked ears, then through his office to the sidewalk outside the Gazette window. He didn't spot anyone, but part of his view to the front door was skewed. Rebecca had left hours ago, and she wouldn't knock because she had a key. They were way beyond normal business hours. In fact, dark had descended without him realizing. He hadn't made plans with Forest, either.

Rising, he strode out of his office, and found Gunner Davis examining the drop boxes Graham and Rebecca had put under the awning on the side of the entryway. He was wearing a white polo stretched across his paunch and khaki pants barely held in place by a belt, indicating he'd popped by after leaving work. As one of a handful of attorneys in town, he didn't practice law often anymore since becoming mayor twenty years ago. Or so Graham had been told. The guy still had an office on Belle Street, even though the majority of his clientele had been in their prime around Vietnam, but he spent more time at his official mayoral headquarters at the courthouse.

What could he possibly want at this hour?

Unlocking the door, Graham eased it open. "Mr. Davis. How are you?"

"Call me Gunner, son." He ran his pudgy fingers through his thinning white strands. "I'm good, thanks for asking. Mind if I come in?"

It was his building, but hey. "Sure. I was just finishing for the day." Graham glanced outside as Gunner squeezed past him. "Or night, as the case may be."

Shutting the door, he watched his boss stroll around, checking out the display counters, racks, tables, and pictures they'd hung. His frequent nodding seemed to indicate approval, but in the couple months Graham had been employed, Gunner hadn't once visited.

"Lookin' great in here. Lots of changes." He pointed to the comic boxes holding copies of old editions. "You get all these from storage upstairs?"

"Yes. It was Rebecca's idea." And a good one.

"Never would've thought to try that, or to turn part of the newsroom into a storefront. It beats this stuff collecting dust upstairs. I like the traces of history in the displays, too." He cinched his slacks. "People tend to forget origins over time. Damn shame, that. What you've done circles back to the Gazette's beginning."

Graham grunted a sound of agreement, unsure if Gunner was here to look over his shoulder or check to make certain he wasn't burning the place to ashes. "Rebecca's handiwork, also. She's got a creative streak that alludes me. Actually, she has kickass marketing skills." Which just happened to coincide with resurrecting the paper.

A guttural laugh, and Gunner shoved his hands in his pockets. "Glad you hired her. I was going to suggest it myself before you beat me to it. She has a lot of marketing skills. You're right

128

about that. You're an honest man, admitting the ideas were hers."

"I wouldn't take credit for something that wasn't mine." Gunner probably wouldn't know that, though. Based on Graham's employment in Minnesota and the way he'd been terminated, he couldn't blame Gunner for whatever assumptions were made. Tension knotted Graham's shoulders as warning knells clanged. He had a six month contract, in which he was two-and-a-half deep. Was he about to get canned? "She's good at what she does and thinks outside the box. I'm lucky to have her."

Gunner nodded. Striding to the display window, he watched the canary for a beat. "Her idea, too?"

Not liking the entire exchange, Graham placed a palm to his gut to calm the jitters. "The whole display. She found the items at a thrift shop. All except the bird."

"Mr. Forester had one like it years ago. I'm sure Miss Rebecca mentioned it."

"She did." He wanted to hammer questions or maybe accusations Gunner's way, but best Graham keep mum, despite the uneasiness of the situation. It was like waiting for the other shoe to drop.

*Nice weather. How you been? I like the new pictures.*
*You're fired.*

Gunner picked up a copy of today's paper from one of the basket racks in front of him, examining the front page. "It pained me to see the Gazette reduced to what it had become. No one seemed to give a darn anymore. We let it fall by the wayside. I'd hoped for this very thing." He turned, holding up the newspaper. "Hoped when I'd hired you to find headlines again and actual content." He stared at Graham, deadpan. "Circulation's on the rise. Numbers are looking better."

"They are." Quite a bit. "Both print and e-delivery. Sales here in the storefront won't amount to much, but it's a little something extra."

"Right you are." Gunner set the paper back in the basket and headed for the door, pausing with his hand on the knob. "I hear you and Miss Rebecca are an item."

Shit. What? "We aren't."

Up went the mayor's bushy white brows. "But you want to be."

Not a question. He stated it as fact.

Graham opened and swiftly closed his mouth. Since he couldn't deny the statement, he just shut up. Let it be known, he did have some brain cells.

"Thought so. Rumors in small towns are typically based on some form of truth. A good amount of our folks are rooting for you." Gunner's lips twitched in what could pass as a smirk. "Best be minding our Rebecca's heart, though. It's been broken a few times too many."

A nod, and the mayor left.

Graham, alone once more, waited for the mayor to pass by the window, then he bent at the waist and blew out a gale force wind.

The hell had that been about? He couldn't tell if he'd been praised, put on probation, or threatened. In five mere minutes. Criminy, he had whiplash.

The jingling of Twain's collar joined Graham's heartbeat, and the dog stuck his head out the doorway of the inner office.

Hands on his hips, Graham sighed. "Thanks for bailing, you sissy. You just left me for the wolves out here."

Twain sat on his haunches as if to say, *sorry, not sorry*.

"I'll forgive you this time." He went to his office to grab his things, petting the dog on his way. "That was completely out of the blue, right? The whole conversation. I mean, weird."

Twain tilted his head like he understood.

Pocketing his keys and phone, Graham stood by his desk, rattled. If he lost this job, there would likely be no other in his field. He wasn't good at anything else. If he had to start all over again in a fresh career, he had zero clue what he'd do. After the scandal, when it became apparent no one would hire him, he'd toyed with different path options, and found squat. But he'd made his bed, and now he had to lay in it. He was damn lucky to have this opportunity.

Until Rebecca, he'd done little more than the motions. She'd lit a fire under him. Got the interest of the town involved. Made changes that were working. Hell, he had ideas and a spark again. Just this evening, after she'd left, he'd written his first article in months instead of just editing or designing the pages for print. Hope had stupidly bloomed.

The visit from Gunner gave Graham the clear impression his boss knew this had all been her craftsmanship. That she was the one making the Gazette thrive anew. And he'd be correct. But what had been the purpose in dropping by? To see if Graham would lie? Take credit? To hint that Gunner was aware of the inner workings and Graham should watch his step? Had it been a warning or precursor?

He just...didn't know, and the uncertainty ate at his gut. He'd moved hundreds of miles from his family and all he knew to take a job in a tiny southern town doing the kind of work he used to baulk at, only to hit a wall. If not for a feisty blonde saving his ass, he'd be fired in four months for no productivity. And after tonight's impromptu visit, he wasn't so sure saving the paper would save his career, seeing as he'd had no hand in it.

Anxiety tripped his pulse. Worry tapped his temples.

Not sure what to do with the restless energy, he whistled for the dog, locked up, and walked down Main Street toward his suburb. As usual, the town square was quiet, and he was left alone with his thoughts. He was beginning to hate his own company.

Maybe the fresh air and stroll would do him some good. It was Friday night. He could call Forest and get a beer. Or change when he got home and go for a run. Read a novel he'd recently picked up at one of the shops. Research material for small town papers and Georgia-specific content. Watch some mindless television. Fix the back door deadbolt that wouldn't catch the latch. Scroll online for patio furniture for the deck. Bake more ridiculous cookies for the mailman. Unpack the rest of the boxes from his old apartment. Paint the spare bedroom. Call his folks. Watch the grass grow that he'd just cut on...

"Hey, everything okay?"

Irritated, he glanced up from where he sat on the top step of the stoop outside his house to the interruption, and was met with familiar blue eyes. Rebecca. She was easy to talk to, didn't judge, encouraged rather than discouraged, both stirred and settled his crazy, smelled great, straddled the cute and sexy-as-hell line, was smart as a whip, and had a great funny bone. Damn if she wasn't exactly what he'd needed. How'd she know?

Actually, after a quick glance around, he realized he had zero recollection of making it home, and it was *her* stoop he was on. Guess that had been his subconscious at play, not her intuition.

He was an idiot. A severely distracted one.

Twain let out an exasperated sigh beside Graham to punctuate the conclusion.

She'd changed clothes since leaving the office. She wore a pair of skinny jeans, sandals with heels, and some sort of flowy green blouse that fell off one shoulder. Her hair was loose from her typical work knot, caramel strands blowing gently in the breeze. She stood, staring down at him, with worry lines creasing her forehead. Probably because he hadn't answered her, not that he could recall what she'd asked.

Slipping a black purse off her shoulder, she set it by his feet on the bottom step and crouched in front of him. "What's wrong?"

Everything. Nothing.

"You look nice." That wasn't exactly an answer, but it was the God's honest truth. She had such a lovely, angular face, accented by those huge eyes. Vastly expressive.

"Thank you." Her expression indicated she wasn't convinced by his evasive comment, yet she rolled with it.

"You're welcome. How was bookclub?"

"It was fun, for the most part." She had Twain move, and sat beside Graham in the dog's place. "Scarlett's mama had her nose in the air about a few changes to the plantation and the fact Aden Abner joined club."

"Who's Aden?"

"An old classmate." She brushed a strand away from her face, smile wistful. "His family used to work for the Taylors. About five years ago, Scarlett sold Aden a chunk of the estate grounds where the barns are located. He built a house there and runs a business that coincides with hers. Horse-drawn carriage rides and such."

He'd thought, or assumed, Scarlett was single. "How long have they been together?"

"Scarlett and Aden?" She laughed, rich and addictive. "They're not. They drive each other up a wall and back down again. On an hourly basis. They're friends. Sort of."

"Sort of, huh?" She was amusing when talking about anything but herself. More open book and less reserved.

"Yeah, it's hard to categorize their relationship. He'd do damn near anything for her, and she respects the heck outta him. She was the one who recognized he should make a go of the business instead of just tending to her horses. They fight like red-headed stepchildren."

Sounded like foreplay in his book. Mighty fine of Scarlett, though. Not only to acknowledge Aden's gifts, but put them to use in way that offered him independence.

"You'd like Aden. We'll get a group of us together one night and introduce you. Might not be a bad idea to join club yourself. Meet some of the townsfolk."

"Maybe." Friday nights could prove problematic because that's when he did Monday's layout. Then again, he could knock it out anytime over the weekend. "We'll see."

"Anyway," she said through a sigh. "We had a lot more people than expected, I think out of curiosity about the library and wanting to hear gossip. Mostly women, but we had about ten gentleman. We settled on a cozy mystery for this month."

He nodded, not having much to add. He'd rather listen to her talk, anyhow. With her being so close, her intoxicating scent was wreaking havoc on his attention span. As in, he had none. What had occurred back in his office this afternoon began playing on a loop through his head. How he'd almost kissed her. The things she'd said.

"There was bickering and fussing over what genre to start with, so finally we just took a vote and—"

"How long is a hot minute?"

Straightening, she snapped her mouth shut, confusion creasing her forehead.

Crap. He hadn't meant to interrupt, but it was driving him bonkers. He'd been having a hard time straddling personal and professional with regards to her. Apparently, half the town, mayor included, thought Graham and Rebecca were dating. And okay with it. Tonight's visit from Gunner had thrown Graham a one, two punch, first with fear for his job and then with the comment about her.

"Um..." Her lips pouted in thought. "In southern terms, it typically refers to a long time, I guess. Could be weeks, months, or years, depending on the context. Why?"

Well, okay. That hadn't clarified anything.

Crawling out of his skin, yet again, he rose and paced the short sidewalk in front of her stoop. "The other night at dinner, you said it had been a hot minute since you'd slept with anyone."

"Oh, that."

Uh huh, *that*. "So, in that context, how long is a hot minute?"

She stared at him, her expression unreadable. "My most recent relationship lasted about eleven months. We broke up almost a year ago."

A year? He thought his dry spell of seven months was bad. He'd been with Felicia going on two years, and she'd flaked the second his career started tanking. Which only proved she hadn't given a damn about him. Frankly, he hadn't been all that upset. Or surprised.

He paced anew, his head a riot. "At the office today, I nearly kissed you, and then I apologized."

She stared some more, and how he wished her typically expressive eyes would give him an inkling of her thoughts. He was batting zero.

Fine, he'd keep going on his bipolar rant. "You said that you weren't sorry I tried." At the time, if she'd given him a lap dance while wearing a dinosaur costume, he would've been less shocked. Or perplexed. "What does that mean, precisely? Could you maybe spell it out?"

This was a very precarious position. He was her supervisor, and though he'd never, not in the realm of ever, force himself on a woman, want them to feel they were being sexually harassed, or coaxed in any manner, he also had to protect himself. His career had already taken a knockout hit. Anything else would be a death blow. And on the flip side, she needed to know she could trust him, that he'd respect her, and that any engagement would be her choice. Without repercussions.

She drew a slow delicate breath, gaze never leaving his, and when she finally spoke, her voice was soft, bordering on feeble. "I'm not very good at this sort of thing, Graham."

Of all the replies he'd anticipated, that hadn't made the cut. "Not good at what thing?"

Her teeth worked her lower lip, and it took everything he had not to erase the distance and do that for her. His skin heated and muscle locked around bone. His fingers twitched in his abject desire to touch her.

A long blink, and she lowered her chin, absently petting the dog. A move so unlike her spirited, straightforward personality that even gravity seemed like a myth.

He needed an aspirin. "Rebecca?"

"Dating." She winced, shaking her head as if berating herself. "I'm not very good at dating or relationships or the flirty banter beforehand. I don't have much experience in this arena. Growing up in a small town where secrets don't exist, there weren't many boyfriend options. A couple, but you get it. All the guys around here had played in the same sandbox. In college, there had been a few interests. Nothing long term. I was more focused on my studies. Same for after I graduated. Some here and there, but I was trying to make a name for myself. That eleven-month relationship I mentioned? It was my longest."

She was honest to a fault. Tactful, usually, but would not hesitate to speak her mind if provoked. She didn't appear to have a deceptive bone in her body. So, as he stood in front of her, hands on his hips, head tilted to be sure he'd heard her right, and gob-smacked straight into Willy Wonka's factory, he had to remind himself of those traits. Because no way, no way in hell, would she have him believe a guy hadn't tried to put a ring on it before now. She was gorgeous. She was kind. She was witty and funny and creative and as real as his attraction to her from the starting gate.

All that aside... "You didn't answer my question."

"I just did."

"But, you didn't." Even the dog was darting his gaze back and forth between them like he was watching a deranged tennis match. "We'll circle back to dating history later. I assure you, there's a heated forthcoming discussion on that topic. For now, answer my question." He gritted his teeth. "Please."

She cast her gaze heavenward as if praying for patience. "What question, Graham? I just said I'm not good at this stuff." She gestured between the two of them. "I don't know what you want me to say."

Alrighty. Stop this merry-go-round. He wanted off.

He raised his palms and spoke in very precise, very articulate, very short sentences. Not because he thought she was stupid, but because the want of her was starting to make him stupid. "I almost kissed you. I said I was sorry. You said you weren't sorry. What did you mean by that?"

"Um, that I wasn't sorry you tried to kiss me," she said slowly, apparently catching on to his daft status.

"Okay." Now they were getting somewhere. "Meaning, it would've been all right with you if I had succeeded in the feat?"

"Yes."

"And you would've wanted me to kiss you?"

"Yes."

"Have you changed your mind about that since this afternoon?" Say no. Please, say...

"No."

Thank Almighty. "Are you feeling pressured in any way or are you uncomfortable with the possibility of said kissing?"

"No."

"For clarification, it was okay that I tried to kiss you, you wanted me to, you still do, and I'm not forcing yes responses." The oxygen backed up in his lungs. "Do I have that correct?"

"Yes. You're being weird and—"

"Pause. That's all I needed." It wasn't all he needed, but he was about to fix that.

Striding the two paces between them, he bent, slapped his palms on the top step beside her hips, and crushed his mouth to hers.

Rejoicing circled the globe.

Angels fell from On High.

Equilibrium was restored to the universe and...

Scratch that. Nope. Point five seconds in, and she knocked him off axis, spiraling toward oblivion.

Her plush, soft lips parted, and a sexy lil mewl escaped her mouth, drifting right into his. His pulse thundered against his carotid and his gut boiled. He tilted his head, went deeper, and stroked her tongue. Long, slow, languid. Drugging.

This was always the best part. Well, not the best, per se, but the most informative. That first kiss was to get to know a woman, learn her style, test her technique to reveal if they were a good match. Discover if they fit. Find out if the chemistry was only on paper.

The two of them? They were the periodic table of elements. And as for the fit? Her puzzle pieces interlocked with his to the point he had the crazy thought she was cut strictly for him.

She met him beat for beat, on equal footing, then twisted the game to Cat & Mouse. Submissive, following his lead. Boom. Her turn, taking the reins. He was dizzy with the desire for her. Pants shrinking, groan-inducing, chest pounding kind of dizzy. The hot, wet cavern of her mouth tasted like mint and she smelled like a pollen-soaked summer afternoon. Honeysuckle and warm woman.

Arching closer, she threaded her fingers in his hair, and...ah, shit. He groaned. Tendrils of need raised the hairs on his nape, sent lightning to his circuits. A war ensued inside his mind.

*Take her.*

*Don't you dare.*

*Yes.*

*No.*

*Too soon.*

*Soon would never be fast enough.*

A whine split the air, unusual in the way it jarred the quiet intensity of the moment. They both paused the kiss.

Not her whine. Or his. Whose? They were alone.

Something cold and wet pressed against his jaw.

She severed contact with a deep-throated laugh. "Hi, Twain." Turning her head, she grinned at the dog, who licked her face. Then, she did the unfathomable and removed her hands from Graham's hair to...*pet Twain instead*. "Who's a good boy? You are."

"I'm a good boy, too," Graham drolled.

"Are you feeling left out?" she cooed, as if the dog was the one needing consolation.

"Yes." Graham nudged her cheek with his nose.

Throwing her head back, she laughed. Her hair cascaded across his hand, which he was unaware he'd placed against the curve of her spine.

As if they needed more cold water splashed, Twain then licked Graham's face.

# Chapter Eleven

"The whole town's buzzin' about you and Graham." Scarlett waggled her brows.

Rebecca sighed and leaned against her car in the parking lot of the library where they were waiting on Forest for a meeting. Sun bathed the grounds while a humid breeze caressed her skin. Cardinals danced between the trees and brown thrashers chirped excited calls. The one thing she didn't miss about Vallantine? The gossip.

She rolled her eyes. "I love how everyone has us married with point five kids, and we haven't even been on a date yet."

Scarlett laughed. "You had dinner together last week."

"A *working* dinner."

Dorothy held up her palm. "How do you have point five kids? That's mathematically impossible."

"That's your take on the situation?" Scarlett set her hands on her hips.

"No, I'm just saying, as an accountant, I don't get it."

Rebecca glanced at the heavens. "I recant my comment. I don't even want kids."

Unless she was talking to present company, that was rarely something she admitted aloud. Most people would say things like, *you'll change your mind*, or think to themselves, *what's wrong with her*? Society often criticized women like her, as if they wouldn't have complete life fulfillment without offspring. It made her so angry. But, in honesty, children just weren't a part of her future plans or something she genuinely desired. She loved kids. She simply didn't want any of her own.

Scarlett grinned. "But you want your boss." When Rebecca didn't reply, Scarlett pounced. "Come on. Give us the dirt. We're your besties."

Tough argument when she was right.

Fine. Rebecca crossed her arms. "Yes, I like him. Yes, I think he likes me, too. No, we're not officially seeing each other. But he kissed me last night." And, geez. Her girly parts were still excited.

Dorothy smiled.

Scarlett went for the jugular. "I knew it. I knew it. How was the kiss? I'll bet it was hotter than a frog in a frying pan."

A laugh, and Rebecca rubbed her forehead. "Let's just say it was a good thing I was sitting down. My legs wouldn't have held me upright."

"Nice." Dorothy flashed a grin. "You deserve some good vibes."

"Agree." Scarlett flipped her hair over her shoulder, obviously not finished with her interrogation. "Like, Alice down the rabbit hole, kinda good kissing?"

Forest's truck pulled in the lot and parked.

"Yes, now hush." Rebecca gave Scarlett the stink eye to behave, then watched Forest exit the truck.

The passenger door opened, and…Graham climbed out.

Lord help her, but he looked darn sexy in a pair of jeans and a gray tee. He normally wore suits to work, which was fine. A well-dressed man was attractive. But give her down-home slumming for the win. His backside filled the denim as if tailored for him and the shirt emphasized the lean, muscular shape of his build. Sunlight changed his ebony strands to something closer to navy. Disheveled and morning bedhead was yummy. Those eyes, though. So vivid green in stark sunlight.

"Well, butter my biscuit," Scarlett teased.

Dorothy elbowed her. Hard.

Rebecca suddenly found herself unsure how to behave around him. Did they act like normal? Nerves pinged her belly and did a waltz. They were in the company of friends. Perhaps she'd just follow the leader and figure it out.

Wondering why he was here, she stayed mute. Graham hadn't mentioned anything about accompanying Forest. Then again, the meeting had been called at the last minute. Something about the Historical Society's verdict on renovations. She had been itching to hear news since the call an hour ago. They all had been on pins and needles, in fact. Their plans for the library depended on what they'd say.

"Hope it's all right I came." Graham smiled, rendering Rebecca's brain cells toast. "I haven't seen the infamous library up close yet."

"You're welcome anytime." Scarlett winked.

"Never mind her," Dorothy said. "She had too much coffee with her sugar this morning. She's not actually flirting. And, yes, we're happy to show you around."

"I think you mean sugar with my coffee."

"No, I meant just what I said." Dorothy squinted, side-glancing their friend.

He nodded, grin implying amusement. "I appreciate the hospitality."

Scarlett fidgeted with her short blue sundress. "I got a baby shower at the plantation in two hours. What's the verdict?"

"Well," Forest sighed. Shuffling papers in his hand, he frowned.

Oh, crap. Rebecca's heart sank. The Historical Society had vetoed the changes. All their ideas and plans wouldn't come to pass. They'd have to draw new ones and submit them again, and there was no guarantee those would get accepted. Those blueprints were what would work the best. All their agony over the past six months...

"They approved everything."

Silence hung, then Forest slowly grinned. Wide.

"No," Dorothy breathed, eyes round. "Seriously?"

"Seriously." He shrugged. "I inserted my two cents by telling them the changes were completely necessary and that our Belles would never disrespect history. Plus, I think Rebecca's plug in the paper showed them how transparent you were being about the renovations."

There wasn't a shadow of doubt in Rebecca's mind that if he hadn't gone to bat for them, this wouldn't have worked out in their favor. He was Vallantine's golden boy, and his word was bond.

"Yes!" Scarlett let out a hoot, fists raised. "I would climb you like an oak if I weren't in this dress, Forest Truman."

"I'm not wearing a dress." Giddy bubbles exploded in Rebecca's chest. "Incoming."

Forest must've guessed her move, because on her way to launching herself at him, he tossed papers at Graham and opened his arms to catch her. Legs around his waist, arms circling his shoulders, she hugged the spit outta him.

"Thank you so much."

He laughed. "You're very welcome."

Glancing over his shoulder, she caught Graham's disapproving expression a half-second before Scarlett and Dorothy swooped in for a group hug.

Forest let out an *oomph*, then laughed again. "If I'd known this was all it took..."

Scarlett lifted her head. "Get in here, Graham."

"Um." He shook his head. "Forest and I don't have a hug-it-out kind of relationship."

Forest grunted. "He's not comfortable in his masculinity."

"Whatever, dude."

A roll of her eyes, and Rebecca extracted an arm. Snatching a fistful of his shirt, she dragged Graham against them, and papers scattered on the ground.

Face smooshed in Forest's shirt, Graham sighed. "Okay, then. Five-some it is."

Dancing in place, Scarlett backed away and squealed. "This is amazing!"

Forest set Rebecca on her feet as the others created a respectable distance once again. He bent to retrieve the scattered paperwork while Graham smoothed his tee with both hands, his cheeks flushed.

"I'm going to call contractors." Dorothy whirled toward her car, then paused. "Is there anything else?"

"No, ma'am. We're good." On what seemed like an impulse, Forest brushed a strand of auburn hair away from her cheek. Dorothy's eyes widened, and he froze. "I'm sorry. You just had a piece of hair, and... Sorry."

Seemingly not breathing, Dorothy shook her head. "Totally okay. Thanks. I'll go now."

"Oh!" Rebecca snapped her fingers. "Anyone have plans tonight? I thought maybe we could get together for drinks or something. Including Aden, so Graham can meet him?"

"That sounds like a terrible idea." Scarlett narrowed her eyes, smiling. "What time?"

Dorothy laughed. "I'm free."

Forest and Graham nodded.

Scarlett's thumbs went to work on her cell. "Graham, what's your number?"

He rattled it off.

"I'll send a group text and we can decide where and when. I included Aden."

"Sounds good. Bye, y'all." Dorothy waved. "See you tonight."

A few minutes later, Scarlett took off, too.

Rebecca sighed dreamily, unable to fight her stupid smiling. Things were finally falling into place, and her heart was full. The library, her career, even something blooming with Graham. It felt surreal.

"Wanna see the library?" she asked him.

His grin was amped to high voltage. "Absolutely."

"You two go ahead." Forest held up the papers. "I'll get these reorganized and wait in the truck."

Graham shook his head. "I'll walk home from here. Head out. I'll catch up with you tonight."

They waited for Forest to leave, then she dug the keys out of her purse.

"Just a warning, it's in pretty bad shape, but now that we're cleared with the Historical Society, we can fix that soon."

His smile softened, gaze sweeping her face. "You look really happy."

"I am." The emotion felt foreign since it had been so long since she'd experienced it.

Reaching out, he lightly tapped a finger to her nose. "You're wrinkling it again. You do that when you're excited or embarrassed."

"Eh." She covered the body part in question. "Bad poker face."

His smile slipped to endearment, his gaze warm. "Could be worse things than honest, Rebecca."

"Very true." Motioning toward the library, she pivoted. "Let me show you my childhood sanctuary."

A nod, and they climbed the porch steps. As she put the key in the lock, he placed a hand over hers to still her motion.

"Hold on a sec."

Before she knew what hit her, he grabbed her waist, spun her around, and had her back pressed to the door. Hands in her hair, he sealed his lips to hers.

And, gosh. Last night hadn't been a fluke. Firm, warm, and cajoling. He kissed like his personality. To the point while listening to feedback. A team player, yet demonstrating knowledge. Tender and direct. Potent.

Ah, geez. That bergamot scent of his. She would gladly drown in it.

A tingle shot through her, and she arched toward him. Heat blasted, and it wasn't from the warm day. Never in her life had she had such a strong reaction to a kiss. Last night or now. It was as if he'd climbed inside her mind to find all her triggers. A brush of his lips. A stroke of his tongue. His hands slid down her back to rest at the curve of her spine and twitched as if he wanted to do more with them. She dug her fingers in his thick, soft hair and clutched the strands. He inhaled. Hard. Her head spun. Too much and not enough.

A groan, and he full body pressed her against the door, aligning their torsos and tangling their legs. Hard and unyielding, he trapped her. And she never wanted to be freed.

He mumbled something she didn't understand and slid his mouth across her jaw, down her throat.

She trembled at the new assault. "Whatever you say."

He chuckled against her skin. "Did you even hear me? I don't think that was coherent."

"No," she panted, lids pinched closed. "I don't care, though. The answer is yes."

Smiling, he lifted his head, and they shared oxygen. "I said, I've been wanting to do that all day."

"What took you so long?"

He laughed, brushing a thumb across her lower lip. "Don't know what I was thinking. Shame on me." He let out a breath, gaze seeking hers. "Does this mean we're dating? A couple? Together? I'm not real clear on logistics."

She wasn't sure, either, but she smiled. "I would like that, if you're interested."

"I'm definitely interested." He paused, gaze assessing. "I think the town already believes we're seeing one another."

"Mmmhmm. Welcome to Vallantine, where everybody is up in your business." The townsfolk had an uncanny way of fueling rumor to become fact or driving persuasion. "It's not all bad."

"I'm just not used to it." He waved the comment away. "We haven't discussed much by way of preferences." He scratched his head, face contorted in thought. "Are there rules?"

The poor guy seemed more lost than her with where to go next. "Like passing Go and collecting two hundred bucks?"

"Smartass. I was thinking more along the lines of avoiding the straight to jail card."

Monopoly references aside, she welcomed the gesture. "Why don't we spend some time together and see where it leads. Play it by ear?" Like she'd told him before, her experience wasn't vast with regards to relationships, but he appeared to need direction, which she could appreciate. "Exclusive, though. No one else in the mix, and we don't let it affect work. If it doesn't pan out, we remain civil."

He nodded, a hint of a smile curving his lips. "Okay."

"Ready to see the library?"

"Probably a better plan than giving the town an eyeful on the porch." Nodding again, he stepped back. "Lead on."

Turning the key, she pushed the door open, and giddy euphoria swamped her. How she adored this place, even if it was in shambles. Mildew and dust coated her throat as she walked to the middle of the room behind the center counter.

His gaze took in the floor-to-ceiling shelves flanking both walls, the chandelier, and the loft before he crossed his arms. "It's bigger than it looks from the outside."

She supposed it did, but the library had been emptied of furniture and books, which could affect first appearances. "We're adding an addition to the back wall there," she pointed, "which will help with space. Upstairs will be a bookstore, while down here will stay a library."

He bumped his chin in approval. "Great plan. There're only a couple places in town that sell books, and one of them caters specifically to rare titles. The other isn't exclusively books."

Their thinking exactly. She smiled. "We'll sell mostly newer fiction in specific genres. We'll also have an Indie book section."

Head back, he kept his gaze everywhere at once. "Amazing building. Seriously amazing. I can understand why the Society was supervising and worried about changes. You just don't find places like this anymore."

How he spoke her language was sexy.

They walked the perimeter, and she gave him highlights of memories with her besties.

Shoving his hands in his back pockets, he grunted. "Is that why they left you three the library? All the time you spent here?"

"Partly." She tilted her head. "When we were in eighth grade, Miss Fillmore was our favorite teacher. She was kinda shy, but she really understood us on a level better than most adults. She encouraged and bolstered us. We wanted her to be happy. Of course, being teenage girls, we first jumped to romance by way of a thank-you. Mr. Brown was awkward in an endearing way. He talked to us like our opinions mattered and tolerated us hanging around. We set them up on a date one spring, and they got married not long afterward. A match made in heaven. Or, in a library."

She sighed, suddenly feeling whimsical. Whether the location or the memories, she didn't care. "Through the years, he tried so hard to save this place. Once, he told us it was like putting a bandage on an amputation. He was the last living Vallantine descendant. You could tell he was torn between familial obligation and the desire to live his life. I think he just hit his breaking point one day. The next thing we know, Dorothy's meeting with Gunner Davis for the deed, Mr. and Mrs. Brown had sold their house, and they'd left Vallantine to roam the country in an RV. I learned via Zoom while in Boston."

Brows raised, he shook his head. "That's insane, and one helluva story."

"It is, and all true." She shrugged. "Their letter said we helped them find love and that no one would love this place better than us. Now, it's ours," she whispered, hardly believing it herself. "We'd had such foolish, idle dreams as girls. This was one dream we never expected to come true."

"I don't know the Browns, but just listening to you tells me they did the right thing."

She closed her lids to the sudden emotion, her throat tight, eyes damp. Somehow, she'd needed to hear that, and not from townsfolk invested in the library's history or waiting for an outcome. Graham hadn't grown up here. His opinion wasn't swayed by sentimentality. Without realizing it, he'd said the solitary thing she'd somehow been waiting for in order to accept the gift she and her besties had been given. Though happy, a strange sort of remorse had surrounded the whole affair, but that guilt no longer sat on her chest.

Turning away from him, she pretended to examine the circular stairs to the loft and cleared her throat. After blowing out a watery breath, she smiled. "Thank you."

"You're welcome."

If he'd noticed her struggle to wrangle her emotions, he didn't point it out, and she was immensely grateful. She'd always been uncomfortable showing a tender side to the world. Even Scarlett and Dorothy hadn't been privy to a lot of her moods, and they would never judge.

"How true are the rumors of haunting?"

Hand to her forehead, she laughed. He didn't seem the type to believe in the paranormal, which made his question funnier. In fact, he'd outright said as much a few days prior.

"I think the rumor started with our parents' generation. Though, to hear Gunner Davis tell the tale, it had been going on long before." Using her arms as leverage, she set her hands on the center counter and hoisted herself onto the edge, letting her legs dangle. "Stories about Katherine Vallantine aren't typical ghost lore. More like they're wrapped in a flowery fanciful myth."

"How so?" Intently watching, clearly interested, he leaned against one of the empty bookcases.

"Well, take Miss Katie, for instance. The peach tree at the center of town supposedly grants wishes. It was the first in town to be planted, and all because she loved the fruit. William and Katherine had an epic love story. Seriously, it was one for the ages. In a time when women had few rights or zero control, her husband's motive for all he said and did revolved around her. It's as romantic as their death was tragic. The pieces of their life they'd left behind serve as a reminder of that love."

A sly smile. "And does Miss Katie actually grant wishes?"

They'd had this conversation a couple days ago, too, but he seemed more open-minded today.

She thought about all the instances where she'd visited the tree as a girl. "I don't know. It hasn't in my case." Not yet, anyway.

A grunt, and he bumped his chin toward her. "And the library?"

"It was built by William for Katherine because she loved books. It survived the hurricane that killed them." She shrugged because he knew that. "She doesn't roam about scaring people or show herself at all. The legend is that she assists all who enter seeking knowledge. I'm unsure how true that part is, but I know when Sheldon and Rosemary Brown were holed up here during another hurricane, back before they were married, they'd fallen asleep on a couch. When they woke, Katherine Vallantine's journal was on the floor in front of them. It had been on the top shelf," she pointed to the twenty-foot shelving unit, "and hadn't been seen since Sheldon's grandfather ran the library. Oddly enough, Sheldon had mentioned the diary while talking about the building's history to calm Rosemary down over the storm."

"Huh." He scratched his chin. "Neat story, if it's true."

"Have you heard about that online challenge going around? While on a date, you relay one truth, one lie, and something you wish were truth or lie?"

"Yeah." He crossed his arms. "Instagram or something, right? A way to get to know your partner better."

"Correct." She paused. "That's based loosely on Katherine and William's courting period. The tradition was handed down. Sheldon and Rosemary played it the night the journal appeared."

"Alrighty." His brows wrinkled. "How'd a blogger get ahold of it?"

"One of my Boston contacts. I told her the tale to get better exposure. She never did write the backstory, though, just the game portion."

"Might be better that way." He winked. "It can stay a Vallantine secret."

"Yeah." Hopping down, she laughed. "Ready to go?" She'd woken up in more pain than usual this morning, and she wanted to take an extra dose of her antioxidant, followed by a nap. Especially if they were going out tonight. Caffeine wasn't touching her fatigue, either.

"Sure." He headed for the door, and waited until they were both on the porch before speaking again. "We should play the truth challenge."

"I'm up for it, soon as we have a first date."

# Chapter Twelve

They'd decided to go to the bar on the outskirts of town instead of The Tipsy Turtle in the Main Square for their night out and celebration. Along the river, the place sat under a lone yellow-tinted streetlight, and the gravel lot was a cluster of cars or trucks with seemingly no order to the parking. It was called Backwater and, well, it was definitely that. The establishment had apparently been in business for over thirty years, catering to locals.

From the outside, the building resembled a large fishing shack, and the inside didn't do much to change Graham's opinion. It smelled like stagnant river water and stale beer. There was no AC. Dark, worn pine throughout. Cracked white linoleum floor. A long bar on the right wall, a small stage with a dance floor in the back, and scarred tables throughout the rest of the space. Oh, and taxidermy. Weird taxidermy. Squirrels, a boar, catfish, deer, and a crocodile, all affixed to the paneled left wall. Lightbulbs with plastic green shades hung from the ceiling randomly by way of illumination. Still, it was dark, somewhat cloudy due to cigarette smoke, and loud. Really, really loud country music.

But, hey. They did karaoke on Saturdays.

If someone had told him six months ago he'd wind up in a bar like this with a bunch of southerners, and enjoying himself, to boot, Graham would've passed out cold in hysterics. As a rule, he tended to steer clear of places where he might need a tetanus shot before entering or where it was likely he'd get murdered walking out. Alas, here he was at a corner table with one old friend and four new ones, waiting on a basket of fried catfish and chips, and drinking warm beer. It was all Backwater served. A fish and fries basket, and one brand of beer on tap.

Rebecca had been right. He did like Aden. He was honest, laid back, and unapologetic. He'd been the last to show tonight, and had promptly parked it in a chair next to Graham, offering a firm handshake and a lopsided smile. They'd been discussing everything from their opinions on the uselessness of golf and their interest in video games to the worst movies they'd seen. He reminded Graham of an aw-shucks, more social version of Forest.

"Be right back," Rebecca announced, rising from her seat.

She wore a tight-fitting blue shirt and jeans. He wanted to peel them off. All her layers. Watching her laugh with her friends and get chatty in a carefree manner half the night had set his heartrate into the next stratosphere. Such a great laugh. More than once, the smile had lit her baby blues, changing the whole schematic of her usually reserved expression. It had actually started back at the library and hadn't seemed to dull since.

Scarlett rose, too, and they headed toward the bar. Probably to get refills for everybody. There was no waitress, so they'd been taking turns.

He glanced at Rebecca's cola. She was the only one not drinking beer.

"She had to take her as-needed pain pill earlier." Dorothy's lips curved in an understanding smile as if she'd known what he'd been thinking. "It's not a narcotic, but she's not supposed to have alcohol while on it."

Pain pill? For what? Worry sank his mood. Before he could inquire, Dorothy pressed her lips into a fine line, realization dawning in her eyes.

"She didn't tell you?" At the shake of his head, she glanced over her shoulder toward the bar and back to him. "She has fibromyalgia. A pain disorder associated with nerves and muscle strain. It's not my place to say anything. I should let her tell you. With you being her boss, I thought she had already."

Aden shrugged. "It's not a secret, either. She was diagnosed, what, five years ago?"

"Yes. She manages it pretty well."

Graham let that fester, worry forming knots in his gut. He'd heard the term before, but he didn't know a damn thing about it. Was it a disease or condition? Was it... "Terminal? It's not terminal, is it? I mean, she'll be okay, right?"

"Oh." Dorothy straightened, placing a warm hand over his, her brows furrowed. "No, it's not terminal. It's not a widely understood condition, but it bears some similarities to lupus. It causes pain and fatigue. Some people have trouble sleeping while others get migraines or have digestive problems. Many experience brain fog, with difficulty focusing. Symptoms are across the map, and not everyone experiences all of them."

Graham tried to absorb the intel, but none of that sounded good. It also didn't seem like the Rebecca he'd met because she was what his grandmother would call a "whirling dervish." Always on the go, helping, working, and staying active. She was sharp as a tack. She never once gave any indication she was hurting.

He scratched his jaw, his stomach a riot. "So, she's in pain?"

Dorothy nodded, but it was Forest who spoke.

"All the time. Some days are better than others, and there's triggers, but yeah. To hear her describe it, she always has pain to a degree."

Damn it. Always? She was *always* in pain? How did she live like that? And Forest had known this, but hadn't thought to tell Graham? Anger battled with anxiety in his head.

"Ask her about it later." Aden finished the beer in his glass. "It sucks, big time, but she's open about discussing it, best I can tell. Scarlett told me way back when Rebecca had been diagnosed, so I texted her out of concern. Of course, she was still up north at the time. We talked for an hour and got caught up on other stuff. It still sucks, yet I felt better after hearing her explain."

Graham didn't think anything would make it better. To know someone he cared about was hurting, and not be able to do a damn thing about it?

Granted, the people around this table were her friends. She'd known them her entire life. She trusted them. Graham had just popped into her orbit. But he really, really wished someone, especially Rebecca, had dropped this bomb sooner. He sure as hell wouldn't have let her haul boxes to and from the attic space above the newsroom or climb to decorate the front window or, hell, even cut her own grass. Did she need to drop to part-time?

Someone behind the bar shouted Forest's name.

"That's our food." He stood and disappeared into the crowd.

Moments later, Scarlett and Rebecca returned with a pitcher of beer. Graham shot to his feet and abruptly took the tray from her, setting it on the table.

"Thanks." Rebecca tucked a strand of hair behind her ear, staring at him like he'd sprouted two heads. "You okay?"

"Yep." But she wasn't. She was *in pain*. Unable to sit still, he told the group he was going to help Forest, and did just that.

After a few minutes, the others dug into their fish and fries, while he stared at his basket. He wasn't certain he could stomach food, never mind something heavily fried.

He watched her instead with freshly opened eyes. Every nuance and tick. But, no. She seemed precisely the same as always. Eating. Laughing. Carrying on conversation. Reminiscing. Sipping her cola because she'd taken a *pain pill* and couldn't drink beer...

Swear to all that was holy, he might lose his shit all over the bar before he ever got the chance to talk to her alone.

"I think it's a great idea." Dorothy nudged her half-eaten basket aside, staring at Rebecca. "Are you ready for that, though?"

Ready for what? He'd been too focused on his thoughts to know what they'd discussed.

"I think so, yes." Rebecca raised her arms over her head to stretch. "It's just... I don't know. On one hand, it's Gammy's house. A place of comfort. But on the other, it's Gammy's house and everywhere I look is a reminder she's gone."

"I stand by my comment." Scarlett raised her palm. "Do some rearranging, repainting, and make it yours. You can keep mementos and personal things, but donate the rest. It really helped me after Miss Maureen died and I inherited the plantation."

Graham frowned. "Who's Miss Maureen?"

"My grandmother." Scarlett rolled her eyes. "She hated the reminder of her age and insisted everyone call her by her name."

Interesting.

Aden set his elbows on the table and leaned on them. "Loath as I am to admit it, she might be onto something, blondie. I'm free tomorrow if you want help."

A chorus of *me-too* sang from the table occupants, Graham included. If he'd caught on correctly, Rebecca was uncomfortable staying at her grandmother's house. Unable to move on, caught up in nostalgia, yet needing to cross that bridge. Grief was a terrible thing. If he could help, he'd volunteer a thousand times.

"You guys really wouldn't mind?" Unshed tears welled in her eyes, and it was like a dagger to chest.

"Girl, please." Scarlett flipped her long cocoa locks over her shoulder. "If it involves decorating, I'm there."

Aden snorted.

"I don't know jack about that, but I can wield a paintbrush." Forest shrugged. "Or move heavy objects."

She gave a watery laugh that twisted the knife in Graham's ribs. "Thank you so much."

The women discussed a sleepover at Rebecca's tonight to get a start on cleaning out Mavis's things and for moral support, dashing his hopes of talking to her alone later. Dorothy, Scarlett, and Aden had driven themselves to the bar. Graham had caught a ride with Forest. Perhaps...

"Would you mind giving me a lift home?"

Setting her chin in her palm, Rebecca smiled. "I don't know. It's out of my way going that whole extra driveway."

Smartass. Even her sarcasm was sexy.

They divvied the tab, paid, and headed toward their cars.

Once on the road, while she followed Scarlett and Dorothy to her house, he managed to make it a whopping five seconds in the passenger seat before unleashing a tyranny of questions.

She laughed. "I'm guessing one of our friends mentioned it?"

That was her reply? Not helpful. "I wish *you* had told me."

Ducking her head in acknowledgement, she apologized. "I should've, yes. It's not a topic I drop in casual conversation."

Okay, that he could understand. They'd just met a couple weeks ago. "So, what is...it, exactly?" He'd already forgotten how to pronounce the condition.

"Fibromyalgia, and no one's truly sure what causes it. Most doctors believe it's an over-abundance of nerve reactions or that it's a form of an autoimmune disease where the immune system attacks healthy cells by accident. Some people experience symptoms after a serious psychological stressor or a bad physical accident, but either way, it's hard to diagnose. There's no imagining or labs that detect it. In my case, it took quite a few years and a litany of tests to rule out other things before my diagnosis."

It sounded horrible. He despised regular checkups, never mind hospitals. She'd been in Boston while her close friends and solitary family member had been here. The thought of her going through that alone tore at him.

"What kind of tests?"

"A lot of labs, mostly. They ruled out lupus, multiple sclerosis, rheumatoid arthritis, spondylitis, Sjogren's syndrome, and Cushing disease because they have similar symptoms, however they checked for other things like diabetes and cancer, too. Eventually, they sent me to an endocrinologist who worked alongside a rheumatologist, and they figured out what was wrong."

That was insane. "All that just to tell you that you have fibromyalgia?"

She shrugged, way more nonchalant than he'd be in her situation. "Those have to be ruled out first before determining it's fibro. In fact, besides symptoms, it's the *only* way to diagnose."

Which brought up concern number two. "What symptoms?"

Humming in thought, she turned onto their street. "Everybody has varying ones, but most have fatigue and a dull widespread pain throughout their body. Others have had headaches, irritable bowels, memory issues, insomnia, that kind of thing. Thus far, I've been fortunate. I just have pain and fatigue."

Just. She *just* had those things, as if it was no big deal.

Pulling into his driveway, she parked. "There're prescriptions that can be taken, but because it behaves like an autoimmune disease, those are the meds for it. I work in a job around people, so I didn't want to be shutting off my immune system. I went the holistic approach since it was best for me. Vitamins, yoga, massage therapy, and herbs to help me sleep at night." She met his gaze, and he found no distress in hers. She shrugged. "I know my limitations and listen to my body. I try to avoid stress, don't push my muscles too hard, rest."

That's what she'd been doing the past few weeks, though. Burying her grandmother, moving home, starting a new job, lifting boxes, redecorating the office. All stressors and physical stuff.

A sigh, and he glanced at her driveway next door, watching Scarlett and Dorothy let themselves into her house. His head was a riot and he had so many more questions.

"Are you okay?"

He laughed without mirth. She had constant pain, and she was asking if he was okay? "Will it ever go away? Or...will you get sicker?"

She was shaking her head before he'd even finished. "It's a chronic lifelong condition, but it's not progressive."

That, at least, brought him a semblance of relief.

Nodding, he studied her. Beautiful oval face, huge blue eyes, full lips, regal neck, blonde hair falling past her slender shoulders. One would never know the struggles she faced daily or the baggage she had to carry. If not for her friends, he wouldn't have been aware anything was wrong. An invisible illness.

Unsure why emotion had him by the jugular, he cupped her face. He'd met her a handful of weeks ago. Yes, he respected the hell out of her, was attracted to her, and adored how their personalities jived despite the differences, but he'd had his dentist longer than they'd been neighbors or colleagues. There shouldn't be an overwhelming sense of empathy on her behalf or the desire to suddenly start slaying her metaphorical dragons. He'd been with Felica nearly two years and hadn't reached this stage. For crying out loud, he'd kissed Rebecca for the first time *yesterday*.

"I'm not fragile." She offered a smile. "I won't break."

Maybe that was it. The culprit. Appearances were deceiving. She was slender in nature and seemed so very delicate. But she was the farthest conceivable thing from weak. Life and circumstances had tried to crush her, yet here she was, still standing. A testament to her nature and strength.

A swallow worked her throat. "If you want to return to just a working relationship, I'd understand."

"That's not what I want."

Her gaze swept his face, more intimate than if she'd physically touched him. "What do you want?"

Honestly? He wanted to take care of her. A concept so foreign to him, it might as well be Greek. And she didn't need anyone to take care of her. She did it just fine on her own.

He went with door number two. "I'd like to carry you in the house and make love to you half the night."

Rearing, her brows went up as if she hadn't expected that answer.

Unable to help it, he grinned. "Damn shame you got company tonight." He exhaled, brushing his thumb across her soft cheek. "For the record, you having this condition doesn't change my desire for you or the curiosity to see where it leads." He got the weird suspicion other men had bolted, and perhaps that's why she had delayed telling him, but his interest only dug deeper the more he learned. "I like you, Rebecca."

A whole heck of a lot. Probably more than was wise.

163

"I'm rather fond of you, too, Graham." She glanced behind him out the window and back again. "But I'm gonna need you to kiss me and get out of my car. My besties are waiting."

He swung his head around, and spotted said besties on her stoop, staring.

Laughing, he returned his gaze to all that blue. "Yes, ma'am."

"Aw, look at you, using southern manners and—"

He kissed her, cutting off her teasing, but he was certain she didn't mind. Her fingers threaded through his hair and she parted her lips upon impact. He lost himself in her for a selfish few seconds and their errant chemistry.

Groaning, he pulled away before they got too heavy and he said to hell with the friends.

She smiled against his mouth, and the sweetness nearly undid him.

"Goodnight, Graham."

Boo. "Goodnight." He opened the door, waved, and strode to his door.

He waited for her to back out of his driveway and into hers before going inside.

After feeding Twain and letting him run in the yard, Graham plopped on the couch, the dog's head in his lap, and pulled up Google on his phone. It took him three tries to get the search or spelling of fibromyalgia in correctly.

For a condition barely researched or one he'd not heard of often, there was a stunning amount of people who had it. Something like four million in the U.S. diagnosed, which was two percent of the population. It affected more women than men, any ethnicity, at any age, though most cases were middle aged.

Sighing, he opened a link to read an article.

The deets mimicked what she'd told him already, however she hadn't mentioned the vast number of people who'd had their pain ignored and how some doctors discredited the condition due to narc-seeking adults. In some medical communities, fibromyalgia was still considered a joke.

Shaking his head, he leaned back on the cushion. To think, Rebecca went through too many tests to get an answer to her symptoms, while others couldn't even get their doctors to listen. Unfathomable.

He glanced at the dog. "She's in pain, buddy. She's *always* in pain." The very idea was causing *him* pain.

Twain whined as if he understood.

Needing to take his mind off what he'd learned, he thumbed through his contacts and connected to his mom.

"Everything alright, honey?"

No. "Yes. Can't I call my mother?" Hearing her voice began calming the tattered fringes of his nerves.

"You absolutely can, but you don't typically do it so late."

He glanced at his screen and winced. It was after ten. "My bad. I know you were awake reading, anyway."

"True story." Rumblings of his father snoring disrupted the background. "Are you feeling homesick?"

Every other instance she'd asked that question, his answer had been *yes*. Oddly, he found his response different tonight, and wasn't sure what to make of it. He'd grown up in Minnesota, had gone to college there, and though he had traveled some, he'd had the majority of his career there. Family. Friends. His apartment. His whole life. Minnesota and Georgia couldn't be more different from one another. Hell, if he looked up the word "opposite" in the dictionary, the two states would be there as an example. He missed home, all the people and places. Always would, but he wouldn't say he was homesick any longer.

Grunting, he wondered when that happened.

"Good," Mom replied, even though he hadn't technically answered. "I'm glad you're finally settling in."

Leave it to his mother to know everything without him uttering a syllable. "How's Dad?"

"Fine. I'm sure you can hear him snoring all the way down there."

He laughed, swiping a hand across his face. "And here I thought it was the pet rhinoceros." When he was a kid, his father had Graham and his siblings convinced a rhinoceros lived in the backyard, and that was the noise they'd heard at night, not Dad snoring.

She laughed, and the sound smacked him with fond memories. "How's work? Is that new hire panning out?"

Ah, Rebecca. "Actually, I think she saved my ass."

He took a moment to tell her all the things Rebecca had done and how subscribers had risen as a result.

"Sounds like she's a keeper."

"Yeah," he said through a sigh, absently petting Twain's ears. In more ways than one, Rebecca was irreplaceable. He'd yet to meet a soul more genuine and honest. "She's pretty, too. Kind. Funny." He hadn't so much as hinted to his mom that he had romantic interest in Rebecca, but now that they were dating, he figured he should.

Except Mom didn't mutter a sound.

"I'm being careful and she's not the type to throw me under the bus. We're keeping work and personal separate."

"Okay," she said at length. "You're a smart guy, Graham. We raised you right. What happened at the newspaper here wasn't your fault. I'd just hate to give your new boss reasons to fire you."

"Agreed." He rubbed his jaw. "It's weird, but I swear the town is rooting for us as a couple, my boss included."

Actually, now that he'd said it aloud, it sounded even crazier than in his head.

"My, my. You *are* living in a Hallmark movie." She made a sound of amusement. "My folks grew up in a small town like Vallantine. It's hard for me to wrap my mind around the concept, but I'm glad you're fitting in. It sounds like an ideal place."

Ideal. Definitely the proper term for Vallantine.

"I think we will come down and visit in a couple weeks, after all. It'll be good to see Forest. I'd like to check out this ideal town of yours and meet your Rebecca."

*His* Rebecca. Just a phrase, but the possession behind the meaning should raise his hackles.

It didn't.

"Okay, Mom."

# Chapter Thirteen

At her kitchen table, Rebecca sat with her knees to her chest, cradling coffee in her hands. Scarlett and Dorothy were still asleep, as it was barely dawn, but Rebecca couldn't fight slumber any longer. She'd done it half the night.

A pinkish yellow glow floated from the open window, bringing the scents of freshly cut grass and spring blooms. She stared idly at the rays and dust motes, fighting dregs of tightness in her neck and shoulders. One of the worst things to set off her fibromyalgia was lack of sleep.

After they'd gotten home from Backwater, her besties thought it a good idea to bag up Gammy's clothes for donation. They were currently on the kitchen floor, staring at her. All of her grandmother's cosmetics and toiletries were tossed in the trash, and certain knickknacks that weren't Rebecca's style were put into boxes. That's as far as they'd gotten, besides discussing redecorating suggestions.

It had to be done. She knew that. It had been her idea. Yet, she couldn't rid herself of the guilt clawing at her belly or swallow the lump in her throat. Gammy was gone. She wasn't coming back. People in need could use the clothing donation, and it did no good sitting here. Repainting or shifting things around would make the house more Rebecca's and less Gammy's. Which she sorely needed in order to remain here. The contradiction kept eating at her, though.

Footsteps padded from the hallway, so she took a sip of coffee to collect herself.

"She'd want you to move on." Dorothy stood in the doorway, leaning on the frame, and wearing an oversized tee she'd slept in. Messy auburn hair was piled on her head in disarray. Her solemn expression indicated she knew where Rebecca's thoughts had been directed. "I know it's hard, but she left you the house for a reason."

Rebecca choked on a sob, covering her face with her hand. Her chest cavity cracked open, and insipid darkness poured from the gaping hole. Months of remorse and gutting anguish pressed against her skull. The grief was so profound it strangled her. Paralyzing.

Dorothy took the mug from her shaking hands and wrapped Rebecca in a hug from beside the chair. Enveloped her, not as a barrier, but as a crutch, like she'd done countless times in their lives. "Let it out. It's going to be okay."

Sometimes, it just didn't seem like anything would be okay ever again. Chest tight, throat raw, she clutched Dorothy's arms, body shaking with a torrent of tears.

After long minutes, she stroked Rebecca's back. "We can wait if it's too soon. There's no rush."

"No." Rebecca sniffed and straightened, wiping her wet cheeks while blowing out a watery breath. "I can't hold onto her things as if she'll come back." They'd kept many mementos, and the house was a reminder of Gammy's life. It would be enough. Rebecca couldn't keep existing in stoic idleness, waiting for something to happen. It was getting to the point where she loathed coming home. "The changes will help to make the place mine, while respecting Gammy."

A gentle smile, and Dorothy claimed the other chair.

Scarlett shuffled into the room, dressed in jeans and a white tee, sleek brown strands in a high ponytail. Rebecca swore she got out of bed looking like a Photoshopped version of a proper belle. Scarlett one-armed her in a hug and went straight for the coffeepot.

Mug in hand, she leaned her butt against the counter. "Second thoughts?"

Sighing, Rebecca shook her head. "Irrational guilt."

"Just so long as you know it's irrational." Scarlett sipped from her mug. "Your grandmother's death wasn't your fault and there's absolutely nothing wrong with making a few changes to the house."

Nodding, Rebecca reached for her forgotten coffee. "I know. You're right." But feelings were feelings, and they weren't always grounded in reality. "I think I'll feel better once we get going or it's done."

"Okay." Scarlett shoved off the counter. "I'll head to the hardware store to get paint before the guys show up." She glanced at her watch. "Aden said they'd be here in an hour."

"Thank you." Rebecca's eyes watered again, the tears hot and cumbersome. "Both of you." She didn't have an inkling of how she would've navigated life, love, and loss without them. The unbearable loneliness was overwhelming as of late. If not for them, she'd have no one.

"No need for that." Scarlett waved her hand. "Now, are you certain you're good with me picking color schemes?"

Rebecca huffed a laugh. "Oh yeah. Go on with your bad self. I trust you." Her bestie had an eye for decorating and making something from nothing. Rebecca would rather put such things in Scarlett's capable hands. "Do you need my credit card?"

"Nope." She set her cup in the sink. "Alrighty. See y'all in a bit."

Once Scarlett was gone, Dorothy sighed. "We should probably get dressed and start taking pictures off the wall."

"Adulting is dumb. Why did we ever want to be grown-ups?"

"Hell if I know, but we're stuck with it now."

Ninety minutes later, Graham was painting Rebecca's old
bedroom a lilac color, Forest was painting Gammy's old bedroom light blue, and Aden was painting the living room but-
tercream yellow. The whole house's interior had been ivory in
tone before. Dorothy and Rebecca were doing the kitchen in a
light gray, which she'd been a little concerned about until they'd
gotten a good amount on the walls. It went well with the scarred
blue cabinets and matched shades in the Formica.

Scarlett had promptly changed the shower curtain from a
plain green pattern to one that had branches with leaves. Somehow, it changed the look of the whole room. Then, she'd taken
off again for more "essentials." What those essentials were, Rebecca had no clue.

By lunch, every room had two coats, and Rebecca ordered
pizza, amazed at how fast they'd gotten stuff done. Had she
attempted the feat herself, she'd barely be through one room,
and she'd most likely have hated the colors she'd picked. They
sat out on the back deck, all but Scarlett, who hadn't returned,
and ate straight from the box.

Rebecca watched the guys laughing, splatters of mismatched
paint on their arms, and sighed. She'd spent so much time alone
in Boston, in her shoebox apartment, that she'd forgotten how
well her inner circle got along. Graham, being new to the group,
had been accepted by the others and fit in as if he'd been here
all along. It warmed her heart. After all he'd been through, he
deserved comfort and camaraderie.

Such a handsome devil. Midnight strands. Emerald eyes.
Strong jaw dusted with whiskers. Lean, corded body. His grin
could level a city to ash. More than physical appearances,

though, he was kind. Understanding in a way that most guys weren't capable and with a bit of old-fashioned consideration she'd thought was long dead. Intelligent, too. Funny. If she weren't careful, she'd wind up falling a bit too hard for her neighbor and boss.

Chewing the last bite of her pizza, she wondered if that would be such a bad thing. He seemed interested in her. She was definitely interested in return. There was chemistry. They worked well alongside each other. He fit in with her friends. Gammy had obviously liked him if she'd made him pie and had let him cut her grass.

Yet, and she couldn't put her finger on what, but something kept nudging her to take heed. Not for the first time, she questioned what would happen if he were to be offered a position at a large syndicate again. If things blew over and the dust settled on his scandal, would a big city newspaper want him on staff? Moreover, would he accept the position? Just up and leave, Vallantine disappearing in his rearview?

Graham caught her staring at him, their gazes locking, and she shook her head to hide the embarrassment.

She thanked the group profusely for today again, but they brushed aside her appreciation. That's what friends were for, she smiled. She'd missed it. Missed them. Having one another's back and helping each other up when they'd been knocked down. Family, not by blood, but chosen instead. Gammy would say her 'cup has runneth over.'

The back door slammed on its hinges, and Scarlett stood on the deck, blowing a strand of hair off her face. "I need some help."

Aden grunted and leaned back in his seat, legs lazily stretched in front of him. "Darlin', ain't none of us equipped to handle the kinda help you require."

Forest laughed, but Graham passed her the last slice of pizza. "Whatcha need?"

They followed her inside and to the living room, where shopping bags were piled on the floor.

Rebecca winced. Though grateful, she wondered how she was going to pay for this. The cost of the paint alone would stretch her savings to the brink. Her first paycheck from the Gazette had dropped in her account yesterday, but she had bills. Knowing Scarlett, she wouldn't let her pay for any of it, and that didn't sit right with Rebecca.

While she was lost in thought, Scarlett had directed the guys to move the China cabinet to a different wall. It had held mostly figurines that they'd packed away last night, but they'd kept the wine glasses and decanter set. Once in place, Scarlett gave Dorothy a bag containing liquor bottles and told her to put them in the cabinet.

Rebecca nodded. In honesty, the piece had been pretty useless once they'd removed the knickknacks. Turning it into a makeshift bar cabinet was a clever idea.

Scarlett had them rearrange *all* the furniture, in fact. Gammy's gold and white plaid couches and yellow wingback chairs were shifted around, and though the pieces were the same, the fresh paint color and moving of objects made the whole room seem like a new one.

"Wow." Rebecca set her hands on her hips. "You weren't kidding. This looks great."

Still Gammy's house, still most of her things, including solace, yet Scarlett had managed to turn it into a space Rebecca could call her own.

"Thank you." Scarlett disappeared into the other room and returned with paintings that had once been in the hallway. She set them along the wall in the living room where she wanted Aden to hang them.

"Yes, ma'am." Aden sarcastically saluted.

They followed her into Gammy's old bedroom, which they were turning into Rebecca's. A change she wasn't sure she was okay with, but she'd try it out.

Once again, Scarlett directed the guys to rearrange, and once again, the paint and shifting of furniture created a completely unique space. Not to mention, she'd bought a new bedspread and matching curtains. Gammy's had been a quilted pattern in various colors with white drapes. Now, there was a blue paisley comforter and navy curtains.

Rebecca had been so worried that she wouldn't be able to sleep in the room, but she should've trusted her bestie. Gammy's bed was queen-sized, whereas Rebecca's had been a full, and Gammy's bedroom was bigger than Rebecca's. Scarlett had turned it into an entirely new room.

Lump in her throat, Rebecca hugged her.

"I told you before. I got you."

She really did, and Rebecca fought tears. "Thanks. I'll write you a check before you leave."

"No need." Scarlett shrugged. "The curtains and bedspreads have been sitting around the plantation for ages. I bought 'em for the guest rooms, but ultimately never could make them work with the color palette. The liquor and cocktail mixes are my treat."

What a relief. "Thank you."

They rearranged Rebecca's old bedroom, and while they were doing that, Dorothy moved Rebecca's clothes to the new room.

Throughout the course of the afternoon, Scarlett had reused the original pictures and frames, but had put them in alternate locations. All the comforts Rebecca had loved were still around, but in a way that she could appreciate them now instead of

KELLY MORAN

bringing her sorrow. She especially loved the family photos lining the hallway.

"Oh." Scarlett glanced at Aden. "There are two chairs in the backseat of my car. Can you grab them please?"

Aden went out the front door, but Rebecca frowned. "Chairs for what?"

"The kitchen table. You only have two. The thrift store had a couple that look similar to yours, so I bought 'em."

Rebecca hadn't thought of that. It had always just been her and Gammy, but extra seats would come in handy for guests.

"Thank you." Overwhelmed, she stood by the front entry hall late in the afternoon, hand on her forehead. "I mean it, you guys. This is amazing. It's like a totally different house."

Graham watched her, his expression solemn. "Yet, still your grandmother's."

Exactly. As if he'd climbed in her head to spit out words, he understood exactly how she felt.

She offered to order dinner as a thank-you, but they all declined and left her to her fresh digs. All except Graham, who insisted on cooking her supper. At her house. She suspected it was to put fresh memories in the kitchen. Or maybe he knew she wasn't quite ready to be alone yet. Regardless, she was grateful.

"Let me run home and shower. I'll bring stuff back with me to cook."

She had every intention of showering herself while he was gone, but she wound up going through one of her boxes from Boston instead and setting out some of her own knickknacks. Then, kitchen items, in case he needed something Gammy didn't already have in the house. By the time Graham and Twain strolled back in, she'd sorted through her third and final box.

He grinned from the doorway to her old bedroom. "I brought the doofus. Hope that's okay."

"Of course, it is." Twain bathed her face in kisses. "Who's a good boy?"

"One of these days, I'm going to get you to call *me* a good boy." Graham sighed and headed down the hall. "Dinner in thirty minutes."

From the floor, she petted the dog and stared at the empty doorway. A wary sense of glee filled her chest and warmed her face. Somehow, her dreadful morning with all the guilt had shifted. It had been forever since she could recall being content or hopeful. Gammy's house was a home again, now with elements to make it Rebecca's, all because of her friends and a pretty great guy next door. Who was cooking her dinner. In her kitchen. Between Boston and moving back home to an empty house, she'd been erringly lonesome. For a really long time, actually. But the house had life again.

*She* was seemingly living her life again.

Confused, she looked at the dog. "I'm not sure what I'm supposed to do now."

A silly comment, but the truth. She was officially unpacked from her move home. The house had been revamped to suit her style. She'd secured a job at the Gazette and helped to get it in a better state to thrive. The library was on its way to begin renovations, so they could hopefully reopen in six to ten months from now. And she'd started a new yet promising relationship with Graham.

Could it be she was finally, blessedly getting her life on track? Heck, she hadn't been in a place where she could admit such a thing since she'd left Vallantine for college. Ten years ago. A sad, pathetic realization.

Whatever. She wasn't going to let the past dull her mood.

Rising, she went into the kitchen, where her legs about gave out on her.

Graham, his back to her, stood at the stove stirring something in a pot. Corded sinew in his arms. Wide shoulders. His hair was damp from his shower, the ends curling. He'd changed into a pair of dark gray sweats and a white tee. Bare feet. That alone could undo her. Lord, bare feet were sexy. Not accounting for an attractive man in her kitchen. Cooking. For her.

Be still her heart.

As if sensing her, he glanced over his shoulder. His grin was just a cheap shot. "Thought you were showering."

She'd rather watch him. "Working up to it. What are you cooking?" It smelled amazing. She walked closer to peer over his shoulder.

She retracted her last thought. *He* smelled amazing.

"Gumbo. I had the base roux made already in my fridge. I'm just adding the rest to the pot." Turning, he wrapped an arm around her waist and swiped a finger down her nose. "You've got paint all over you."

"Eh, I tried to keep it on the walls."

His low chuckle vibrated her ribs. "Adorable." He smacked a quick kiss to her lips and returned to the pot. "This'll be done soon. Go shower."

Sigh. She'd rather watch him, but fine.

Making her way back down the hall, she went into her old room out of habit, then backtracked to her new one. It took her a few tries before she figured out where Dorothy had put her items in the dresser.

Shower complete, leaving her hair to air dry, she returned to the kitchen. He had bowls of gumbo on the table waiting, with cut French bread piled on a plate.

"I could get used to you cooking for me."

He laughed, turning from the stove, and froze. Slowly, his gaze drifted down the length of her and up again. "Damn."

"What?" She glanced down at herself. She'd put on a pair of hip-hugger pink boxers and a white tee with a cupcake on it. Unsure what he'd cursed for, she sent him a questioning glare.

"You look good enough to eat, that's what."

"Oh." Well, geez. Blow her over with a feather. His low, coarse, guttural admission seemed too sincere to be a random comment.

Setting the oven mitts aside, he strode to her. Languidly. Seductively. Hunter seeking prey. Pausing in front of her, there wasn't any oxygen between them as he looked down at her.

"Hi," she lamely said, unclear what his intentions were, but very certain she'd do whatever he asked. Her heart thumped erratically behind her ribs.

"You are an incredibly attractive woman, Rebecca."

Aw. "Thank you." Her voice had come out closer to a choked whisper, but she put the blame on him.

"You're welcome." He bumped his chin toward the table. "We should eat before I get other ideas instead."

Call it curiosity or a flat out rise in gumption, but she challenged his statement. "What kind of ideas?"

He inhaled. Hard. His eyes heated as they narrowed to slits. "Ideas not acceptable to mention in polite company."

"I don't see any company." Lord, what had gotten into her? Before today, she couldn't flirt if her life depended on the task for survival.

As if siding with him, Twain barked.

Throwing her head back, she laughed. "You win."

They sat, and she dug into his gumbo.

She'd seen the hearty soup or stew made countless ways. Correctly and incorrectly. However, as a northerner, Graham seemed to nail all the right ingredients for proper southern gumbo, and color her surprised. Onions, bell peppers, celery, okra, shrimp, sausage, and chicken. Oh, and the flavor? Amazing. The perfect blend of spices. Gammy had made hers with cayenne and black pepper, dry mustard, paprika, sage, cumin, bay leaves, thyme, and parsley. Rebecca had watched her multiple times. Graham's version was very close, though she was used to it over rice instead of with a side of bread.

"This is delicious." Wide-eyed, she looked at him. "Seriously delicious."

One corner of his mouth curved. "You sound shocked."

"Don't take this the wrong way, but I am. I've had gumbo in Boston or surrounding areas more times than I have fingers and toes to count. It was never good."

Nodding, smile faint, he reached for a slice of bread. "My folks vacationed in New Orleans one year when I was a kid. Dad tried gumbo for the first time, and demanded to learn how to make it." He laughed. "They went to five different restaurants, where he wormed his way into the kitchen for a brief cooking lesson. This is his recipe."

"That's hilarious." And dedicated. "I like him already." She took a few more spoonfuls. "Please tell him I'm impressed, and he can move south to cook for us anytime."

Up went his brows. "No props for the chef. I see how it is." Humor in his eyes, he winked. "I have all his recipes. Say the word, and I'll cook for you."

"The word."

He laughed. Rough, coarse, and from the gut, causing her insides to heat, and not from the stew.

After a beat, he sighed. "I'd kill for your grandmother's peach pie recipe. She never did tell me her secret."

Full, she nudged her bowl aside. "Not many know her secret. It's written down around here somewhere, but I know it by heart. I'll teach you sometime."

He pointed at her with his spoon. "I will hold you to that." Rising, he set their bowls in the sink. "My parents are coming down for a visit next week."

"Are they? I'll bet you're excited to see them." He'd been uprooted from everything he'd known when he'd accepted the job in Vallantine. If it were her, and it had been not so long ago, she'd miss the people and places from home.

"I am." He set the large pot on a cooling rack and filled the sink with soapy water. "I know a few tourist spots here, but maybe you could help me show them around?"

"I'd be glad to. Don't you dare do the dishes. You cooked. I'll clean."

"Yes, ma'am." He turned off the water and eyed the pot. "This will need to cool before we can put it in the fridge."

"Okay." A tingle shot through her. There was something sexy about hearing him *ma'am* her like a southern boy. "Want to watch a movie? Or do you need to get home?"

"Nowhere I gotta be." He straightened as if remembering a detail. "You have a flatscreen on the floor of your old bedroom. Would you like me to connect it in your new bedroom for you? You've got a TV in the living room already."

That's right. She'd forgotten. "I brought it back from Boston with me. Haven't gotten around to setting it up yet. You don't mind?"

"Nope." He offered a sly grin. "Show me your bedroom, Rebecca."

# Chapter
## Fourteen

While Rebecca laid on her bed, cuddling with his damn dog, Graham connected an ethernet cable to her flatscreen on the dresser. After plugging in the TV, he glanced over his shoulder. "Try it out."

She picked up the remote and pushed a button. "Yay." She pushed another button, and Netflix filled the screen. "I'll have to unbox my Blu-ray player one of these days, but we can find something on here to watch."

Guess that meant they were staying in her bedroom.

He walked around to the other side of the bed and lay beside her, crossing his feet at the ankles. The intimacy of the situation wasn't lost on him, but she seemed nonchalant, flipping through the menu. He about choked on his tongue earlier when she'd emerged from her shower wearing the equivalent of panties and a tight tee. From the second he'd spotted her at the curb outside their homes weeks ago, he'd been avidly attracted to her. Getting to know her better and learning her personality had only amped his desire.

But her in that outfit? Hell. He was but a mere mortal man, for crying out loud.

"What are you in the mood for?"

He turned his head to look at her, figuring this was a female trap, but she'd meant movies, not where his dirty, dirty thoughts had plummeted. Pity.

Clearing his throat, he rationalized a proper response. "I'm up for anything."

Which was becoming a literal statement with her so close, laying in a bed beside him, and smelling like sweet honeysuckle. Long legs. Acres of fair, smooth skin. Blonde locks still damp from her shower. Damn, but he didn't think he'd wanted a woman more in his life. An itch yet to be scratched. Oxygen through his bloodstream. The thunder in his heart.

Anticipation just might kill him.

"Anything, huh?" She smiled, cindering his brain cells. "Dangerous, that."

She hadn't the foggiest.

Sighing, he focused on the screen. "Okay, smartass. Action, horror, or comedy. Your choice."

"I accept all three suggestions. Love a good ghost story, my-self."

Excellent. Maybe she'd get scared and seek...him for protection. She could defend herself, but he was delusional enough to hope.

She hit Play on some haunted house flick, then rose from the bed. Her perfect round backside swiveled as she closed the curtains, then she moved to his side of the bed. His pulse jacked, but she turned off the lamp instead of climbing on him, dashing his fantasies.

Eerie music played during the opening credits, and he re-trained his gaze to the screen. Though the sun was nearly set, she'd cast the room in full darkness, adding creepiness to the atmosphere for the flick, but it only served to make the cozy room more intimate.

She reclaimed her spot on the bed beside him and lay down, the dog now on her other side instead of between them. "I've not seen this movie, but it looks like it's scary enough to get my heart going faster than green grass through a goose."

Unable to help it, he covered his face with his arm and laughed. Dear God, she didn't drop southernisms often, but when she let 'em roll, he about died. His side ached. Actually ached.

"You laughing at me?"

"No, ma'am." He hadn't necessarily adapted to the 'yes, ma'am/no, sir' manners of the south, but the few instances he'd sarcastically done so with her, she'd seemed to like it. As in, flushed cheeks, parted lips, hot-and-bothered kind of liking it. Any weapon at his disposal he'd willingly use. "I wouldn't dream of it."

"Uh huh. Don't make me bless your heart."

"Yeah, about that." He rolled on his side, propping his head in his hand. "Explain to me how the phrase appears to be both an insult and a sentiment."

She laughed, sultry and rich, then shifted to lay on her side, matching his pose. "It depends on the context. There's the *oh, I genuinely feel sorry for you/that's terrible* kind of bless your heart, which is generally sympathizing for another, then there's the equivalent of a *fuck you* version."

He'd not heard her curse before. It was strangely cute. "Makes zero sense."

"Unless you're from the south."

No kidding. "So, what you're saying is, I need to read the room and body language to interpret meaning."

"Precisely." Her warm smile lit her baby blues as she swept her gaze over his features. "*Kiss my grits* is an alternate way to say *kiss my ass*."

Shaking his head, he grinned wider until his cheeks ached. "I don't know how you southerners can eat grits. They're gross." Made of finely ground hulled corn, they were grainy in texture and had the consistency of cream of wheat with less flavor. Blech.

"Another regional difference. Northerners tend to not like them because they expect the dish to have a lot of taste, but it doesn't. It's a tradition in most southern states, especially in low-country, because of the proximity to the sea. Fisherman found it a quick, yet filling breakfast and often added shrimp. Some prefer just butter while others use brown sugar. There's a thousand ways to cook it. The dish actually originated from Indigenous Native Americans, though. Tribes served it to Colonists."

"Your mind is fascinating." He shook his head as his gut heated into a hot ball. Seriously. Brains were sexy. Specifically, hers. "I love these tidbits you throw my way." Since they'd met, she'd done that very thing. Found ways to logically explain things so he could adapt and understand.

She narrowed her eyes as if suspicious.

"Relax. I'm not pulling your leg."

She made an uncommitted sound he couldn't decipher. "I enjoyed learning as a kid. Weird, random facts. Gammy said I was a sponge for meaningless trivia. I don't realize I lecture sometimes. I think I started doing it in Boston to justify some of our ways when co-workers made fun of us. My ex got annoyed by the habit. Eventually, I quit doing it."

Which meant she was comfortable enough with him to pick it back up again. Good. She should always be free to act like herself, not some version others expect.

"Well," he said through a sigh, "I don't mind. He can kiss your grits."

Her laugh penetrated his skin and wrapped around bone. "Absolutely."

"Why did you two call it quits?" He'd been itching to ask more personal questions, and she'd left the opening for him to eek past.

"Eh." She rolled to her back, arms crossed over her face in clear avoidance. "We didn't really have a lot in common. I think he was expecting me to advance in my career, getting irritated when I didn't. He also wanted kids, and I don't."

Hmm. They were in the beginning stages of a relationship, but they probably should've brought up that topic before tonight. "I don't, either."

She turned her head. "Really?"

"Yeah. I mean, I'm more indifferent to the concept than outright against it. I just..." He frowned, attempting to formulate the right words. "I don't know. Never had the urge to start a family."

"What about marriage?"

He wondered if she was fishing or just that good at communication. "I'm all for wedded bliss, so long as it's actual bliss. Relationships take work. I get that, but I don't think I'd leap unless I found the right woman."

She nodded. "Ditto, except with a man." She winked.

Utterly adorable. "Your ex had unrealistic expectations of your career and your womb, thus the split. Were there other factors? What'd he do for a living?"

"He was a bigwig at a marketing firm. As for the breakup, I also don't think I..."

They'd circle back to her job, but for now, he wanted the last half of her sentence. "Don't think you what?"

"This is embarrassing." She scrubbed her hands over her face and moaned. After a heinous pause, her arms dropped to the mattress. "I don't think I satisfied him."

Um, no. That couldn't be the case. Granted, they hadn't gotten more physical than kissing or heavy petting, but she was warm and affectionate. No way would she be unsatisfying to any living, breathing male.

She must've taken his silence for agreement because she made a motion to rise.

He grabbed her hand and tugged until she was facing him again. He slid her closer and trapped her with his arm. If she showed signs of distress, he'd let her go. For now, they needed to hash out a couple things.

Staring at her pretty face, the way she bit her lower lip was enough to turn him on. Just her presence, her scent, or the whimsical sound of her laugh. Her body. Her wit. The feisty way she liked to put him in place...

"If he was sexually unsatisfied, he should've discussed it with you to find ways to fix the issue. In saying that, I highly doubt you were the problem."

She stared at him so long, the earth rotated, and four seasons came and went. Dramatic music from the movie drifted in the room, but he ignored it.

He raised his brows. "You don't believe me?"

"Forgive me, but no. I don't believe you. I was in the relationship. A woman can tell when a guy is bored."

Nodding, he silently agreed. "If things go stale, there are a number of factors. Lack of chemistry can't be laid solely at your feet. That's nature. Some people are compatible, others aren't." And since he had the sinking suspicion she blamed her feminine wiles for the disconnect, he decided on brutal frankness. "You turn me on sixteen out of twenty-four hours a day."

She blinked, yet said nothing.

"I know what you're thinking." He very much didn't. "Why only sixteen hours? Because for the other eight, I sleep. You can't be responsible for those."

Blink, blink.

"Your scent has managed to turn something sweet and innocent in nature to an X-rated fantasy that belongs behind closed doors."

Blink, blink, blinking.

"I find you attractive as hell, including your mind. Not accounting for your temper." *Uhn*, her temper. "I want to taunt you just to hear that sexy little southern drawl that emerges when you're angry."

Blink. Silence.

"When we kiss, my head explodes." What he wouldn't give to have her do just that. Right this second. Kiss his damn brains straight out of his head.

Still, she said zilch.

"Believe me yet?"

Her mouth opened and closed twice before she summoned words. "That's very kind of you to say."

*Kind*. Kind of him? Not a syllable had been etched from kindness. Consideration went a long way and was ingrained in his DNA. Respect, for sure. But his admissions weren't due to either. Lust? Definitely. Truth? Undeniably.

"I wasn't trying to be kind." She was driving him up a wall and back down again, only to repeat the process without having moved a muscle. A special talent of hers.

"Please don't feel obligated—"

"It's not obligation." He drew a steady breath. "I am feeling something, though. You started your response correctly."

"Okay." Her delicate throat worked a swallow. "What are you feeling?"

He'd rather demonstrate. He'd never been good at the former part of the Show & Tell game.

Sealing his lips to hers, he wove his fingers through her damp hair and shifted to roll her beneath him. She made a sexy little mewl of surprise that traveled from her mouth to his.

Keeping his weight on his forearm, he kissed her with the patience of a saint while waiting for her cues. His skin was tight, and his muscles strained with the want of her. Having their bodies horizontal and aligned wasn't helping. He vaguely wondered if it bore no end, this rampant desire she invoked.

Their tongues mated in a dance that resembled the salsa. Rhythmic. Teasing, taunting, stimulating moves meant to entice. Nothing more. A precursor. Foreplay. Yet, he desperately hoped for more. That she was just as enthralled and needed him with the same fervor. He may never get over it otherwise.

The bed shifted, indicating the dog jumped down, and the skittering of nails on wood meant he'd vacated the room. Their movie continued to play. All white noise to Graham, at this point.

Her fingers skimmed up his sides, the first instance she'd touched him since they'd locked lips, and his muscles rippled like a caged beast. She'd not had many relationships or lovers. By her admission, it had been part situational, and the rest chalked up to uncomfortable inexperience. She'd said she wasn't good at it.

He disagreed. With every fiber. As her hands roamed—up his back, down his sides, across his pecs—he all but vibrated with need.

Deepening the kiss, he tilted his head, and began an exploration of his own. Smooth, taut skin. Slight curves. To which she reacted by arching under him, silently seeking more.

Gladly.

Breaking the kiss, he latched onto her throat, swirling his tongue and losing his mind in her sweet scent. He cupped one firm breast, small enough to fit in his hand, and something about her size undid him. Restraint was becoming a thin tether as her nipple beaded against his palm. Shifting lower, he brushed his lips across her collarbone and peeked up at her to verify he was hitting her hot buttons.

Head back, lips swollen from their kiss, she moaned. Emboldened, he pulled her nipple into his mouth through the soft cotton of her tee. She arched again, just like that. A puppet on his string, yet she seemed to have all the control. Shoving her fingers in his hair to hold him, her lids parted, and their gazes locked. Hers were heavy with lust.

He moved to her other nipple, repeating the ministrations, and her lids drifted shut again with a flutter of her lashes. Gripping the back of his shirt, she tugged at the material, insisting its removal.

Okay. They were doing this.

Hell to the *yessssss*.

By the hem, he removed her shirt before his own, exposing a blue lacy bra shades darker than her eyes. Hair spread over the pillow, she stared at his chest. Fingernails lightly scratched over his abs, her gaze following the path, and his dick throbbed.

"I'm glad you shared your feelings."

He only half-listened to her words since her fingertips had been tracing the waistband of his sweats. Panting, braced over her with his elbows locked, he wrenched his brows in confusion.

"I asked what you were feeling." She gripped his shoulders, and in a move that would probably have him bowing in covenant later, she bent her knees, dipped her toes in his waistband, and tugged his sweats down his legs. "I'm glad you did."

The nimble little minx.

Tit for tat, he shoved the pants off the rest of the way and did the same for hers. Have mercy, her panties matched her bra, but with way less material.

She sat up, unclipping her bra. Unceremoniously, she tossed it to the floor. Part of his restraint went with it. Small, pale, perky breasts. Pink, hardened nipples. So damn beautiful. As she reached for her panties, he shook his head.

"I got you." Palming her hips, he hoisted her off the mattress, and she fell backward onto her pillows, feet in the air. More slowly than he could withstand, he slid the blue lace torture device down her legs. It joined the bra on the floor.

Between her thighs, watching her, he bent and pressed a kiss to her navel.

She inhaled, lids at half mast, cheeks flushed.

Oh yeah. He adored her avid response to him. Still watching, he kissed his way lower, and her pupils swallowed her irises. Inner thigh. Kissing one, then the other. Her lips parted as if oxygen was in short supply.

And then he buried his face in her short golden curls.

She gasped, fisting the pillow.

Smiling, he flicked her tiny little nub with the tip of his tongue, parted her wet folds, and groaned against her. Responsive, she bucked, seeking more, to which he was only happy to oblige. He learned her body, her pleasures, and relished every moan, gasp, and tremor until her body went rigid. A sharp cry, and she threw her head back, limbs vibrating as she came.

Hard, throbbing, he shucked his briefs while she recuperated. He climbed over her on all fours before she'd opened her eyes and sucked her nipple between his tongue and the roof of his mouth. Another tremble, and her hands were back in his hair, fisting the strands. Groaning, he kissed his way to behind her ear, slid his hands between her perfect backside and the sheets, and thrust against her swollen wet folds. She emitted the most delicious, detrimental to his well-being sound of inclination he'd ever heard.

Needing inside her, he crushed his mouth to hers, aligned his hips, and thrust.

Stars. He actually thought he saw stars, until he realized his eyes were shut. Damn, she was... Tight. Hot. And made just for him, the fit was that right.

He paused, giving her a moment. Or maybe he needed one. Regardless, he buried his face in her strands and tried for all he was worth not to say or do anything stupid. Breathing labored, he skimmed his hand up and down her outer thigh, cherishing the feel of her under him. Around him. Inside him, it seemed, now that they'd taken things to this level. She was all he could breathe, hear, or see. All he could taste or feel.

But then she moved. That thin tether he'd had earlier snapped as her legs wrapped around him, her arms held him, and she ground her hips, seeking more.

He had the stray thought he'd give her everything as he withdrew achingly and methodically from her. Only when he thrust anew did he seem to find purchase amidst the firestorm in his head. Pleasure ran rampant through his system, unlike anything he'd known before. The connection between them heightened the experience, put them in sync. It was too much and not enough.

She kissed his jaw, trailed her lips to that tender spot between his neck and shoulder. He pumped harder, rolling his hips to ground her clit, while she assaulted his nerve endings. So beautiful, the way she moved. Languid and graceful. Submissive, but wielding all the power. Giving and taking.

They seemed to fuse, and not just their bodies. Becoming one, yet not even close to similar. Joining. Merging.

Just when he thought he couldn't hold out much longer, she bowed, bringing them even closer, and her walls gripped him in a vise. She trembled, emitting a cry of satisfaction that penetrated his ears and reverberated in his skull.

A tingle shot up his spine, and he followed her over the edge. He tensed, mouth open over hers, as he came undone. His arms gave out, and he collapsed on top of her, fighting for oxygen exchange.

Moments passed while he tried to recover. She held him, warm hands stroking his back, and their legs tangled. It should be the other way around. He should be holding her, but she offered a sense of reprieve he hadn't felt since his life erupted in Minnesota. Comfort, safety, and peace. Gratification. Selfishly, he took it, in case it never came again.

Toying with the ends of her hair, he tried to recall what they'd been discussing before she'd had the brilliant idea of asking what was on his mind. Wait. No, she'd asked *how he'd felt*. A sluggish, methodical laugh rumbled in his chest, emerging as a tired chuckle.

Turning her head, she pressed her lips to his forehead. "What's so funny?"

"You're not unsatisfying in the sack. Your ex is an idiot. The biggest idiot in all the land."

She paused her stroking across his back, and he could all but hear the gears turning in her head. "Thank you." Combing her fingers through his hair, she let out a quiet sigh. "Maybe you're just better at it."

What? Nuh uh. He lifted his head. "Maybe?"

She grinned, leveling kingdoms. "No maybe about it." She brushed her knuckles across the whiskers on his jaw, gaze following the movement. "At the risk of sounding cliché and going to reporter hell, that was pretty amazing."

His inner caveman wanted to pound his chest and preen. He settled for accepting the compliment as she'd done. "Thank you."

"You're welcome. Most guys clam up or tuck tail and run for the hills when asked about their feelings." The teasing amusement in her tone and illuminating in her eyes was cute. Playful with a side of sass.

He hadn't actually spouted feelings, though. He'd shown them instead. And there were definitely feelings involved. What they were precisely, he didn't know yet, but they were present. Hovering in his peripheral. Poking at his chest. "Stereotypes are yesterday's headlines."

A laugh, and she covered her face with her hand.

He rolled them to their sides, still facing one another, and brushed a strand of hair from her cheek. It had grown quiet in the room, and he glanced at the TV. The title page was floating around the screen, indicating their movie had ended.

He grunted. "Great film."

She laughed again, and he figured he wouldn't mind spending an eternity getting her to do it often. Every hour on the hour. "It was great. We should watch it again."

"Inuendo accepted, Rebecca." Wasn't she a gem. "I need to let the dog out. Give me some time to recuperate."

They got dressed and went out onto the back deck, watching Twain mill about the yard. A cool humid breeze brought varying scents of the river, magnolias blooming, and night jasmine. Stars littered a pitch black sky, unmarred by the city lights to which he was accustomed. Crickets chirped, but it was otherwise silent.

"It's so quiet here," he mused.

She hummed a sound of agreement and claimed an Adirondack chair. "I don't know which was harder to get used to, the city noise or the stillness."

"For me, I'd say the quiet, but I was raised in the city." He plopped in the chair next to hers, tilting his face toward the sky. "I think I'm used to it, and then the hush just hits me."

"I was the same way after leaving for college. Just when I thought I had adapted, a fire or police siren would wail on the street or a party would start down the hall."

The conversation reminded him of a thread he'd meant to unravel. They'd already dealt with her ex. "You mentioned how your career didn't advance in Boston." She'd skirted the whole truth in her interview, but they were much closer now. "What happened?"

Laying her head back on the seat, she drew her knees to her chest and stared at the heavens. "I'm not sure if it was one thing or many, if I'm being honest. They hired me straight out of college, and I just assumed Obituaries was a starting position. My first week on the job, I was in a bathroom stall when two ladies from higher up the food chain came in, talking about me. They made fun of me and my accent. Worst part was, I'd worked dang hard in college to drop most of my southern dialect."

Not completely. He'd caught traces when she was in regular conversation, but it went from a trickle to a flood when she was animated or angry. Nevertheless, she shouldn't have had to hide it from anyone, and said as much.

She shrugged. "A lot of people equate southern with stupid. Figured I'd just prove them wrong. I applied for three positions in three different departments after my first year. None of them even bothered to consider me. It was a huge paper with lots of staff, but I suppose word got around. Sometimes, I'd spot a good story and write it up, forwarding it to the proper department head. All I ever received was polite formulated rejections. I just...never fit in."

Twain walked up to her, and she absently petted him. "I had a couple acquaintances in my apartment complex or at work, but not anyone I would consider a friend."

It sounded terrible to him, and he could relate. He'd moved here, sight unseen, at the lowest point in his life. At least he had Forest. "Why didn't you leave? Put your bid in at other newspapers?"

"I did. Probably should have sooner, but I kept holding out hope that they'd see my skills and promote me." She shook her head. "First year was settling in. Second was a wash. I dragged my heels most of the third year. I sent my résumé out to quite a few companies, but after seeing I was employed at one of the largest syndicates in America, without advancing, they passed. Smaller bloggers and newspapers couldn't match my salary. I could barely afford my apartment as it was, so even if I got offered a position, I couldn't take it."

She slanted him a look from the corner of her eye. "Lord, I hated that place. The job and the apartment. It was a studio with a kitchenette. Seven hundred square feet."

He winced. "Ouch."

The thought of her alone, proverbially beaten down by life and luck, and wasting her talents, tore a hole in his gut. She was outgoing, friendly, and smart. A rare, gorgeous flower among weeds that had choked the spirit out of her amazing attributes. Not for the first time, he wished he'd known her back then. Or sooner.

"Would you go back?" Scratching his jaw, he stared at his house next door to hers, wondering what his answer would be if she asked him. A month ago, it would've been an unequivocal *yes*. He'd merrily return to the city, his family, his life, and his career if given the chance. He hesitated to think it over now, and that surprised him. "If they offered you a better position and higher pay, would you take it?"

Distractedly, she shook her head, but her tone brooked no argument. "No. I'm grateful for the learning experience and opportunity. It taught me a lot about the world and myself. I used to beat myself up over failing or not fulfilling my dreams, but I believe all roads led me back here for a reason, even if it's not where I expected."

# Chapter Fifteen

Rebecca padded back into her bedroom and climbed under the covers. Graham lay sleeping beside her, lightly snoring, and with the sheet draped across his waist.

He'd spent the night. As in, slept over. After an epic night of sex and conversation.

Color her crazy, but it had never been like that for her before. Sure, she'd been in relationships and had lovers, but this seemed different. Felt different. For one, the sex had been fantastic. Like he'd been so in tune with her body that pleasuring her had been automatic. No thought or research required. And then there were the discussions. Before and afterward. Intimate, open dialogue where there had been no judging, no shame. Even when they'd disagreed, it had been a respectful exchange. She'd said things she hadn't even admitted to her besties. Details she hadn't let escape from the dark corners of her mind.

Shaking her head, she smiled. He was kind and honest. Open and willing. Present and able. They'd formed a connection in such a short period she'd never achieved with other partners. They just...clicked. It almost seemed too simple. Well, maybe not simple, but fast. Perhaps she was jaded, but she wondered if this was a honeymoon period, and if so, how long it would last.

He hadn't said much after she'd answered his question about going back to her old job in the city if given a better opportunity. Would he? If the scandal blew over and he was given the chance, would he take it? Merely get up and leave? The thought had crossed her mind more than once.

Forget it. She wouldn't let doubts pop her euphoric bubble.

She shoved skepticism aside and stared at him while he slept. Something she used to find creepy, but now she willingly understood the hype. Unbidden, walls crumbled and pretenses didn't exist while watching someone in slumber. No guards. Just him. And he appeared to be the same while asleep. Which said a lot about his character. It meant he didn't hide anything or blanket his thoughts. No ulterior motives.

For the most part, his expressions were easy to read when they'd been together, and she'd greatly appreciated that characteristic. Once they'd gotten better acquainted, anyway. Throughout her adult life, she'd had difficulty in relationships because her communication barrier erected a wall with the inability to understand her partner's needs. Guys tended to be black and white in the majority of things, but the shades of gray halted her in her tracks. Even when she'd tried to ask, she'd failed, and the relationships dissolved.

Graham was such a handsome devil. Ebony hair that curled slightly at the ends. Angular face. Jaw dusted with dark scruff. Full lips. Eyelashes that any female would maim to possess. Though closed, his eyes were a shocking shade of green, and she could stare into them for hours, yet never fully grasp their hue. Expressive, to boot. Wide shoulders, defined abs, light sprinkling of black hair trailing to his goody zone...

Le sigh. Definitely a looker.

He stirred and turned his head, but didn't open his eyes.

She smiled, watching from her pillow, and wondered if he was a morning person. Typically, she required two cups of coffee to have any sort of function. She'd bet he was the grouchy type. Adorably so.

He emitted a half-groan and rolled onto his side. As if by afterthought, his arm looped around her waist and he drew her flush in front of him. *Rawr.* He'd done that last night during the movie, too. An alpha-male action without rendering her weak in the demonstration. She was slender by nature. She knew that, but how he physically manipulated her body to his whims was downright panty-drenching.

Nuzzling her neck, he mumbled something she couldn't decipher.

She threaded her fingers through his hair. "What?"

"I said, you smell good."

"Thank you." So did he. Warm male with lingering traces of his bergamot cologne. "It could be the coffee I brewed."

"You are the perfect woman."

Laughing, she kissed his temple.

"How long have you been awake?"

"Just a few minutes. I started coffee and let the dog out." And hit the bathroom to relieve herself, did a few of her yoga stretches, plus made sure her hair wasn't finger-in-light-socket crazy.

He picked up his head, and grunting, set it down again. "I'll need to run home to feed him in a while. But first..."

Taking her with him, he rolled to his back with her sprawled on top of him. She'd put her tee and panties back on after they'd come inside last night, but he'd slept naked. Deliciously, gloriously naked. As she straddled him, his long, thick erection ground against her, and just like that, she was aroused.

His large hands sprawled over her belly and slid north. "You're overdressed."

"Am I?"

"Yup."

201

Off went her shirt. He sat upright, mouth nibbling and licking her neck. Those amazing, skilled hands of his were traveling her body like a backroad map. In her hair, down her spine, cupping her backside. Over sensory stimulation, and still not enough. Her skin grew feverishly hot, her core throbbed, and she ached from a place so deep, she hadn't known it existed before him.

"How attached to these are you?" His fingers dipped into the waistband of her panties.

"Um..."

"Never mind. I'll replace them."

A tear of fabric rented the room as he ripped them off. At the seams. Just ripped off her panties.

And then, he lifted her the slightest bit. When she came down again, he was buried inside her. She barely had the chance to acknowledge the full, magnificent hardness filling her, and his mouth closed over hers. Demanding, desperate strokes of his tongue matched the rolling motion of his pelvis as he moved.

Ah, yes. *So dang good*. Like last night, he brushed her clit with each thrust, sending lightning through her nervous system and zings of intense pleasure everywhere. Heavenly friction. From the roots of her hair to her toenails and back again. She prayed he'd never stop, so she could latch onto this amazing sensation forever. Desperate for release, yet not wanting it to end. Hovering in that place only he could take her. His corded, taut muscles against her softer curves clicked like a piece completing a puzzle.

Last night hadn't been a fluke. They were just that dang good together. Harmony and bliss.

Tension built low in her abdomen, and she broke free from the kiss to throw her head back. She tried to siphon oxygen, but it was futile. Rocking her hips in a rhythm to match his, she rode him, spine arched for better momentum. Faster. Harder.

He held her by the back of the neck, his breathing labored, as his other hand closed over her breast. Kneading. Manipulating the nipple until it was hot, and the slight ache added to her arousal. Desperate guttural noises of pleasure quietly rasped his throat, something he seemed unaware he was doing, and added to her kindling. Stoked the fire within her.

Her orgasm was a slow build, the best kind, and when it peaked, light blasted behind her lids as she quaked. A sharp inhale wedged in her lungs while she spiraled, catapulting her across the waves instead of merely riding them. Tremors wracked her system, but before she could collapse or fall backward, he dragged her to him and held her against his chest.

"You feel so damn good," he muttered, his body going rigid like when he'd come last night.

Yeah, she sure did feel good. Great, actually. Stupendous. Except, he meant something else, and she smiled against the crook of his neck.

A couple more pumps, and he grunted, stiffened, and choked out a satisfied sound that ruffled her strands. His arms banded tighter as he shook. Then, he went still for a moment.

Panting, he eased his hold on her and pressed a kiss to her shoulder.

Sluggish fulfillment pulled at her, making her lax. Sated, she nuzzled his neck. "Good morning."

A rough chuckle, and he inhaled as if he'd not done so since waking. "Damn good morning, indeed."

And then... *Then*, he did the sweetest dang thing. He lifted his head, smiled lazily at her, and smoothed her strands, holding her face in his hands like she was a treasure. A caring, tender action no one on earth had ever done for her. Simple, yet it leveled her to rubble.

Throat tight, eyes damp, she stared at him, wrangling her emotions.

His brows wrenched in concern. "You okay?"

She nodded, not trusting her voice. It had been so very long since someone had held her or had shown consideration to this degree. Besides Gammy or her besties, she'd not been cherished.

If that's what this was, anyway.

"Did I hurt you? Your fibro, I mean. I'm not sure how it works or what sets you off. You'd tell me if—"

"You didn't hurt me, and I'll let you know if there's an issue." Lord, this man. How had she gotten so lucky? Her ex hadn't had any interest in learning about her condition and would display frustration if she'd been too tired or sore for going out or making love. In Boston, most days, just getting through work was all she could handle between the weather, stress, and bouts of depression causing flareups.

Reaching for the covers, he wrapped the blanket around them, but remained sitting. He studied her expression, gaze roaming, and eventually sighed. "What's it feel like? The pain. Where is it?"

"Mostly, it targets my upper back, shoulders, and neck. On rare occasions, my thighs. Average day? It's like the early stages of the flu. Fighting sleepiness and a general, dull ache. When it flares up, the pain is more of a throbbing. Have you ever had a Charlie horse?" At his nod, she shrugged. "The pain feels like that on bad days, all over."

His eyes widened. "That's... Shit, Rebecca. That's horrible."

No truer words. "It can be. You never really get used to it, but I've grown accustomed and adapted. I try to avoid situations that set it off and take preventative measures."

"Like what?"

"The climate here helps. My fibro would get irritated by extreme weather shifts. The snow and cold were awful in winter in Boston. I make sure I sleep, do massage therapy, stretching, take antioxidants, and try not to get stressed."

He huffed a dry laugh devoid of humor. "As if stress can be avoided."

He was correct on that account, too. "It is what it is."

Resting his forehead to hers, he sighed. "That sucks. I wish you'd told me sooner. I wouldn't have let you do all that moving around at the office."

"I know my limits, and I refuse to let it take over my life. Everything we did at the Gazette helped the newspaper and was within my scope. I was a little more sore than normal afterward, but not a big deal."

He studied her anew, like trying to assess the honesty in her answer. "You say 'we' a lot when referring to the Gazette."

Um, yeah. "Because we're a we. *We* shifted things around, utilized what we had, and built it back up again."

"You did all that. I just went along for the ride."

The stubborn man. "Did you tell me no? To stay in my lane? Pull the boss card? No, you didn't," she said before he could refute. "A good boss listens to their employees, takes into account their wishes, and considers constructive criticism. You knew I had more knowledge of the town and what the residents would want. You listened to me and respected the newspaper's history. You had ideas of your own we implemented. Since the initial changes, you've written great articles that are among our highest clicks on the site. You also edit everything that goes in the paper and design the layout to make sure we go to print on time."

She exhaled, her shoulders sagging. "So, yes. I say *we* because *we are* a we."

What had begun as a droll expression at the beginning of her rant wound up morphing into something resembling shock and ended with veiled awe. Wide-eyed, lips parted, he stared at her as if she'd belted out a showtune while twirling a flaming baton.

Silence stretched. And stretched.

Maybe she should change the topic? "I'm hungry. Want to go grab some breakfast at The Busy Bean? They have the best croissants. And coffee."

Unmoving, he did little more than blink.

"Take over the world?" She grinned for effect.

Still nada.

What exactly had she said to render him catatonic? Was he angry? This was one of those rare instances where she couldn't read him, and her belly cramped. Needles of concern pricked her nape.

Okay, enough. "Are you all right?"

"Yeah, I..." Sighing, he narrowed his eyes. "Sometimes, I just don't know what to say to you."

What did that mean? "Are you upset with me?" She'd tried to bolster him, not hurt him.

"No." He tucked her hair behind her ears. Tone apologetic, he shook his head. "No, not at all. Journalism is very cut-throat, and your personality is the opposite. I have to be honest. Most people in your position would take advantage, go after my job, and not hesitate to look at the trail of dust behind them. But, here you are, conjuring ways to show my worth and doing nothing except supporting. I just...wasn't expecting you."

Oh. Well, geez. "I'd never do something like that, even if we weren't romantically involved."

"I know." The corners of his mouth curved in a smile. "That's my whole point."

Before she could reply, he smacked a quick kiss to her lips, and stood, taking her with him. "Let's go get you a croissant."

Alrighty. Discussion over.

They dressed and took Twain next door to feed him. She waited outside, letting sunshine bathe her face. Humidity clung to a warm breeze while birds chirped. Cut grass and pollen wafted in the air, reminding her of her childhood where she'd grab a book, climb a tree, and read half the day. She should do that again soon. Maybe minus the tree part and sit under one instead.

Walking toward and down the Main Square in a comfortable silence, townsfolk nodded and smiled knowingly at them. As if others knew something they didn't, and were leaving bread-crumb hints by way of grins. She'd nearly forgotten the aspects of small towns when she'd been swallowed by mediocrity in a big city. A community. Friends, neighbors. Part of her had wanted that escape. Having almost no privacy and tired of rumors, she'd fled.

And had lost nearly every aspect of her identity.

Outside The Busy Bean, he paused. "Okay, seriously. Did you color on my face with permanent marker while I was sleeping? What's with all the stares and smiles? It's creepy."

Laughing, she tucked a stray strand of hair behind her ear. "It's their way of saying they know about our relationship, and they approve."

"Huh." He scratched his jaw. "That was quick."

"Could be worse." She shrugged. "Take it as a compliment. They like you, or else they wouldn't accept us together." He was a transplanted Yankee and not born one of them. Backwards as the mindset was, it was truth. Proof that her town was kind once they got to know someone. Acclimation wasn't just his process.

"All right. *That* I take issue with." Hands on his hips, he frowned. "We shouldn't need approval from anyone. If we wanna be together, we'll be together."

Ah, there was the grumpy goose she'd met at the curb not long ago. The northerner unacquainted with the ways of the south and frustrated to no end.

"Why are *you* smiling at me like that?"

She hadn't realized she was, but that didn't stop her. "No reason."

His eyes narrowed to slits.

"Okay," she said through a sigh. "At the risk of sounding condescending, you're cute when you're mad. And, you're right. We shouldn't need approval from anyone. But, it's a good thing that they like you. It means they've noticed your character and attributes, and accept you as a good partner for me. This place is your home now. I want you to be comfortable. Besides, it's not that different than meeting your family. Do they have to like me in order for us to stick? No, but it would make things less difficult."

A grunt, and he crossed his arms. "Point taken. It's still archaic."

She huffed a laugh and opened the door to the coffee shop. "Let's consume caffeine."

"Stop that." He darted his gaze around as if checking for spies. "They see you holding a door for me and I'll become a pariah."

Propping the door with his foot, he nudged her inside, letting out a comical breath of relief.

"You're my kind of dork, Graham." Laughing, she looped her arm through his and stared at the board above the counter. "Me thinkst you need a double shot."

"A triple, me lady."

The shop wasn't very large, like most in the Main Square, but it was tastefully decorated with Italian tile floors, artistic pencil sketches of coffee in frames, and latte colored walls above a white chair rail. White iron tables were scattered throughout the lobby, nearly all of them occupied.

Candy, owner of the shop and two years Rebecca's senior, smiled politely as she waved them forward. Stout build with a cherubic face and short brunette bob, she reminded Rebecca of a nicer, more subtle version of the character Janice from the *Friends* TV show.

"What in the Lifetime movie is going on here?" She eyed Rebecca and Graham. "My ears have not deceived me. You two *are* an item!"

"Hi, Candy. We sure are." Rebecca dug her wallet out of her purse. "How are you?"

"Just dandy." She straightened, eyes wide. "I adore your new Health Column in the Gazette. I've learned a lot and it's very helpful. Oh, and the Town Beat, too. It's so nice not having to look up activities on ten different sites. And the Recipes addition? I tried one at home the other day. Delicious!"

Rebecca eyed Graham with a told-you-so lift of her brows.

"Thank you." He cleared his throat.

"What can I get for y'all?"

"I'm gonna need three million croissants and a caramel cappuccino." Rebecca glanced at Graham. "What would you like?"

Laughing, he shook his head. "She means two croissants, and I'll take an espresso, please."

He shoved her behind him, blocking the counter when she tried to pay, and dug his wallet out of his back pocket.

She pouted. "I really did mean three million. Candy's croissants are the best thing you ever put in your mouth."

He muttered something under his breath she couldn't decipher, but she'd bet it was naughty.

Amused by their display, Candy grinned as she rang up the order. "Sweet as you can be."

"You take that back." Rebecca huffed. "You'll ruin my reputation."

"Your secret is safe with me." Candy handed Graham a bag with the croissants, then turned to fill the coffee order. After a minute, she passed Rebecca the cups. "Have a blessed day."

"You, too." Rebecca nudged her chin toward the door. "Eat outside?"

"Sure."

They walked and ate, while he muttered sounds of appreciation.

"Damn, these are good."

"Right? I tried to tell you. Should've gotten three million."

He laughed, tossing his garbage in a can by the curb as they passed.

Winter pansies in the flower boxes along the cobblestone road next to the cast-iron old world lampposts had been replaced by begonias and violas, adding splashes of red, purple, yellow, and white from the blooms. Pink cherry blossom trees had already dropped, scattering petals on the sidewalk. Green leaves budded on the branches in their place. Varying food scents mingled with late spring caught the breeze. Even the hummingbirds had made their way back, sipping from feeders under a few awnings. Busy little things that buzzed like bees, yet twice as anxious. They were entertaining to watch.

Gammy used to have a feeder. Rebecca would have to look for it in the shed later. And maybe do something about Gammy's decrepit tiered garden boxes in the backyard that had gone unattended for too long.

"If all I need to do is feed you croissants and cappuccino to get you to smile, I'll do it daily."

The adorable man. "The company isn't bad, either. Or the morning wakeup activities."

They came to the end of the Square, not far from the library, and he wrapped an arm around her waist until she was snug against him. "Gonna have to agree with you." His gaze swept across her face, his smile fading. "Are you happy? Right now, I mean. With us? In Vallantine?"

Unsure where his question had originated, she brushed her thumb across his lower lip. "I'm quite happy." She chewed the inside of her cheek. "Are you?" He'd asked for a reason, and she had to wonder if it was because he *wasn't* happy. Or satisfied. Or content...

"Very." He inhaled, and even that seemed measured. "For the first time in a long while, I think I'm actually happy."

"Relocation can take time to acclimate." In her case, she never had adjusted to Boston. She'd stuck it out way too long.

A slight shake of his head, and he glanced over her shoulder, his expression distant. "It's not only the move down here. Whatever success I had at my old job seemed trite with no one to share it with. I was just another reporter bringing them stories, until one of those articles created problems. Then, I was dispensable. My relationships, too. Not my family, but in my love life. It just... I don't know. Feels different."

Accomplishments and successes mean so much more with a supportive tribe encouraging you. Same for when you're down on your luck and everything goes wrong. The people around you matter. But what she thought he was getting at was that perhaps he was starting to see Vallantine and the townsfolk as home. No matter how far she'd traveled or ventured, this was always home to her.

She smiled. "Different isn't necessarily bad."

One corner of his lips curved in a half-assed smile. "No, it sure isn't."

# Chapter Sixteen

Graham's folks had landed in Atlanta on the seven-thirty flight Monday evening, and rented a car to drive the ninety minutes toward Vallantine. He'd introduced them to Rebecca this morning at the office, where she insisted she'd cover the fort so he could take them to lunch. They'd spent the majority of the day hanging out at the Gazette listening to his parents tell stories from his youth, and Rebecca laughing. While working, he'd not noticed one lapse in conversation, nor had things gone stale.

They liked her. They genuinely seemed to like Rebecca.

Through the years, as girlfriends or lovers had come and gone from his orbit, his folks had appeared mostly indifferent. Mom, especially. They'd been pleasant, if not distanced. Cordial. Their parenting style was not invasive, allowing him to make his own choices, and offering advice when warranted or requested. Essentially, they'd stayed out of his love life. If they'd known his previous relationships wouldn't work out, they'd kept mum.

This was different. Entirely. He wasn't certain what to make of it since it was new territory. On one hand, an overwhelming sense of relief flooded his system that they got along with her. Enjoyed her company. Were as smitten by her as he seemed to be. On the other, he felt like he'd been dropped in a 'Mayberry' episode of 'The Twilight Zone.'

Alone, while his parents tuned in to something on the living room TV and doted on the dog, Graham stood at his kitchen window, watching Rebecca in her backyard. She'd bowed out on their dinner offer, too, claiming she needed to get caught up on gardening. Not once since she'd moved home had he spotted her doing anything of the sort. He figured it had been a paltry excuse if not for the fact she was actually...well, gardening.

Their modest quarter acre lots didn't allow a lot of leeway for landscaping, and hers had a slight incline toward the rear. Mavis had installed a three-tiered layered wooden garden box that ran the length of the backyard long before he'd moved next door. Up until this evening, it had been overgrown with weeds.

Rebecca had made quite a bit of headway since leaving her shift at the Gazette. Not that he was surprised. Blasted woman could work circles around ten men. Regardless, the weeds were gone and overfilling a garbage can near the house. Empty disposable pots were strewn about the yard, a result of her having planted the top two tiers with varying bushes or flowers. More than twenty bags of mulch were piled on her other side.

He wondered how she'd gotten all that in her car. Maybe the nursery had delivered. If not, that was easily five trips.

Her blonde locks were up in a messy knot and her have-mercy pink shorts were molded to her perfect ass. She also had on a white tank top which, had she been facing him, might have resulted in him ditching his folks to slip next door. Peel off her layers. Get dirty in the figurative sense versus literal.

Vast oranges and reds of sunset played with the mood's lighting, casting her in romantic hues which belonged at the end of a camera lens. Or a poetry collection. A punch of emotion hit him out of nowhere and smacked his chest, creating reverberations. He wasn't sure what the feeling was, other than fondness, but damn was it profound. His throat grew tight, and he attempted to figure out the mystery of his lil southern belle.

Lovely and funny. The obvious. Smart, creative, and patient. More duh. All reasons he'd be interested or attracted to a woman. But what made *her* different? What was it about Rebecca Moore that rendered him putty? Smitten by a smile? A sarcastic comment? A sigh? Hell, just by her breathing?

Normally, he liked puzzles, wading through the deets to get to the heart of a subject. Except, this mystery was driving him to the brink and back, coupled by the fact that he had no clue where they were headed in the relationship.

Uncertainty was not his favorite bedfellow.

At any given moment, one or both of them could get an employment offer outside of Vallantine. She'd mentioned not wanting to leave again, that she'd preferred home. In turn, he hadn't known how to reply. The only home he'd ever known was hundreds of miles north, and that had stopped feeling less like comfort and more like a safety net over time. He'd failed there. In every sense. And Vallantine wasn't exactly what he'd envisioned for himself. He may never climb out from under the scandal, but was that a reason to settle?

"You're going to burn a hole through the glass watching her that hard."

Smiling, he glanced at his mother's profile. Shoulder-length black hair, pointed jaw, and round cheeks. It had seemed like eons since he'd seen her last, but she looked the same. Age was beginning to show in the creases around her mouth and eyes, a testament to a life lived in laughter and love. One couldn't ask for more.

"Maybe," he said through a sigh, casting his focus outside again. Rebecca had put the last of the plants in the bottom tier and was now staring at the mulch bags with her hands on her hips. Probably trying to work up the energy to begin. Worry cranked in his gut. "She's going to put herself in traction."

"A little yardwork never hurt anyone. Besides, she's doing a great job. The garden looks amazing."

It did look awesome. Rebecca had alternated red and coral rose bushes with white gardenia on the top tier, yellow jasmine and pink honeysuckle vines on the second tier with trellises, and purple coneflowers with blue delphinium on the bottom tier. All perennial, so they'd return every year. Smart of her because all she'd have to do from there was light weeding and mulch replacement. It was colorful and eye-catching. She'd mixed small, rounded holly bushes in between flowers on all tiers, assumingly to keep something growing year round in the off-season since they were an evergreen variety. The only reason he knew all the plant variations was because of his father's green thumb, and by listening to conversation between Dad and Rebecca at the office earlier.

He wasn't even surprised by how much had brushed off on him without him realizing.

And a "little gardening" might not be much for the average person, but it *would* hurt Rebecca.

He internally debated whether or not to tell his mother, and decided Rebecca wouldn't mind. She wasn't ashamed of her condition, not that there was a reason to be, and she didn't use it as a crutch, which his mother would respect. Best he could tell, she was also very open about it when asked, indicating her diagnosis wasn't a secret.

"She has fibromyalgia." Crazy how quickly he'd learned the term, pronunciation, and definition in such a short span. It didn't exactly roll off the tongue. "Ever hear of it?"

Mom nodded, her gaze out the window, a frown curving the corners of her mouth. "One of the paralegals in the firm was diagnosed last year. I never would've known had she not said something. Invisible illnesses are tricky and often ignored in the medical community."

He grunted in agreement. "She mentioned that very thing. It took them forever and a litany of tests just to tell her there was nothing they could do." Or almost nothing. "I mean, she looks fine."

But she wasn't. At some point, he needed to figure out how to cope with that. He wasn't doing a very bang-up job of it yet. Like now. He was all but crawling out of his skin wanting to march over there and do the work for her. She'd crucify him for it. Rightfully so.

Another nod from Mom. "I had lunch with Janet a few weeks ago to go over a case. That's the paralegal I mentioned. The topic of her condition came up, and she said something that stuck with me. I don't think I'll ever forget it." She turned to face him, arms crossed, and the troubled weariness in her eyes had his gut sinking. "She said the level of pain she lives with every day would cripple most people, and no one has any iota there's a thing at all wrong."

Well...*shit*. Why didn't she just pummel his face with a sledgehammer? That would've hurt less.

He pressed his forehead to the glass, closing his eyes. It didn't help. All he pictured was his dear, feisty, affectionate Rebecca. *In pain*. It caused agony of his own. In his head. His chest. Every damn where.

"You know, Mom, I could've gone the rest of my natural life without hearing that tidbit, thanks."

She carried on as if he hadn't been split in two. "I asked her how she dealt with it, and she replied with the darnedest thing. Just shrugged and said, what other choice was there? She either lived her life or let the disease take it from her. People have jobs and hobbies and friends and family. If they focus only on the symptoms, then they'd never get out of bed."

Yeah. "Sounds like Rebecca, all right."

A warm hand settled on his back and rubbed in soothing circles. Her faint scent of rosemary knocked him back to childhood when she used to comfort him this way. "Remember a few years ago when your dad was having chest pains and they did all those tests at the hospital?"

He huffed a laugh. "I remember you threatening to sue the hospital into oblivion if he didn't make it."

"Not my best moment," she mumbled, then shook her head. "My point is, when we love someone, their pain is our pain. Their struggles, their joy. Love isn't always sheer bliss, but if you're lucky, the good outweighs the bad. Sometimes, the best you can do is be there to support them, so they know they're not alone, and offer to help when you're able."

A long-winded sigh, and he rubbed the grit from his eyes. "I don't recall saying I loved Rebecca."

"MmmHmm."

"Didn't imply it, either."

"MmmHmm."

He narrowed his eyes on her. "Is this one of those reverse psychology parent tricks? I know you like her, but that's beneath you."

Dad chose then to stroll into the room, the dog on his heels. He glanced out the window, around the kitchen, and back to them. He scratched his head, disrupting his salt-and-pepper strands. "We having a family meeting?"

"No. Our son thinks I'm using ploys to get him to fall in love with Rebecca." She smiled at Dad, weaving her arm through his, and winked.

"That would be a feat. Besides the fact that one cannot make a person fall in love with another, he was already in love with her before we got here."

She raised her palm in emphasis. "Exactly."

"Really, son. Your mother is an amazing specimen, but you give her too much credit."

Sighing, Graham eyed the ceiling. "Y'all are a barrel of laughs."

"Oh boy." Dad cleared his throat. "He's been in the south too long. He 'y'alled' us."

Crap. Had he? Graham rolled his response around in his head and...yep. He had.

Whatever. When in Rome...

"I think he's been here just long enough." Mom's grin had slid from cheeky to endearing. She searched Graham's expression, nodding as if she'd found what she'd been looking for, and him being no wiser in what the quest had been. "Indeed."

Blowing strands of hair out of her eyes, Rebecca glanced at the five remaining bags of mulch, then at the tiered garden. Dang, it looked so much better. But, geez. Her body was irrevocably pissed off right now. Tightness and tension had a chokehold on her shoulders and neck. Thighs and lower back, too, proving she'd done too much. Exhaustion weighed on her from a bone-deep level. Fatigue forced her to hunch over or faceplant on the lawn.

It had to be done, though. Gammy's gardens had looked sad for too long. Rebecca was sick of being sad. The sight of color and life again would've made Gammy so happy. Plus, it was, for the most part, self-serving once Rebecca got finished. She wouldn't have to consume this kind of effort again.

Twilight had fallen, stars aplenty, as a cool breeze wafted across her skin. Scents from the roses, gardenia, and vine blooms scented the humid air. She was worried if she sat down or stopped, even for just a quick rest, she'd never get up again. Five bags seemed like five hundred with her current pain level.

Giving herself a mental peptalk, that there were only five bags left, and they were for the garden's lowest tier, she bent and cut a bag open. A deep breath, and she hauled it to the garden.

A screen door clacked from the direction of Graham's house, and she glanced over.

His mama walked toward Rebecca, a smile curving her lips. Not for the first time today, she spotted a resemblance to Graham in the eyes, the shape of the woman's chin. Rebecca had thoroughly enjoyed hanging out with them for a stint today. His folks were funny, warm, and down-to-earth people. They'd been by the office earlier, and not wanting to be a third wheel, Rebecca had declined lunch and dinner. It was also supposed to rain the rest of the week, so she'd wanted to get the garden finished. She hoped his mother hadn't taken offense.

That, and Rebecca looked like hell warmed over right now. Sweaty, dirty, and in clothes not fit for company.

"You did an amazing job. It's lovely." Mrs. Roberts bumped her head toward the new plants, making the last legs of her trek, and stopping beside Rebecca.

"Thanks." She grinned, eying her progress. "Quite the workout, but I think Gammy would've approved the choices. Coneflowers were especially her favorite." She sighed. "How was dinner?"

"Oh, it was wonderful. I'm so full."

She laughed. "Pizza My Heart's put me in a food coma more than once. I can relate."

Mrs. Roberts nodded, her expression whimsical. "I'm sorry about your grandmother."

"Thank you. Me, too."

"Do you have any other family to help you with things?"

Rebecca knew his mama meant well, and judging by the way she eyed the garden, Graham had probably told her about the fibromyalgia. It felt like a get-to-know-her fishing expedition, though, which Rebecca understood. She was dating the woman's son, who'd up and left home a handful of months ago. Mrs. Roberts probably just wanted to make sure the person he was dating lived up to par.

"I don't, no. My parents died in a wreck when I was young. Gammy raised me. I'm an only child."

Any hints of whimsy that had been present dissolved. Mrs. Roberts pressed a hand to her chest, eyes wide and beseeching. It was like looking at an older, more feminine version of Graham. "I'm so very sorry. Graham hadn't mentioned it."

"That's okay. Vallantine is like family, and I've known my besties since birth. I've had nothing but love in my life." Except when she'd left home. It felt, sometimes, that she'd abandoned all forms of love from her rearview while chasing dreams. Not for the first time, she wondered what had taken her so long to return. Sheer stubbornness, she supposed. It was actually downright pathetic how accustomed to being alone she'd become while in the city. Everybody needed a someone, but she'd had no one. Not close by, anyhow.

"A wonderful way to look at it." Mrs. Roberts nodded as if Rebecca's response had been a test she'd answered correctly. "I'd like to meet your friends one day."

"That can be arranged. Just take Scarlett with a grain of salt." She laughed at her own joke as a case of nerves rattled her. She wasn't sure why.

"Graham said as much, that she's Scarlett O'Hara made over, except with less selfishness."

Rebecca barked a laugh, wiping her brow with her forearm. "If that ain't a proper description."

A hum in her throat, and Mrs. Roberts smiled. "And Dorothy?"

Interesting that she was asking about Rebecca's friends. Perhaps she was worried about her? "Dorothy has all the courage in Oz, but the patience of a saint. She always does the right thing, even if it's hard."

"Ha. You three were aptly named by your parents, it sounds like. With a twist." She tilted her head. "Tom Sawyer's Rebecca was beautiful, clever, and resolute. You didn't pick up her slightly prissy ways, nor are you prone to excessive displays of emotion. It's as if the three of you chose the prominent parts of the fictional personalities and left out the less endearing traits."

That was... Heck, that was extremely kind. "Not certain we had a choice, but thank you. I've never heard us described quite so eloquently before. Maybe you missed your calling as a writer."

"Nah." She waved her hand. "I'll leave that to you and my son." She pulled over a patio chair and sat like she was staying awhile.

Um... "Can I get you something to drink?"

"No, but thank you. Go ahead and finish what you were doing. We can chat at the same time."

Relieved, because Rebecca just wanted to get the task accomplished, she hefted the bag she'd cut. "When are y'all heading back to Minnesota?"

"Trying to get rid of me?"

Since there was no malice or barb in the question, she laughed. "No, ma'am. I like you two quite a bit." A grunt, and she dumped the bag, spreading it around the plants with her feet. Her legs were itchy from the wood shavings, but she'd shower soon. "I was wondering if you're free tomorrow night? I can cook us dinner. I'm not as good as Graham or his daddy, but I haven't poisoned anyone to my knowledge."

A quiet chuckle rose from behind her as she grabbed another bag.

"I see why my son is besotted with you. We rather like you, too, Rebecca. We leave the day after tomorrow, and dinner sounds lovely. How about we order in? Not because you might poison us, but since you've been out here all afternoon and evening, you might be extra sore tomorrow."

She straightened abruptly to look at Mrs. Roberts, and nearly lost her balance. Graham had obviously told her about the fibromyalgia, which Rebecca didn't care about, but most people didn't know a lot of what the condition entailed. Thus, either Mrs. Roberts was more educated than most, or she was hunting for a reaction.

Resolute sympathy and understanding stared back at Rebecca, and she wasn't sure how to reply. It had been a severely long time since someone not in her inner circle had shown any kind of grace without suspicion looming on the fringes. A lump formed in her throat and her eyes welled.

Stupid fibro. Flare-ups made her more emotional, and she despised it.

Angry at herself, she turned and dumped another bag, clearing emotion from her throat. "We can order in if that's what you prefer. I don't mind cooking, though. I'll leave it up to y'all. I appreciate you offering, nonetheless."

"We'll play it by ear, see how you feel. We're adaptable people, and so is Graham. You can be honest with us. We'll never judge you for it, or ask anything you're not capable of giving. Should you ever need help with anything, all you ever have to do is ask."

Halfway through the woman's diatribe, Rebecca's chest hitched, and her ribcage cracked open. Hot, outlandish tears fell unbidden onto her cheeks. She'd met these people mere hours before, had only tidbits of conversation with them, yet they treated her as if she was a part of their family.

And it hurt. So badly, it hurt. Yes, Vallantine and its towns-folk were home, and yes, she had her besties. But she had zero family to speak of left. They were gone. All gone. Buried in the Vallantine Cemetery with the town founders and everyone else who'd been a part of the community. Sometimes, the emptiness inside her was a cavern. Endless. Bottomless. Hopeless.

Overwhelming.

Arms came around her. Comforting. Just like Gammy's had been. They absorbed the pain instead of taking it away or shrugging it off. The scent of rosemary surrounded her as sobs wracked her sore, tired, aching body.

After she didn't know how long, she straightened, mortified. "I'm sorry. I don't know where that came from."

Mrs. Roberts smiled, tucking Rebecca's hair behind her ears, and wiping her cheeks with a tissue she'd produced from who knew where. "No need for apologies. You did nothing wrong. We all need a good cry now and then." She took a step back to give Rebecca breathing room. "Besides, it was my fault, poking at wounds, and especially after you've exhausted yourself out here." She glanced next door and back again. "I think I made my son freak out a smidge."

Rebecca glanced over, and yup. There stood Graham at the property line, arms crossed, and expression wrenched between who-do-I-need-to-murder and oh-crap. The poor man.

She pathetically waved. "I'm good. Your mama is torturing me with stories from your early writing days. It's terrible. Please take her home."

Mrs. Roberts laughed, and patted Rebecca's cheek. "Oh yes, you'll do nicely." She strode back to Graham's yard, said some-thing to him Rebecca didn't hear, and then went into the house.

Moments passed. Long moments where he seemed so tense, a feather would snap him in half.

Finally, he shook his head and walked toward her. He studied her expression a beat, and shook his head again. "Go in the house. I'll finish this."

"But—"

"Go. Ten minutes, and I'll be right behind you."

"I can do it."

"I know." A swallow worked his throat. "I'm fairly certain you could solve the energy crisis or relocate Stonehenge if you set your mind to it. Can and should are two different things, and in this case, you don't have to. I'm here. I'll finish."

She sighed, her shoulders sagging. Guilt battled with pride until she realized she was too tired to care or act. "Thank you."

"Not a problem."

"My hero."

"And don't you forget it, but let's not go overboard."

"I like your mom."

"She's fond of you, too."

"And your dad."

"Same answer."

She chewed her lip, still hesitant. She was unable to read his mood. He seemed to be straddling angry, tired, and confused. "Are you mad at me?"

Closing his eyes, he furrowed his brows. A shake of his head, and he opened his eyes, emerald gaze piercing. "I am many things. Mad isn't one of them."

Anything more would be poking the bear, so she went inside. But instead of showering, taking pain pills, or warming her heating blanket to help her muscles later, she stood by the window to watch him.

And she fell in love with him.

Right then and there, perhaps weeks ago. She hadn't a clue, yet she was consciously, vividly aware of it now. She was in love with Graham. No questions asked, he'd demanded to finish the garden, recognizing she'd been stretched beyond her means. He'd researched her condition so he could better understand her triggers. He'd given her a job and reins at the office to help them rebuild the once great newspaper. He got along well with her friends and shared the same interests. He was funny. He was sincere. He was smart. He was sexy. He was charismatic, brave, and honest. He made her chest burst with emotion whenever he was near, her girly bits zing with only a kiss or glance. He simultaneously took care of her while allowing her to stand on her own.

She'd never been in love before. It was kinda scary, actually. Enlightening, exciting, freeing...and terrifying. What was she supposed to do?

He came in the back door, locking it behind him. A once-over, and he sighed. "Did you take anything for the pain?"

"No."

He nodded, eating the span of the kitchen in a few strides. Opening the cabinet, he shook out a pain pill from the prescription bottle and her antioxidant from another, passing them to her.

In a daze, she took them, swallowing them with the glass of water he held out.

"Wait here."

He disappeared, and the sound of bathwater running filtered toward her. Moments later, he returned, wearing only his boxers.

"Up you go." An arm behind her back and another under her legs, he lifted her and made his way through the living room, down the hall, and into the bathroom, where he carefully set her on her feet.

Be still her heart.

He'd laid out her pajamas on the vanity and put bubbles in the running bathwater.

Dang, but her chest hitched again, and she nearly sobbed. He was taking care of her. Like her parents used to. Like Gammy used to. Rebecca could take care of herself. If anyone knew that, it was Graham. But sometimes, it was nice to have someone else do it for her. Or care enough to try.

Through a watery haze, she stared at him. "Thank you."

A solemn nod, and some of the tension eased from his features.

He undressed her, lifted her into the bath, shed his boxers, and got in behind her. It was a tight fit in such a small tub, but the intimacy threw her for a punch. As if she could handle any more surprises, he washed her hair, her aching body, helped her dress, and put her to bed, where he cuddled with her until she fell into a deep, exhausted sleep.

# Chapter

## Seventeen

A couple days later, Rebecca stared at her screen in the Gazette office, tweaking the article Mrs. Roberts had suggested she write regarding fibromyalgia. Per her, it might help bring awareness to the condition within the parameters of town and make people more understanding. Graham had thought it a great idea, too, and had gotten quotes from a few medical personnel near Atlanta.

She rolled her head to stretch her neck. Her body had calmed down since her afternoon of gardening, but the ever-present achiness was always there. Especially because it was due to rain again this afternoon. Springtime in the south. It still beat fall, winter, or spring up north.

After his parents had headed back to Minnesota yesterday, Graham had been acting normal. Less brooding and troubled, more like his affable self. She wasn't sure what discussion he'd had with them that might've set him off, but she hadn't gotten the impression he wanted to talk about it.

Thus, they hadn't.

Yet, her revelation about falling in love with him hung in her peripheral, waiting to be addressed. She'd spouted the three words in past relationships to a couple partners, but in honesty, she knew now she'd been lying, if by complete unawareness. What she felt for Graham, how they were together, was like realizing she'd been dating with her eyes shut before him. Still, she didn't want to rush him or make him feel pressured to say it back.

Worry ate at her esophagus he might not feel the same.

Maybe she should call her besties to hang out tonight. Hash it out with them first.

The front door chimed, and she glanced up from her computer in the back of the building. It was too soon for Graham to be back from picking up food, and she'd just flipped the storefront sign to Closed during the noon hour.

Gunner Davis strode in, hiking up his trousers and looking around.

Interesting.

She rose, wondering what on earth the mayor was doing at the Gazette in the middle of the day. "Hello, sir. What can I help you with?"

He wiped the sweat from his brow with a handkerchief and repocketed it as he walked to her desk. "Hello, darlin'. Graham around?"

"No, he went to grab some sandwiches from What A Pickle." They'd probably be backed up with orders this time of day, plus Graham liked to take a walk during lunch. She glanced past Gunner through the window. The sky still threatened rain, but it hadn't let loose yet. "He might be awhile."

Plucky II chirped as if to confirm her statement.

"Good." He dragged a chair from Joan and Jefferson's station, pulling it beside her desk. He set his briefcase on the floor.

"Wanted to run something by you." He deposited his girth into the chair and rested his hands on his knees, winded.

Alrighty. She reclaimed her seat. She hoped to all that was holy it didn't involve interviewing him for an article. There wasn't a soul in Vallantine who didn't know the mayor or his life story. She couldn't listen to another of Gunner's 'back in my day' lessons without wanting to rip her ears off.

"Been thinking about The Gazette and what to do with it."

Her gut bottomed out. Gunner had given Graham six months to turn the paper around. He still had a little over a month to go, but he'd done what Gunner wanted. Graham had raised subscribers, revenue, and interest in their fledgling little paper. Advertising was through the roof from the independent shops. What was there to discuss?

Unsure what to say, or even if she could force out words, she kept mum. She stared at his thinning, neatly combed white strands, at the green polo stretched across his paunch, at his clean-shaven jaw, and wondered why he'd been relieved Graham wasn't here.

Nothing was adding up, nor sounding optimistic, and her stomach started eating itself.

"Library renovations are coming along?"

Seriously? What next? Nice weather we're not having? "Dorothy's scheduling the contractors. It looks like they'll be starting sometime in the next six weeks."

He nodded because he obviously knew that intel. Forest ran everything for the Historical Society through the mayor's office. She really wished Gunner would get on with it.

"Are you planning on sticking with the Gazette after the library reopens?"

"Yes." Expelling a breath of relief, she leaned back in her chair. That's what he was worried about. Her leaving an open position at the newspaper. "Between the three of us, we're working out details for how to balance work and the library."

He nodded again. "And what if I were to offer you the paper?"

*Offer her the...* "What?"

Graham was editor. Not her. What in tarnation was going on up in here? Gunner didn't seem to know whether to check his ass or scratch his watch if he thought she'd take the job from Graham.

"I do believe you heard me, Miss Rebecca." Up went his brows.

"Explain. What do you mean by offer me the paper?"

"Just how it sounds." He straightened, casting a glance around before resettling on her. "You did all this, from the framed art to the canary."

"I helped."

"Per Graham, it was all your idea."

She had a horrible, horrible feeling where this conversation was going, and her belly was rejecting the coffee she drank this morning as a result.

Carefully, she pulled a deep breath and let it out. "I had ideas. So did Forest, Scarlett, Dorothy, and Graham, the latter being the one who tabulated all those ideas into data for execution. He has a mind for business and a critical editorial eye. I'm simply more creative. Both are needed."

He never took his gaze from her, just kept bobbing his head slowly like a demented toy on a dashboard. "You're one of us."

That's what this was about? Graham being a Yankee? "So is he, you know. He owns a house, supports the small businesses, and pays his taxes here in Vallantine. Discrimination doesn't look good on anyone, especially a mayor. I was gone almost ten years. Does that mean I'm not one of you anymore? There's a big world out there, and getting stuck in a small town mindset would hurt The Gazette, especially accounting for tourism. For years, the newspaper was in the red. He got you out of that rut. We got it thriving again."

A smirk lifted one corner of his mouth, indicating he'd not only expected, but appreciated her reply. Or he found her amusing. So, what the hell, then? Why was he here? Irritation tapped her temples as she narrowed her eyes.

"What happens if this little affair of yours goes sour?"

Now he was overstepping, and it was sticking in her craw. "My personal life is none of your concern. I do my job, and I do it well. So does Graham." She leaned forward. "Our relationship will not sour, but if we do happen to go our separate ways on some distant day, we're both adults enough to be professional."

Gunner cleared his throat and puffed his cheeks. After a beat, he rose and replaced his chair. "There was a time, Miss Rebecca, you would've battered and deep fried me for a question like that."

She gritted her teeth. "Trust me, I'm still thinking about it."

"Good to know." He smiled, and for the first time since he'd entered, it reached his eyes. "You were a lil spitfire of a thing as a young girl. I watched you grow, hoping the world wouldn't douse your flame. No matter what life threw, you were always able to dust yourself off. Some folks could learn a thing or two from you. I'm mighty proud of you, and Mavis would be, too."

Well, crap. How was she supposed to stay mad? Emotion tightened her airway, so she focused on arranging her pens.

He glanced around anew, arm draped over the top of her cubicle. "I assume that's a no to my offer?"

He hadn't actually offered her the job, though, had he? He'd skirted around the topic as if gauging her skin in the game. Regardless...

"That's a firm no, and I'll elaborate a step beyond so there's no confusion. Graham goes, I go. He stays, I stay. None of which has anything to do with personal feelings."

Brown bag of market sandwiches in hand, Graham stepped out of the deli onto Main and glanced at the sky. Angry black and greenish clouds hovered over the town like a shroud. They'd been calling for storms all day. Luckily, nothing serious, but the static in the air was palpable. Hopefully, it'll have cleared out by the time he and Rebecca had to head home. Neither of them had driven today.

Townsfolk had started to thin on the cobblestone sidewalks in preparation, but there were a few stragglers, Mrs. Boone included. The mayor's secretary looked up from digging in her purse and smiled at Graham. Her lime-colored dress seemed to make the salt-and-pepper coifed hairstyle appear green, too. Or maybe that was the clouds overhead.

"Can I give you a hand with anything?" She seemed aflutter.

"No, but aren't you a dear! Mr. Davis wanted me to grab his lunch for after his meeting with Rebecca. Honestly, why he couldn't just get it while over here, I'll never know. That man!"

"Right," he mumbled, distracted. Gunner Davis's little red sportscar was parked outside The Gazette across the street, about five shops down. Rebecca hadn't mentioned a meeting. "What's he want with her?"

He was more than a little concerned Gunner would try to throw his weight around. He'd assured Graham he wanted no hand in things when it came to the newspaper, that he'd stay out of the business end, but after that impromptu drop by last time,

Graham wasn't so sure. The mayor had been cryptic and...well, weird. It hadn't sat right in Graham's gut ever since.

"Oh, about taking over The Gazette, of course!" She fumbled in her purse, muttering about a wallet, while his stomach landed somewhere near his knees. "There it is. You have a blessed day. Stay dry, young man."

"You, too," he managed, staring at The Gazette's window.

The Earth could've rotated the sun and they developed a cure for cancer in the amount of time he stood at the curb, frozen. A hollow fissure formed in his chest, just below the knot in his trachea.

A meeting implied scheduling. Which meant, Rebecca had known Gunner would be by, and during lunch when Graham typically left the office.

Taking over The Gazette? His worst nightmare. That Gunner would replace him or stop the press altogether had been looming over Graham for months. He had nowhere to go if this didn't work out. No one would hire him. What had Gunner's secretary meant by that statement? Was he being fired? Replaced by Rebecca?

*Had she known?*

The worst, the absolute worst part, was the possibility she'd been in on it from the start. Had they used him and his skills to get the print in the black again, and then planned to toss him out? Had their romantic relationship been a ruse?

No. That wasn't like her. He dismissed the errant thought immediately. She didn't have it in her to hurt another or be deceitful, to any degree. She was more honest than any ten people he'd come across in his career. What they shared was real and vivid and potent. But...

He straightened, cold to the bone.

*But*, would she accept his job if it had been offered to her?

After mulling it over, he didn't think so, nor did he think she'd have known what Gunner was up to before today. She had done nothing but defend Graham since he'd hired her. She hadn't succeeded out in the big bad world. His career had nosedived straight into a flatline. And when push came to shove, she was a local, him merely an outsider, which would matter to Gunner.

Shit. There was only one way to find out what was going on, but his feet weren't cooperating.

Whatever. Checking for cars, he crossed the street and strode to the office, yanking the door open.

Rebecca, still at her desk, peeked over her monitor. Next to her, Gunner stood with his arm resting on her cubicle, a never-may-care expression as he glanced at Graham.

He set the sandwiches on the entryway table. "What's going on?"

She rose and opened her mouth, but Gunner got the jump on her.

"I was going over some Gazette business."

Graham tilted his head despite the oh-shit pummeling his innards. "Wouldn't that involve me being present?"

"Not in this case."

Temples throbbing, Graham looked at Rebecca to gauge her response. She could be quite expressive when her guard was down, and he desperately needed reassurance. The chewing of her lower lip and wrench in her brows indicated nothing short of being caught red-handed.

Brick by brick, his world began to implode a second time. Except, this time, he'd not done anything wrong. Pointedly, he stared at Gunner, waiting him out.

"Whelp." Gunner dropped his arm and strode to the front of the room near the display stand. "I came to ask Miss Rebecca her thoughts on taking over the Gazette."

Graham nodded once. He'd heard that much from the mayor's secretary. What he hadn't heard were the words straight from the horse's mouth. How petty, immature, and underhanded.

And Rebecca? They'd been intimate. Were co-workers and, he'd thought, friends. Neighbors. Lovers. Her betrayal cut deeper than his former editor not having his back, than his career abruptly being cut short, or than the woman he'd been dating at the time walking out on him instead of offering support.

Attempting to swallow, he glared at Rebecca, keeping his voice deathly low. "And what did you say?"

It took point five seconds to realize his mistake.

Centimeter by centimeter, she straightened to a position so erect, it made his spine hurt. Her expression flatlined into an unrecognizable version of the warm, affectionate woman he'd come to know over the past few months. Lips thinned, gorgeous blue eyes narrowed, she shook her head in blatant disbelief and unadulterated rage.

Her initial reaction to Gunner's blanketed admission hadn't been guilt, as Graham had assumed. It had been worry etched in her features and concern about Graham or his job, not because she'd had remorse for stabbing him in the back. He'd been too stunned and angry to notice or correctly read her cues.

But it was too late. The damage had already been done with his accusation wrapped around a question, and spoken to her in a tone where nothing she could say would be believed.

He was a fucking idiot.

"Rebecca..."

She lifted her palm, halting anything he might've spouted.

Closing her laptop, she shoved it in her bag, grabbed her purse, and wove around her desk. She paused a mere moment to pin those big blue saucers on him, shrouded in ice. "Bless your heart."

As the door closed behind her with a quiet click, it may as well have been a resounding thud to him. An urgent need to go after her battled with the flagrant desire to set the record straight to his boss. None of this was okay. Not one damn thing.

He pinched his eyes shut, sighing.

"She said, if he goes, I go. If he stays, I stay."

Opening his eyes, Graham stared at Gunner, debating who he should punch first, his boss or his own face. Neither would solve anything or take back the past five minutes.

The man shrugged, as if he'd said the grass was green. "In case you were wondering, that was the answer she gave me about taking over the paper."

Graham had hit his limit. Stick a fork in him. "I gave you everything. All my experience, my time, my knowledge. Granted, you took a chance on hiring me, and I appreciate that more than you know, but I moved a thousand miles to accept this position. I utilized what we had, sought advice and proper help, and rebuilt this paper. Sales and subscriptions are up. Content is precisely what the town asked for and more. Advertising is a continuous steady stream. I stay late and show up early every single day."

Letting out a gale force wind, he slapped his palms to his thighs. "And you repay me by going behind my back to the woman I'm romantically involved with, whom I hired, to offer her my position without bothering to show me the respect I deserve or fire me to my face. Hell, I can't blame you for the decision. She's sharp as a tack and can do the job better. She deserves the promotion. None of my success would be possible without her. But, damn. I gave you everything I had left in me, Gunner."

"Now, son. Not once did I say anyone was getting fired."

Splitting hairs. Graham had ejected verbal diarrhea, and the man was splitting hairs.

He grabbed the paper bag of sandwiches and strode to his office. His appetite was gone. Rebecca was gone. His job was gone. What the hell was he supposed to do now?

When he was nine years old, he'd fleetingly wanted to be an astronaut. Perhaps NASA was hiring.

Tossing the bag in the fridge, he slammed the door shut.

Gunner had followed him and leaned against the doorway, hands shoved in his pants pockets. "I didn't go behind your back, either."

Exhausted, his give-a-shit gone, Graham dropped in his chair and kicked his feet up on the desk, crossing his ankles. "The last nerve I have left is on fire, Mayor."

A huffed laugh, and Gunner shoved off the frame. He went to Rebecca's desk, where he pulled a file out of a briefcase on the floor, and returned to Graham's office, easing into one of the chairs across from him.

"I had my reservations about you." Gunner cleared his throat. "You had experience, but I didn't know if you'd make a good fit or could pull off the job having not been a Vallantine native. Sometimes, a person's gotta hit rock bottom before they can climb out again. That's where you were when I offered you the position. Rock bottom, son. You started to claw out when you hired our Rebecca."

He pulled a handkerchief from his pocket, wiped his brow, and repocketed it once more. "My mind was set on you that evening a couple weeks ago when I visited to check on things. You didn't take credit for her work when I asked about the changes. Know what else you didn't do? You didn't ignore her suggestions or brush her aside. The big city chewed up our girl and spit her back out again, but instead of adding to her beating, you picked her up. That's the measure of a good man."

Shit. At a loss, and suddenly, stupidly emotional, Graham swiped a hand over his face. Throat tight, chest pinched, he stared at the ceiling, trying to gain composure.

"She keeps things close to the vest unless someone's lucky enough to earn her trust. I attribute that to her folks' passing while she was so young." Gunner shifted in the chair. "I wanted her alone to poke at her without you lurking. That's why I came today, and she answered exactly how I figured."

Leaning forward, he tossed the file he'd been holding onto Graham's desk, bumping his chin toward it.

"What is this?" Graham reached for the file, opening it. And about fell outta his chair.

He blinked, then blinked again. He couldn't possibly be seeing what he thought.

"I never wanted The Gazette. I bought it because no one else did, either, and history needed preserving. I'm not firing you, Graham. I'm giving you the newspaper outright. Both you and Rebecca."

Holy, holy shit.

Graham flipped through the legal pages, which he'd have to read in detail later, but yeah. It appeared Gunner had drafted documents to transfer The Gazette to Graham and Rebecca. All files, contents, physical products, and even the building.

It was dated yesterday, too, meaning his first gut reaction on the sidewalk about her having no clue had been correct. One second. He'd second-guessed himself and her for *one* second, but it may cost him everything. Owning the newspaper or remaining in Vallantine meant squat without her.

Gunner rose and went to collect his briefcase, then backtracked to Graham's doorway. "The two of you look those over and get back to me. If you're in agreement, sign the last page." He lifted one corner of his mouth in a smirk. "If you can get her to talk to you, that is. Might want to start with, *I'm sorry*. Flowers wouldn't hurt. Or begging."

In a stupor, Graham watched the man's retreat.

Quickly, he dropped his feet to the floor and leaned forward. "Gunner."

At the door, hand on the knob, the mayor turned.

"Thank you." Graham didn't know what else to say. Not in his dreams or expectations had he expected this kind of gesture. It wasn't only a fresh start, but a leg up. Something to call his own and no one to answer to. "Thank you."

# Chapter Eighteen

Rebecca had no sooner made it to the end of Main Street, and the sky let loose. A torrent of fat, cool raindrops doused her, the road, and everything else within seconds. The *whoosh* as the storm hit Vallantine was a roar against her ears and heaviness settled in her chest.

Cursing, she cut left toward the library instead of her neighborhood since it was closer. Ankle-deep puddles had already formed since the rain was coming down faster than the ground could absorb. Her shoes squished in grass as she crossed the lawn and bounded the porch steps. Fumbling with the key, she let herself in, shut the door, and...

Screamed. She screamed. A frustrated, angry, gutted bellow because it was all she was capable of doing to vent. Long, loud, and rattling her ribcage, she let it rip until there wasn't any air left in her lungs.

Damn Graham Roberts, anyway.

Heaving oxygen, she glanced around. The already dismal light in the library from very few windows as a natural source was made darker by the storm. Shadows creating shadows. The tall, vaulted ceiling and empty shelves made the patter of pouring rain echo throughout the space. The electricity had been cut to prepare for renovations, so she couldn't use the overhead chandelier. For some, it might be a location for an epic horror flick, but to her, it was welcoming. The place was built out of love, and love had kept it standing.

Setting her purse and laptop bag on the center station, she wiped water from her eyes and pulled out her phone. With shaking hands, she roused it from sleep mode, grateful it hadn't been damaged in her back pocket from rain.

She sent an SOS text to her besties. *Emotional Emergency: I'm at the library and fit to be tied. Please bring alcohol and dry clothes.*

She paused after sending the text, then swiftly sent another. *If you can. If you're busy, no worries. I'll deal.* Worst case, she'd put her phone in the bag and walk home. Take a hot shower and read until her mood and the storm passed.

She really didn't want to be home, though. She wasn't sure the reason, other than Graham would find her there. If he bothered to come look for her, anyway. Judging by how he'd treated her at The Gazette, maybe he wouldn't.

Clenching her teeth, she stalked the creaky floorboards, trembling with pent up rage. How dare he? How dare he accuse her of vying for his job? Of going behind his back with the mayor? As if she'd ever be that sneaky and underhanded. He'd looked at her as if they'd not shared secrets, their hearts, and a bed. Like he'd not known her at all.

Her phone pinged multiple texts.

Scarlett: *Whose ass I gotta kick?*

Dorothy: *We'll be there in under 30 mins.*

Scarlett: *What she said.*

She thumbed a *thank you*, and set her phone down to pace some more.

Twenty-eight minutes later, she was no calmer when her besties rushed through the door, both smart enough to wear raincoats.

Thunder clapped overhead, followed by flashes of lightning. How Rebecca despised storms. Her parents had died during one just like this. Ever since, they made her edgy and uncomfortable, as if she needed that on top of her current mood.

"What happened?" Dorothy set a thermos on the station and shrugged out of her coat. "Why aren't you at work?"

Before Rebecca could reply, Scarlett handed her a duffel bag. "Yeah, spill it. You have us more than a lot worried."

Dry clothes, thank goodness. Cold plus wet did not equal a happy body with regards to Rebecca's fibro.

"I'm sorry." She set the bag on the floor and peeled the wet garments from her body. They hit the ground with a *thwap.* "Graham Roberts is what happened and why I'm not at work." She stepped into a pair of pink sweats and a matching hoodie, then tried to balance to apply socks. Rummaging in the bag, she was grateful they'd thought of shoes, too. Hers were soaked, like everything else. "I could murder him."

"I have plenty of land to bury a body," Scarlett professed.

Tempting.

Turning around, she noted Scarlett had spread out a blanket on the floor with a battery-powered lantern in the middle. A muted yellow glow encased the small area.

Dorothy poured mixed drinks from the thermos into disposable glasses, passing one to each of them.

Rebecca downed hers in one swallow, not even tasting the Georgia Sunset cocktail.

"Well, goodness." Dorothy took the empty cup and refilled it. "It must be bad."

She sat with Scarlett on the blanket while Rebecca paced anew. From the door to the back wall, passing the floor-to-ceiling shelves, and back again. Her skin itched and her face burned and she shook with rage.

Where to start? "First, Gunner Davis came into the office, while he knew Graham was gone for lunch, and offered me The Gazette—"

"Hold it." Scarlett tilted her head. "What does that mean, he *offered* you The Gazette?"

Rebecca threw her arms out and let them drop. "Heck if I know. It came out of nowhere. The way it was presented struck me like he was checking my reaction more than what he actually said carrying weight. I assume he wants me to take over Graham's position as editor."

Dorothy hummed a sound of disagreement. "As if you'd do that."

Whirling on her, Rebecca pointed. "Thank you! I would never take Graham's job out from under him, even if he wasn't doing it right. Which he is. He's an amazing editor."

Dorothy crossed her legs. "What did you tell Gunner?"

"To take the offer and shove it. Not in those words, but anyway." She resumed her pacing. "I said no, thank you, and told him if he fired Graham, I'd leave, too."

Scarlett nodded approval. "Well, there's a stand for you. Good girl. The both of you have done a bang-up job of bringing The Gazette back from the brink."

"Why are you angry at Graham, then?"

Rebecca paused by the window, watching sheets of water pummel Main Square. "He walked in on the tail end of the conversation."

"Ruh-roh." Scarlett took a sip of her cocktail. "Let me guess. Graham overheard Gunner's offer?"

"Worse. When Graham asked what was going on, Gunner just spit it out. *La la la, offered your lover and subordinate your position. How's your morning?*" She growled. "Poor Graham looked like his head might blow off, and that was after thirty seconds of the someone-kicked-his-puppy expression." The memory made her nauseous all over again. "Then," she laughed without mirth, "in a pissed-off tone, he asked me what was my response to the offer. And let me tell y'all, it was a rhetorical question."

Dorothy bared her teeth in a clear *eesh* reaction.

"Oh, hell no." Scarlett flipped her hair over her shoulder, obviously as affronted as Rebecca.

"Oh, yes." She downed her glass and set it on the windowsill. Physically and mentally drained, she leaned her butt against the frame and slouched. "How could he believe that of me? After all we've been through, how could he believe I'd betray him? Our field is so cut-throat. He's experienced it. I've experienced it. Neither of us liked that aspect, and vowed to help one another, to work together instead of against. There was only the two of us with no one else to compete against."

"Is that why you left Boston?"

She whipped her gaze to Dorothy, and found abject curiosity wrapped in sympathy staring back at her. Still, she couldn't push words past her lips to reply.

"Is it?" Dorothy gently prodded. "Is the cut-throat atmosphere why you left?"

Tears stung her eyes, but Rebecca attempted to shove them aside. "No. I left because my throat had been cut on day one, and I was merely a ghost walking around mimicking a human that mattered. I was just too stupid to notice." For almost ten years.

Lord, feeling it and saying it aloud were entirely different things. Only in the dark recesses of her mind had she allowed herself to admit that fact. She'd told Graham, but to bear the truth, her brutal truth, was eviscerating. Shame sliced through her midsection.

"You're not stupid." Scarlett glared at her. Hard.

Rebecca stared at her, at Dorothy, and could only shrug. No, she wasn't stupid, but she hadn't followed her instincts or made something of herself, either. It had been something she'd battled for a long time. She'd failed. Over and over. Day after day. Month after month. Year after year.

Until she barely recognized herself in the mirror.

"It took guts to try." Dorothy set her drink on the floor beside her hip. "A small town like Vallantine wouldn't prepare you very well for the rest of the world. You had goals and a dream for yourself, and you tried. That took grit and determination and guts. If you didn't catch a break, if they didn't give you one, that's their loss, and our gain. Most people never would've made it out the front door."

"She's right." Scarlett drew a breath and let it out, her gaze searching. "I know you feel disappointed in yourself, but we don't. Never have. If the Rebecca from our childhood had met the you of today, she wouldn't, either. You made it on staff at a newspaper, and now, look at you. You're practically your own boss. You were just offered an editor position. You write what you want, when you want, and there's twenty-five hundred residents anxiously awaiting your words every morning."

Rebecca nodded, some of the weight in her chest lifting. Her besties were right, but it would take a bit for belief to sink in. Wounds didn't heal overnight. Not even self-inflicted ones.

"Based on what you've told us, Graham has battled his own demons." Dorothy leaned back on her hands. "It doesn't excuse his behavior, but what Gunner did probably fed into Graham's insecurities, and he lashed out at you."

She was right, yet again. They'd hash it out later when Rebecca wasn't so raw.

Up went Scarlett's brows. "Bettin' he regrets it."

Rebecca smiled despite the turmoil in her chest. She'd talk to him later. If need be, she'd accept the offer from Gunner, then hire Graham so they could continue the same roles they'd had the past couple months. Something. She didn't know, but she needed space to think.

"You love him, don't you?" Scarlett grinned. "The kind of swoony, head-over-heels love we'd made up stories about as girls on the couch back there while Mr. Brown rolled his eyes."

"The kind of stories *you* made up," Dorothy corrected.

Rebecca huffed a laugh and tilted her head to stretch her neck. The achiness was more pronounced, but she'd worked herself into a tizzy, and it was storming.

"Fine." Scarlett dramatically waved her hand. "Don't answer me."

"I do love him." It was jarring, admitting it to another soul.

Rebecca sighed, recalling the happily-ever-afters Scarlett had profusely touted in her dreamy tone in this very library. Fiction, nothing more. Or so Rebecca had thought, until they'd played matchmaker for their favorite teacher and their favorite librarian. Fairytales hadn't seemed so unrealistic once they'd proven their theory and succeeded. But love wasn't about throwing two people together. They required proper pairing, chemistry, interests, and respect. They had to be the correct fit for it to work.

She had zero doubt in her mind Graham was her fit, her missing puzzle piece. Had she not chosen now to come home, had Gammy not passed away, had Graham not been exposed in a scandal that wasn't his fault, they may never have met. What an irrevocable shame that would've been, them not coming together or ever crossing paths.

Perhaps Scarlett had been correct, after all. Vallantine had some magic to it.

"I'm not sure he feels the same, but I love him."

"He does." Dorothy winked. "When we were setting up The Gazette, making copies and such, I caught him watching you more than once. And when he found out about your fibromyalgia, I swear, he was in just as much pain. He might not know it yet, but he loves you."

One could only hope. Then again, he treated Rebecca with kindness and reverence like he was invested, like she mattered to him an awful lot. He tried to take care of her. That was the other thing about love she was coming to discover. Sometimes, the proof was in the details.

Scarlett glanced around Rebecca. "The rain stopped."

A check of her watch had Rebecca realizing a couple hours had passed since the besties had come to the rescue. No wonder she hadn't noticed the storm had passed. The air was still sticky with humidity, but the tangible pressure had abated.

She smiled. "You two can head out. Thank you for coming."

They got to their feet.

"You sure?" Dorothy asked.

"Yeah. We can stay as long as you need."

How Rebecca adored these two. What would she do without them? "Yep. I'm going to stay a bit. I'll clean up. Go on. Thank you, though. Seriously."

A hug, some more quick witty banter, and her friends left.

The silence was both cumbersome and welcome. So sudden, it seemed like someone had flipped a switch. Yet, the sanctuary of the library wrapped her in its arms. No matter how long she'd been away, it understood. It would heal her hurts and mend her heart, and it would stand like it had for centuries long after she was gone.

Melancholy, she glanced at the blanket, noting the besties had left the thermos with their Georgia Sunset mix on the floor beside the lantern. She grabbed her wet clothes and shoved them in the bag, then threw away the cups. Switching off the lantern, she set it by her purse on the counter and decided to fold the blanket in a moment.

She wasn't ready to go yet, and she'd done her best thinking here as a girl. Ideas and whimsy. Perhaps she could stand for more of that in her life again. Reality hadn't been nice.

Walking back to the window, she gazed at the town center. Dusk would descend soon, and the lampposts would cast a romantic yellow glow on the wet cobblestone street. For now, the cobalt sky shone its last legs of late day, fluffy clouds drifting as remnants of the storm moved on. Flowers in the curbside boxes and leaves on the cherry blossom trees reflected sunlight off the rain droplets. People milled about again, in and out of shops, stopping to chat.

She wondered how many times Katherine Vallantine had stood here in the library her husband had built for her, staring at townsfolk and the bustle. There were sketches of the town the way it had looked back then, but Rebecca hadn't seen them in years. The Historical Society had possession of them at the mayor's office if memory served. There certainly hadn't been as many shops, colorful awnings, or decorative additions, for sure. Time marched on.

Which was what Rebecca needed to do. Let go of past aspirations and carve new ones. Remain true to herself, yet grow. Expand. The perimeters of Vallantine weren't as small as she'd recalled when she'd left. Her besties had been right. She should give herself more credit. She had achieved most of what she'd desired, but she'd done it within the confines of home instead of elsewhere, and through the eyes of an adult more versed in the world than with the ones of an altruistic child.

How would she do that, though? How could she shuck whatever doubts or regrets lingered to blend old dreams with new ones?

A noise came from behind her. Delicate. A rustling, noticeable only because the library was vastly somber. A sound that she'd recognize if deaf, dumb, or blind.

*Pages flipping.*

The fine hairs on her arms rose, and she slowly turned around.

Notebook pages, at least twenty of them, littered the blanket. And they'd appeared from nowhere.

Expelling a shaky breath, she walked closer and glanced around. No white mist, shadows shifting, or spooky vibe. She was alone, just as she'd been before, and she didn't sense any sort of malice. In fact, traces of a lingering scent of roses wafted over that of dust and mildew.

"Katherine?" She swallowed, her pulse thumping. "Katherine Vallantine?"

Had to be. Rosemary and Sheldon Brown had experienced something similar. Many generations of Vallantine descendants, actually. A book or something would appear just when they'd needed it most. An answer to what they'd been searching for. Rebecca always waffled on whether she believed the legend or not, yet it was hard to dispute this. She'd been alone, and standing by the window, next to the only entrance or exit. These papers certainly hadn't been there before.

Utterly surreal.

"She assists all who enter seeking knowledge," she whispered to herself. What did Katherine want Rebecca to know?

Kneeling, she grabbed one of the pages.

*Why Kittens Are Better Pets Than Dogs by Rebecca Moore*

Nuh uh. She'd written these in one of her blogging phases. Gammy hadn't had the money to buy a computer back then, so Rebecca had written "articles" on notebook pages and had hidden them in books throughout the library. Old school media via a kid. There were still creases from where she'd folded them in half. The paper was slightly yellow-tinged, the ink faded. Gosh, she had to have been twelve, maybe thirteen. She'd completely forgotten.

Laughing, she gathered the rest, reading the titles and shaking her head at her penmanship. Little hearts to dot every other lower case "i" and underlining certain words for emphasis. She cringed at the amateurish musings. My, how far she'd grown in ability. Her stories were obviously more targeted for blogs, not journalism, as they were personal jots of random opinions with some information thrown in.

Sitting on her haunches, she stared off into space, the papers in hand. Even when she'd gone away to college, her goal had been to make it big. Win awards, gain recognition. Breaking news stories that would stand the test of time. Many of her professors had tried to steer her towards creative writing, but she didn't have the skill or interest. Yet, the articles she'd turned in had been much like these. Come to think of it, so had a lot of the pieces she'd tried sending to editors in Boston. They had edge, distinction, but too much...heart.

Had she been heading in the wrong direction from the start? Admittedly, she'd hated the competitiveness of reporting. Climbing over colleagues to get to the top. The back-stabbing. She'd never had it in her to betray someone. It might've been one of the reasons she'd never earned her way out of the Obituaries section. She wanted to inform, educate, but not at the expense of others, and not while losing herself in the process. There was an abundance of depersonalization in journalism, and being from a small southern town, she hadn't adapted to taking character out of the story.

Perhaps she hadn't failed, after all. Maybe she'd merely succeeded in staying true to herself, her nature, and listening to her instincts.

When she and her besties had first learned the library had been turned over to them, while still in Boston, Rebecca had reached out to an acquaintance about the myth. A bigwig blogger with thousands of followers. She'd told her how, during their courting period, William and Katherine Vallantine had played the Truth/Lie game. The objective was to get to know a person on a deeper level. Tell one truth, one lie, and something they wished was truth or lie. The other person had to guess which was which. Her acquaintance had made the game go viral, starting with Instagram, and branching out from there.

At the time, Rebecca had been pretty peeved the game had been the blog's focus, and not the history behind it. William and Katherine's love story, how the library came to be, her spirit who haunts it, and the Miss Katie wishing tree in the center of town were all absent. They'd all been left out. Her besties had told her to write it, tell the tale, but she'd dismissed them. She hadn't been in a good headspace to do anything except exist.

She could now, though.

Chewing her lower lip, she pieced together the ideas into creation for proper execution. Start a blog, ride the game hype by tying it in to the real origins, gain followers from that, and when she wasn't at The Gazette, write about whatever she wanted. Books, the town, her medical condition. Anything. She'd need a name that would encompass her vast topics. Or something vaguely catchy where it didn't matter.

Sighing, she glanced at the pages in her hands. Katherine hadn't been wrong yet. Clues had been leading Rebecca here. It was about time she listened.

Rising, she went to the center station and grabbed her laptop bag, then reseated herself on the blanket. While it booted, she rolled around the pros and cons of an actual site or a free blog, deciding on the former.

For the next few hours, she got a site up and running, with a bio page and links to her socials. Since it was a blog, she changed her Instagram name to the new blog name and made it a professional account. As her fingers flew over the keyboard writing her first piece, a sense of euphoria washed through her. Finally, she was in the right space, at the right time, doing what she was meant to do. It was crazy how at peace she felt with her decision.

Laughing, she closed the laptop and stood to stretch.

And realized how dark the library had become. As in, pitch black.

A glance toward the window, and she pressed a palm to her forehead. Night had fallen without her being aware.

She packed her things, and checked her phone. The besties had texted an hour ago to make sure she was okay. She replied, apologizing for taking so long to respond. Graham had messaged, too, roughly an hour after she'd left The Gazette. She hadn't noticed.

*I'm sorry about earlier. We need to talk about the newspaper and us.*

Alrighty, he'd apologized. That was a start. Yet, her belly grew uneasy with the other part. Typically, that kind of blanket statement preceded a breakup. She didn't want to end things.

Opting not to text back, some things were better done in person, she slung her bags over her shoulder, thinking maybe she'd stop by to see Graham if he was still awake. They could discuss what had happened and work it out.

Hopefully. Worry clawed her belly that he might not believe her about Gunner's offer.

If he didn't, then he never really knew her at all.

At the door, she took in the darkened confines of the library from the threshold, and smiled. "Thanks, Katherine. I promise, we'll make you proud with the renovations."

# Chapter Nineteen

Unable to sleep, Graham rose from bed well before the sun and showered. After feeding Twain, he checked the forecast, noting it would be clear skies today. He hoped that was an omen for all things, and not just the weather report.

Regardless, he could take the dog with him to work. Which technically didn't start for another six hours. Three a.m. was not his friend.

He'd texted Rebecca.

She hadn't replied.

He'd knocked on her door.

She hadn't answered.

And the lights had been off all night at her place. A fact he knew only because he'd been stalking the house from his window. Unapologetically. She'd probably spent the night at Scarlett's or Dorothy's, having a men suck rampage. He wasn't sure where else she'd go.

Despite realistic assurances in his mind, anxiety cranked his gut.

She had every right to be angry. He'd implied an ugly accusation of her, even when he'd known better. He'd stuck his foot in it. A habit he'd done often with regards to her, but that ended now. She was not the crux of his mistakes. She hadn't been the one to leave him for the wolves in Minnesota. She was not a representation of all the bad luck he'd faced.

It was time he let go of his baggage.

From day one, she'd bolstered him. Baked cookie advice regarding issues with the mailman. Menu suggestions at the bar on the cusp of him insulting the town. Feeding him ideas about The Gazette. Killing herself helping him to transform the newspaper. Offering encouragement. Translating southernisms. Listening with an unbiased ear about his scandal. Charming his parents. Hell, charming his damn dog. Aiding in getting his mojo restored. Introducing him to her friends so he felt less alone in a new town.

Frankly, if not for her, he'd be screwed. She'd made him human again, had reminded him of his worth, and gave him his life back.

He was wrapped around her little finger, and he didn't care. He was...happy. She made him happy. Which was something he'd not been able to claim for far too long.

He'd hurt her yesterday, and it was inexcusable. He couldn't grovel if she kept ignoring him, though. It was driving him out of his damn mind.

Pouring coffee into a travel mug, he eyed the dog. "Let's go for a walk before we head to the office."

Twain danced in circles.

Laughing, he grabbed his keys and phone. "Come on, then."

It would still be a couple hours before daybreak, and he enjoyed the quiet as they departed the subdivision, heading toward town, Twain trotting beside him. Everything was still, not a soul about, and once again, Vallantine enchanted him. It was an interesting mix of tourism and small town living. Quirks, but not the kind he'd stereotyped in his head.

Well, some, but not all.

Leaves shushed with a gentle breeze, and everything still smelled of rain. Fresh. Clean. Stars winked overhead, too many to count, and it blew his mind how he'd not paid attention to what he'd been missing. In the city, he'd never had a panorama like this.

They got halfway down Main and stopped in front of The Gazette. He didn't want to go in yet, and the warm, humid temperatures kept his feet moving.

"We'll backtrack to the office in a bit."

Twain looked at him, then ahead, going with the flow.

At the end of the road, he paused, eyeing the infamous peach tree and courtyard designed around it. Rebecca had told him the history, and if what she said had any truth, it was an amazing feat the thing was still around.

What the hell. "Let's visit Miss Katie."

If he lived a hundred more years, he didn't think he'd get used to calling a tree by a formal name.

Parking his butt on one of the benches, he glanced around. Twain jumped up to sit beside him, seemingly doing the same.

Brick was laid around the courtyard's circumference and a black wrought iron fence around the tree, which sat on a slight grassy noll. Shorter lampposts encased the perimeter. He hadn't realized before today, but there were spotlights aimed up at the trunk. A few iron signs telling the myth were posted.

Admittedly, what he knew about belle peaches or their trees couldn't fill a thimble, but he trusted what Rebecca had said as factual. The thing was almost twice as big as others of its variety, and ten times as old. Branches were growing upward, as if reaching, and the shape neared a rounded crown. More decorative and ornamental in his opinion, if not for the size. Leaves had almost finished filling in from the dormant winter, dark green and shaped like the foliage from birches in his parents' neighborhood. Gorgeous red blooms dotted the tree, but those would be gone by summer.

When he'd asked, Rebecca said she'd wished on the tree as a girl, like so many visitors and townsfolk. He'd not done frivolous things as a kid like cast wishes on stars or dropped pennies in a well. He wondered if that was solely a female thing, but perhaps he should. She hadn't steered him wrong yet.

"What do you think, Twain? Should I make a wish?"

The dog lifted his paw in a motion to shake, and Graham chuckled. He supposed that was a yes.

Crossing his arms, he leaned back and thought about it. Six months ago, he would've asked for his career back or another legit offer from a syndicate. He didn't miss the hectic pace, or the bullshit associated with the job. Constant travel, deadlines, ten reporters behind him gearing for his position. Meals from a sack and heartburn. Sleepless nights.

If someone had told him, at any point in his life, he'd be his most content editing a small town newspaper in the south, he'd assume he was being pranked. Not accounting for an offer of ownership, but there it was in a nutshell. He still wrote important pieces. It just wasn't on a massive scale for political junkies or business moguls, and without someone looking over his shoulder. It took him awhile to realize the material they put in The Gazette was important to the people in Vallantine. The patrons may not run for high office or be the latest celebrity or operate a pharmaceutical company, but they did represent the average everyday consumer. They mattered.

He'd been a snob, and no better than the jerks who'd shunned Rebecca in Boston. That changed now, too. He'd do better.

A sigh, and he scratched his jaw. He had no desire to win the lottery, stay young forever, or be best friends with Jason Momoa, though the actor did seem like a cool guy. Graham shook his head. He had a job, a roof over his head, food in his pantry, a great family, and wonderful supportive friends. There wasn't a solitary thing he wanted.

Except Rebecca.

They had a great thing going, and he hoped to hell he hadn't mucked it up. There was an ache in his chest that wouldn't abate since yesterday. He missed her. It had been less than twenty-four hours, and he missed the daylights out of her. All he could think after Gunner's offer was to go to her and celebrate. She would understand how much it meant to him, besides the fact she deserved it just as much. It was her triumph, too. He'd told Forest and his folks, but the victory was nothing without her by his side. Without him by hers. She was the embodiment of everything he never knew he'd been missing. He couldn't envision a future without her.

"I wish she'd forgive me." Huffing a laugh, he swiped a hand over his face, not even a little surprised he'd said the wish aloud. To a tree. Because Rebecca had told him it granted wishes. "I wish she'd forgive me and come back."

His phone pinged, indicating he had an email on his personal account. He thought about ignoring it, but he dug the cell out of his pocket anyway.

Rebecca? They'd exchanged personal emails, but she'd not sent one yet. He scanned the message, confused. She started a blog?

Clicking the link, her site opened to a lavender and bright green design. In the header was a beyond adorable close-up picture of her with her head inclined, eyes crossed, and the tip of her tongue sticking out between her teeth. Waves of her caramel-colored hair cascaded around her shoulders. She'd named the blog "Because, Becca!"

He smiled at the play on words like she was calling herself out. She didn't care for the nickname, he knew, but it would give her a small sense of anonymity, thus it was a good choice.

Her biography page listed her writing attributes with links to The Gazette and her socials. He clicked those and followed, along with following the blog. She had quite a few followers already. At the bottom of the page, she'd posted some screenshots of what she described as her first blogs as a young girl, claiming she'd just found them again. She was something else. Cute and crafty.

The only blog piece she had so far was titled "The History of Truths & Lies." She'd mentioned the popular trending game having originated in Vallantine with William and Katherine. It was brilliant to open with that since she'd get a lot of clicks based off hashtags and word of mouth. The article was articulate and funny, to boot, which people would gravitate toward, and it wasn't so long that it would bore the reader.

"Look at our girl, killing it online." He was so damn proud of her.

Putting his phone away, he stared at the tree, the courtyard, and the horizon while petting the dog. Whisps of red and orange were fighting the dark off in the distance for sunrise. Birds were already chirping, as was the sorrowful call of a whippoorwill.

"Aren't you a postcard, sitting there with your dog, watching the sunrise."

Flinching, he shifted toward the voice.

*Rebecca.* Thank all the holy creatures. She stood off to the side of the courtyard, dressed for work in a blue sundress that matched her eyes and her laptop bag slung over her shoulder.

The breeze caught wisps of her hair framing her face that had escaped her ponytail.

He hadn't noticed her coming, and neither had Twain, but the doofus's tail was wagging happily to see her. Graham's would be, too, if he had one.

He tried to find his voice, but couldn't. He could've wept at the sight of her and sheer relief.

She came closer, sitting on the other side of Twain, so the dog was between them. "You look like you've been rode hard and put up wet."

He shook his head to clear it, but...nope. "What?"

Smiling, she turned in her seat to face him. "You look tired."

"Oh. I didn't sleep. At all. I texted and went by your place, but you weren't there." He wanted to touch her so badly, he had to fist his fingers to resist the urge. "I'm sorry. I'm so damn sorry about yesterday."

"Forgiven."

Wait. Just like that?

And while he was on that thread, she seemed different. Happier. Content. As if the weight she'd been carrying around had been unburdened.

"Still, it wasn't right. I knew, *I knew* you had nothing to do with Gunner's offer, but..." He shook his head. Anything he said would sound like an excuse.

"But you've been burned before, were blindsided, and ever since, you've been waiting for the other shoe to drop."

Expelling a hearty breath, he rubbed his eyes. "Yeah." Leave it to her to understand the psychology behind his actions. For the past six months, it felt like he'd been walking on eggshells, biding his time until his last hope was dashed. "It doesn't justify taking it out on you. I am sorry."

"I know." She petted the dog, staring ahead. "I've been think-ing about Gunner's visit. Maybe I should accept the position to—"

"No." Bless her heart, but no. She obviously had no clue what had happened after she'd left, and he wasn't certain how she'd take the news. "Gunner wasn't offering you the editor position. He doesn't want the newspaper. He was trying to unload it on us. As in, full ownership. That was his offer, he was merely gaging your reaction to scenarios to cement in his mind he was making the right call."

"What?" Eyes round, she gawked at him. "He wants to hand over The Gazette, just like that?"

"Yup. Trust me, I was just as shocked. All this time, I thought he was waiting to shut it down or fire me. The papers are on my desk. Three drafts. One for both of us to sign, one for you if I don't want it, and the last for me if you bow out." Pausing, he waited for a reaction, but she just continued to stare at him in an adorable, dumbfounded manner. "What do you say? Want to go into business with me?"

Covering her face with her hand, she bowed her head and laughed. By the time she lifted her head, the laughter was near hysterics. "I'm as confused as a fart in a fan factory. You've got to be kidding me."

Was that a no? Damn southernisms. "I'm not joking."

"I know." She fanned her face. "Whew. I know," she repeated, sobering. "Our mayor sure knows how to bury a lead. Are you certain this is what you want? Small southern town. Lil ole newspaper."

He'd never been more sure of anything in his life. "Yes."

"Really?"

"Yes. Why does it sound like you're trying to talk me out of it?"

"I'm not." She shrugged, studying him. "I wouldn't want you missing out on something bigger or better if it comes along."

He nodded, finally understanding. "It took me awhile to figure this out, but I'm where I'm supposed to be. There's nothing bigger than co-owning our own newspaper and intimately knowing the people who read it. Faces we pass everyday and who are part of a community. And there is nothing better than you."

Straightening, she pressed a hand over her heart. "Aw, if that isn't the sweetest—"

"I love you." No sense in beating around the bush.

Her perfect pink lips parted, and those big blue eyes widened.

"I do. I love you. That has no bearing on my decision for the newspaper. Hell, if Gunner had fired me, I'd find something else. Maybe put my bid in the race for his job next term. I don't know. Start a lawncare business. Moot point, but I love you. From the lilt in your voice when you drop your guard to the way you wrinkle your nose when embarrassed. You're the most selfless person I've ever met. You're funny, clever, and brave. I mean, you're sexy, too, which doesn't hurt."

She laughed, her eyes welling, and slowly shook her head. "I love you, too."

Funny thing, he hadn't noticed his heart quit beating during his diatribe because he'd been terrified she might not feel the same, or wasn't on the same page yet. But there it went, thundering in his chest.

"Just remember who lead with the story first."

Another laugh, the sexy, rough, smoky one that hit him below the belt, and she got on her knees. Leaning over the dog, she cupped his face in her hands and kissed him.

Hell, yes. They needed to ditch work today. They were the bosses. They could do that.

Tilting his head, he went in at another angle, deepening the kiss, stroking his tongue with hers. Her sweet honeysuckle scent invaded his orbit, and he groaned. Joy, untainted imaginable joy, spread from his chest, and encompassed his entire being.

He brought his arm up to wrap around her, tug her closer, but he got a fistful of...

Dog fur.

He broke from the kiss and glared at Twain.

The doofus licked his chin, then hers.

She laughed, scratching Twain's ears. A pinkish glow lit her features as the sun crested, bathing her in light. "Who's a good boy?"

"Once more with feeling, I am. *I'm* a good boy."

Throwing her head back, she laughed harder. "Yes, you are." She scratched behind his ears. "You're a good boy, too."

Fine. She wanted to be a smartass? Plucking her from her seat, he lifted her and deposited her sideways in his lap. Nothing between them.

Damn, but she was beautiful. He cupped her cheek, stroking it with his thumb. "I liked your blog. Great opener to kick things off."

She smiled. "Thank you. I had an epiphany in the library last night."

"Is that where you were?" All he had to do was walk a couple blocks to find her?

"Yes. Time got away from me." She abruptly straightened. "You'll never believe what happened."

She became a whirlwind, hands flying, spouting a tale about lost blog pages and a ghost visiting her. By the time she finished, she was panting.

"Are you trying to have me believe Katherine Valantine's spirit pulled blog pages you wrote as a kid from multiple books in the library and tossed them to you?"

"Well, when you put it that way, it sounds preposterous. But, yes."

He laughed.

Her eyes narrowed. "You don't believe me?"

Coming from anyone else, he probably wouldn't. "I believe you." He glanced at the tree behind her, golden rays of dawn filtering between the branches, and grunted. He'd be damned. "I made a wish on the tree earlier."

Up, up, up went her brows. "You're a true Valantine resident. Grats!"

He rolled his eyes. "Aren't you going to ask me what I wished for?"

"No. That's between you and Miss Katie."

Perhaps it was. Regardless, he smiled at her, brushing his thumb across her pouty lower lip. His sun rose and set with her. His whole world, in fact. His little belle.

"It came true." This odd sense of fullness encompassed him, until it seemed he'd burst. "My wish came true."

### Gammy's Peach Pie Recipe

**Crust:**

- 2, ½ cups flour (all-purpose is good, unbleached is better)
- 6 tablespoons of unsalted butter (cold and sliced)
- 2/3 cup of vegetable shortening (cold)
- 1 teaspoon of salt
- ¼ cup ice cold water
- 1 tablespoon of sugar (for dusting)
- 1 egg (for glaze)

**Filling:**

- 8-10 ripe peaches
- 1 tablespoon of bourbon
- ¼ cup sugar
- 1 teaspoon of vanilla extract
- 6 tablespoons of water

**Make the Crust:**

- With a fork, press the butter cubes and shortening.
- Mix the salt and flour, then add to the butter/shortening.
- Mash the ingredients until it becomes dry/crumbly.
- Add the cold water. Mix again.
- Take dough out of the bowl and knead it a few times in different directions with the heels of your hands (like when making bread). It will have chunks of butter and shortening. This is fine.
- Split the dough into equal halves. Cover in plastic wrap and put in the fridge.

**Make the Filling:**

- Peel and slice the peaches. Set aside in a bowl.
- In a saucepan over a low heat, add the sugar, vanilla extract, water, and bourbon until it boils, stirring constantly, then remove from heat. Pour it over the peaches and gently stir until coated.

**Make the Pie:**
- On a floured surface, roll out both crusts on both sides.
- Place one crust in a 9 inch pie pan.
- Spread the peach filling inside.
- Add the second crust and crimp the edges.
- Cut 4 slits in the top of the crust for ventilation.
- Beat the egg. Brush a thin layer of the egg over the top crust.
- Sprinkle lightly with sugar.
- Bake in a preheated 400 degree oven on the middle rack for 45-55 minutes. The whole crust should be golden brown.
- Cool on a wire rack. Refrigerate leftovers.

*For extra yumminess, you can add 1 package of raspberries to the sliced peaches during that step, or add vanilla ice cream when serving the pie warm.

Check out the opening novella for *Heart of Vallantine* NOW!

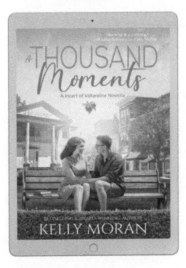

More *Heart of Vallantine* books coming soon!

*Y'all come back now, you hear...*

Want to help an author? Please consider leaving a review
and tell others about the great romance you just read!
Continue to read more about Kelly!

## ABOUT THE AUTHOR:

Kelly Moran is an international bestselling author of enchanting ever-afters. She gets her ideas from everyone and everything around her and there's always a book playing out in her head. No one who knows her bats an eyelash when she talks to herself. She is a RITA® Finalist, RONE Award-Winner, Catherine Award-Winner, Reader's Choice Finalist, Holt Medallion Finalist, Book Excellence Award Finalist, Amor Book Award-Winner, and landed on the "Must Read" & "10 Best Reads" lists in USA Today's Lifestyle section. She is a former Romance Writers of America® member, where she was an Award of Excellence Finalist. Her books have foreign translation rights in Germany (where she is a Spiegel Bestseller), the Czech Republic, Romania, Russia, France, and the Netherlands. She is the owner and founder of Rowan Prose Publishing. She also writes horror under the name Kelly Covic.

Her interests include: scary movies, all kinds of art, driving others insane, and sleeping when she can. She is a closet coffee junkie and chocoholic. Tell no one. She's originally from Wisconsin, but she resides in South Carolina with her significant other, her three sons, their wily dogs, a bearded dragon, tree frogs, and their sassy cats. She loves hearing from her readers.

www.AuthorKellyMoran.com

Milton Keynes UK
Ingram Content Group UK Ltd.
UKHW041419070524
442338UK00001B/16